little

· IT'S ...

Dea... ...le Black Dress Reader,

... ...r picking up this Little Black Dress book, one
... th... great new titles from our series of fun, page-turning
...om... ... novels. Lucky you – you're about to have a fantastic
... ...ad that we know you won't be able to put down!

... ... you make your Little Black Dress experience
... better by logging on to

www.littleblackdressbooks.com

where you can:

♥ Enter our **monthly competitions** to win
gorgeous prizes

♥ ...t **hot-off-the-press** news about our latest titles

♥ ...ad **exclusive** preview chapters both from
... **favourite** authors and from brilliant new
...ng talen...

♥ ...up-and-coming books online

♥ ...up for an essential slice of romance via
...**nightly email** newsletter

We l... ...g more than to curl up and indulge in an
addi... ...nce, and so we're delighted to welcome you
into ... ... Black Dress club!

With love from,

The *little black dress* team

Five interesting things about Janet Gover:

1. I grew up in a small Queensland town which I believe is the only place in the world with a memorial dedicated to an insect.

2. While working as a television journalist in Brisbane, I once rode my horse to work and tethered it on the helicopter landing pad.

3. People ask me why I left Australia's sunny shores for England. The reason is about five foot ten inches tall, with green eyes and he plays guitar.

4. Despite working at Pinewood movie studios during the making of four James Bond films, I have never seen Pierce Brosnan or Daniel Craig. I did once see the gorgeous Johnny Depp and was incapable of coherent speech for hours afterwards.

5. While shooting a television report about the demise of an exclusive men's club, I was filmed playing on the billiard table – which almost gave one member a fit. Women were not even permitted in the room – far less allowed to play. The club was closed the next day and the building was torn down. I guess that says it all.

By Janet Gover

The Farmer Needs a Wife
The Bachelor and Spinster Ball
Girl Racers

Girl Racers

Janet Gover

little
black
dress

1

Cataloguing in Publication Data is available from the British Library

ISBN 978 0 7553 4717 9

Typeset in Transit511BT by Avon DataSet Ltd,
Bidford-on-Avon, Warwickshire

Printed and bound in Great Britain by
Clays Ltd, St Ives plc

Headline's policy is to use papers that are natural, renewable and
recyclable products and made from wood grown in sustainable forests.
The logging and manufacturing processes are expected to conform to the
environmental regulations of the country of origin.

HEADLINE PUBLISHING GROUP
An Hachette UK Company
338 Euston Road
London NW1 3BH

www.littleblackdressbooks.com
www.headline.co.uk
www.hachette.co.uk

For Dad . . .
we had such fun in your little red sports car.

Acknowledgements

Before I started writing this book, I almost knew what a carburettor was. Almost. My thanks go to my brother Kenneth for sharing his rally experiences with me, letting me play with his cars and answering many, many questions.

This has been a bit of a family affair. Thanks for the eagle, Clare.

As part of my research, I spent a wonderful week touring the Cooma-Monaro region, the Snowy Mountains, the Riverina and Canberra. I want to say a big thank you to all those people who made that trip such a delight – the tourist information centres and the pubs, the Old Tin Shed in Dalgety, the campsite at Old Adaminaby – and others too numerous to mention. A special thank you goes to Tim and Amy for their fabulous bin-diving in Gundagai.

John – thank you for the website, the proofreading, the patience and the many, many cups of tea.

On a daily basis, I receive much support and encouragement from my friends and fellow writers in the Romantic Novelists' Association, especially the girls in Reading, London and Oxford. Thanks, ladies. I love you all to bits.

And finally – my heartfelt thanks to the team at Little

Black Dress, especially my editor Leah, for taking such wonderful care of my stories.

A lex lay on her back and wondered just how easy it would be to kill a man with a spanner.

'Hey! Come on. Are you asleep or something?' The owner of the voice prodded her leg with his toe.

She was definitely going to have to kill him. It shouldn't be that difficult. She looked at the heavy tool in her hand. Hit him hard enough in the right place . . .

'Look, mate. I haven't got all day.'

Alex sighed and placed the spanner on the ground. Taking her weight on her elbows, she wriggled out from under the car and got to her feet. This was the moment when she should have shaken out her long blond hair to cascade in slow motion around her beautiful face; then stretched her shoulders to show off her spectacular bosom. The surprise on the man's face would turn to shock with a touch of lust. The problem was . . . her hair wasn't blond. It was a particularly bright shade of copper better known as orange, and it only just touched her shoulders. No one had ever called her breasts spect- acular, and lust was not an expression she was used to seeing on men's faces; certainly not when she was wearing dark blue grease-stained overalls.

She simply raised one eyebrow. 'Were you talking to

me . . . mate?' she said, slowly and deliberately.

The harassed official shook his head in disgust.

'Damn, I have to speak to the driver. Alex Reilly. Is he about?'

It happened so often, she really couldn't be bothered getting annoyed any more.

'I'm Alex Reilly,' she said.

The official's face duly registered an appropriate amount of surprise. He looked from her face to the papers in his hand, then shrugged.

'Okay. You need to have the car ready for scrutineering by nine thirty tomorrow morning.'

'Tomorrow morning?' It was Alex's turn to be surprised. 'I thought I had until late afternoon.'

'We're starting early. If there's a problem, talk to the chief steward.' He thrust some papers at her and turned away, looking for his next victim.

Alex flicked through the forms. The organisers of this rally were not all that organised. That wasn't surprising. Everything was difficult the first time, and as the banner in the distance proclaimed, this was the inaugural Snowy Mountains Classic Race. She should expect a certain amount of confusion. She would just ignore it, get past it and win. Because that was what it was all about . . . winning. And if she had to have the car ready a day early, she would.

Alex ran her eyes over her car. It was beautiful. A symphony in red paint and gleaming chrome. An expert would recognise it as a 1967 Lotus Elan 26 R – one of the finest factory race cars ever built. That same expert would know that only forty-five of them had ever been made, and that Alex's gleaming machine was worth a considerable sum of money.

Anyone who wasn't an expert would simply see a low, sleek and very, very sexy red sports car.

Alex loved her car. She enjoyed the powerful throb of the engine and the rich smell of the leather seats. She adored the graceful curve of the bonnet and the taut resistance in the gear lever. But most of all, she simply loved the way the car made her feel when she drove hard and fast, with the top down and the wind in her hair.

She pulled a rag from the back pocket of her overalls and wiped her hands. Racing her lovely little car meant conforming to the rules and regulations, something she wasn't always good at. She glanced at her watch. She had to present the Lotus for inspection in less than fifteen hours. And there was still more work to do. All around her, other drivers and mechanics were carrying out similar last-minute preparations. There was some tough competition ahead of her. On either side of her were two Porsche Carreras. Behind her, a couple of very nice Alfa Romeos. She had seen at least one Ferrari and there was even an Aston Martin DB5 – the classic James Bond car. Alex guessed that every one of the other drivers had spotted her car. Even in this company, the Lotus was something special. Some of them might also have spotted her. And written her off. The race was five days and thirteen hundred kilometres of pretty wild country. This was a man's world, and no woman was going to win. At least, that was what the men thought. Alex was going to do her best to prove them wrong.

But before she could do that, she had to finish getting the car ready. She did most of the mechanics herself. There were very few people in the world she trusted, and even fewer she was willing to let near her most prized possession. But she couldn't do this alone. She did need a support team. Well, not exactly a team. There was just Mick, the mechanic. Alex had bumped into him, almost literally, three years ago, as they both looked under the bonnet of another Lotus at a car show. Their shared love of rare cars had turned into friendship, and he was the only person she allowed to work on the Lotus. His girl-friend Sarah, another car nut, was Alex's navigator. Their share of the prize money would help them finance their car restoration business and they wanted to win as badly as Alex did. Well, almost as badly. Alex hadn't seen either of them in the past hour. But if she was going to be ready for scrutineering tomorrow, she was going to need Mick's help. She slid her toolbox out of sight under the Lotus, locked the car door and set off in search of her errant mechanic.

The rally headquarters had been set up in the Canberra showgrounds, where there was ample room for cars and drivers, mechanics, officials, reporters, caterers and all the confusion of a major motoring event. The cars were parked in rows, according to their classification in the race, and most were receiving the full attention of their drivers and support crews. All the other competitors seemed to know each other, but Alex met nothing more than polite and distant nods. She wasn't a regular competitor. In fact this was her first race, but she was ready for it.

When she wasn't lying under the Lotus, Alex was a lawyer. She never walked into a courtroom unprepared. Each case required exhaustive research, which she did herself, trusting no one to do the job as well as she could. A car race was no less cut-throat than a courtroom, and Alex was equally in control here. She had checked and double-checked every detail herself. She'd learned long ago never to rely on anyone else. It was her race. Her responsibility. Her fault if anything went wrong and her victory if she won.

She finally spotted Mick hovering near the food area. His acne-scarred face was creased with concern.

'Mick!'

He jumped as if bitten. Mick was only twenty-one, but he was a pretty steady character, not given to nervousness. Something was bothering him.

'Oh. Hi, Alex,' he said.

'Where's Sarah?'

He waved a hand in the direction of the ladies' bathroom. 'She's still feeling sick.'

'God. I hope she's not coming down with something,' Alex said. Sarah had been ill that morning as well.

'Me too.' Mick looked worried.

'Well, here's some real bad news,' Alex said. 'We have to be ready for scrutineering early tomorrow morning.'

'Shit!'

Alex raised an eyebrow. The vehement exclamation was not characteristic of her mild-mannered friend.

'They moved the inspection forward?' Mick asked.

'Yes. I've fixed that exhaust bracket, but I want to have another look at the brakes.'

Mick didn't answer. His eyes were on Sarah, who had just emerged from the bathroom. In a flash he was at her side.

'Are you all right?' Alex asked. 'You look terrible.'

'I . . . I think I should go to the doctor,' Sarah said hesitantly.

She certainly looked like she needed a doctor. Her face was very pale and her hands were shaking. Alex fought down her exasperation. Sarah wasn't being ill on purpose, but she certainly could have picked a better time.

'Go,' she said. 'Mick and I will work on the car.'

'I'll come with you, Sarah,' Mick said. 'You don't look like you should go on your own.'

Alex opened her mouth to protest that she needed Mick. But then she looked at Sarah again. The girl's brown eyes were bright with tears. Mick was right. Alex could take care of the car. She needed to be certain her navigator was going to be all right.

'Go, both of you,' she said. 'Let me know what the doctor says.'

They left, Mick putting a protective arm around Sarah's shoulders as he led her through the crowd. Alex felt a fleeting pang. No one did that for her. Of course, she told herself, she didn't need anyone to look after her. She had always looked after herself.

The enticing smell of coffee wafted past her, and she set out in search of some caffeine before she had to get back under the Lotus. She had just procured a large cup when she noticed a media gaggle among the car lines. Intrigued, she walked over.

The woman at the centre of the spotlight was tall and blonde and beautiful. Like Alex, she was wearing blue overalls, but hers seemed to have been designer-made. They fitted like a couture gown, outlining her slender body. Among the grease-stained mechanics and rumpled drivers, she stood out like a thoroughbred among carthorses. Alex had a feeling this woman would look amazing whatever she wore. Something about her was vaguely familiar.

'Lyn! Look this way,' a photographer called.

Lyn? Alex suddenly understood the media interest. The woman was Lyn Stanton, supermodel. No wonder she looked familiar. Alex must have seen her face in dozens of magazines and television ads. In the flesh, she was just as stunning as in her photos. Alex felt her hackles rising. Lyn Stanton was everything Alex was not. It wasn't just that she was tall and blonde and beautiful; she was also perfectly made up. Not one of those long blond hairs was out of place. Somehow, in what was effectively a huge garage, she was completely clean. From the tips of her bright red fingernails to the toes of her immaculate black boots, not so much as a smear of grease marred her perfection. She looked like she had just stepped off a catwalk.

By contrast, Alex looked, and felt, like a grease monkey.

Alex almost snorted. Looking like Lyn Stanton was all well and good, but she would bet good money the girl couldn't even change a tyre, much less tune an engine. Not that she would ever have to. When you were paid the sort of money Lyn got just to walk around looking good, you hired someone else to do the mucky bits. Someone else to do everything ... including the thinking, Alex added grumpily to herself. Lyn was the classic blonde bimbo. She probably had an IQ in single digits. And now she was holding centre stage – as she no doubt always did. Not that Alex cared. She had no great love for reporters. She certainly didn't want them bothering her. But she had expected to be the only female driver in the race ...

'Lyn, can you get on the bonnet?' one of the photographers shouted.

Lyn obliged, draping her long limbs across the gleaming paintwork of a Ferrari Dino, while camera flashes exploded around her. She moved gracefully from one pose to another. Alex frowned. That was no way to treat a car. Certainly not a Ferrari. A car like that deserved respect.

'Where's your lucky driver?' a reporter yelled.

So that was it, Alex smiled grimly. The supermodel wasn't driving. She was a navigator. It was probably just some sort of publicity stunt. Still, a navigator's job was demanding. They had to think fast and react fast. To win a tough race, even the best driver needed a good navigator. Alex certainly wouldn't want someone like Lyn Stanton sitting beside her.

'Oh, he's around here somewhere.' Lyn's voice was unexpected. Low and soft. Alex had expected something more . . . girlie.

'How do you think the two of you will do in the race?'

'We'll be great,' the model smiled. 'He'll just have to get used to handling a different kind of horsepower.'

The reporters laughed. Alex guessed it was a joke that she didn't understand.

'So, when are we going to meet him?' another reporter said. 'Maybe he got lost without you to give him directions.'

'I don't get lost that easily.' The deep male voice came from just behind Alex.

She froze. Her breath caught in her throat and her gut clenched.

No! Please God. No.

She felt movement in the crowd. The reporters and cameramen were all turning towards her. No – they were looking at the man who was standing just behind her.

It couldn't be. Not here. Not now. Not ever. Please.

'Excuse me.'

He was so close; she felt his breath on her skin as he

spoke – as she had done so many times before. His voice was deeper and richer, but unmistakable.

Keeping her head averted and her eyes on the ground, Alex took a step sideways. She felt him next to her – not a memory this time, but tall and solid. He began to move past, then something made him stop. She could see his boots as he turned towards her.

The world around them shrank to just two people. The hubbub of noise faded and everything dimmed. Knowing the whole world was about to change, Alex slowly raised her eyes and turned her head.

Deep brown eyes met hers and the coffee cup slipped from her frozen fingers.

In the gentle darkness of the night, Alex ran her hands lovingly around the gleaming steering wheel. Like any kid brought up in the outback, she'd been driving farm vehicles since her legs were long enough to reach the accelerator. The big Jaguar was something entirely different. She could hear the subdued purring of the powerful engine as it waited her touch to roar into life. The rich scent of fine leather filled her nostrils, and her heart pounded with the excitement of doing something forbidden.

She had stopped the Jag just inside the wide gateway that marked the border of her father's empire. This side of the gate, she was Alexandra Reilly. The boss's daughter, a princess and untouchable. On the other side of the gate, she would be just a sixteen-year-old school kid joyriding in her father's car. Unlicensed. Illegal. And in real trouble if she was caught.

But she wouldn't be caught. Her father had been called away on another business trip. Her mother was on one of her regular shopping expeditions to the city, and wouldn't be back until the end of the week. None of the staff at the big house would rat on her. There was more danger of being spotted by one of the 'plant workers', as her mother called the employees at the abattoir, or by one of the stockmen who worked at the huge cattle feed lot. But it was dark now. The feed lot and the meat-packing plant had closed for the day. The workers had all gone home long ago. She wasn't going to get caught.

She pressed gently on the accelerator. The engine responded instantly, the soft purr turned to a low throaty growl and the wheel under her hands began to vibrate gently with suppressed power. Alex closed her eyes. God, how she loved this car! It was beauty. It was speed and power. It was escape. She pressed the clutch to the floor, and reached out for the gear shift. Even with her eyes shut, her hand found its way unerringly to the right place. Her fingers closed around the lever, and she slid it easily into first gear. All she need do now was drop the clutch, and all that power would be unleashed and at her command. She opened her eyes.

He was standing about a metre in front of the car, watching her.

'What . . . ?'

Alex threw the gear shift into neutral and lifted her foot from the accelerator. The engine noise dropped instantly. She gripped the steering wheel firmly with both hands. She had been so close to . . . Another second and the car would have leaped forward right over the top of him.

He was still standing in front of the car, as if the danger had never even occurred to him.

She had never seen him before. He must be one of her father's stockmen. He was young, but he had the look of a man who worked hard for his living, and spent a lot of time on horseback. His jeans were faded to a pale blue, and fitted him like a second skin. So too did the T-shirt. He was lean and fit and held himself with an easy, almost graceful assurance. He couldn't be more than a year older than her. A wide-brimmed hat was tipped back to reveal a slight smile on his lips. He was looking through the windscreen straight at her. He wasn't handsome. His face was too strong, too rough for that. But something about him made her heart pound. Or maybe it was just the realisation that she could have killed him.

After an eternity, his eyes moved away from her, taking in the lines of the Jaguar. A slow step brought him right to the front of the car. He reached out his hand, but didn't touch the metal. He moved slowly towards the driver's door, his fingers a breath away from brushing the object of his attention. He caressed the gleaming dark blue paint without touching it. He worshipped it without leaving a flaw on its perfection.

Alex watched his hand, mesmerised as it moved closer to her up the long, elegant slope of the bonnet. It was a strong hand for one so young. The skin had been burned a deep brown by the sun. She knew his palm would bear the calluses of many hours of hard work. The long fingers would be firm and strong.

He stopped moving. Alex forced herself to breathe again as he leaned down to look in the window.

His eyes were the colour of chocolate.

'Nice car.'

'. . . Alex?' The voice that called her back to the present was the same, but not the same. 'I said – nice car.'

He had found her. Of course he had. After dropping the half-full cup of coffee at his feet, she had fled before he could speak to her. Before she had to speak to him. Instinctively she had returned to her car. She was safe there. She was always in control when she was behind the wheel. Disturbing images from the past could be pushed to the back of her mind. She had tried to lose herself in a close examination of the engine. Tried to focus on the present and on the near future. It hadn't worked. The past had come looking for her.

She dropped the polishing cloth on the bonnet of the car, and turned slowly.

The compelling boy had grown into a handsome man. He was much taller now. Solid. The defensive, almost arrogant tilt of the head had been replaced by strength and confidence. He was wearing a set of race overalls, no doubt for his press call. They were tight-fitting, as race clothes had to be, revealing a trim waist and hips, and broad shoulders. He was clean-shaven. His black hair, though, was quite long, with just a slight hint of early grey at the temple. That curl still fell over one eye. It was all she could do not to reach out and push it aside as she had done a hundred times before. But that was a long time ago.

For a few seconds she felt she would lose herself in the dark velvet of his eyes. She swayed away from him, feeling the comforting solidity of the car behind her.

'Kier. It's been a while.' The tremor was barely audible.

'Yes. It has.' His voice was deeper than it had been when they were teenagers. It was the touch of suede and the scent of a log fire on a cold rainy night.

He was too close to her. The force of his presence wrapped around her, holding her to him as if he held her in his arms.

'The Lotus – you finally did it.'

Kier had been the only person she had ever trusted

with her dream. She was the tomboy daughter of a father who wanted a son to follow in his footsteps and a mother who longed for a debutante to follow in hers. Kier Thomas worked for her father. He was a kid from the wrong side of the tracks. He knew about being an outsider. He knew about disappointment and fear and longing.

'I found her a few years ago.' The last thing Alex wanted was to talk about her car.

'She's beautiful.' He wasn't looking at the car. His dark eyes had not left hers for a second.

How many years? How many lost dreams and regrets? How many tears?

'Thank you,' she said.

'I guess we're competitors,' he said.

'I guess we are. You're driving the Ferrari?' She didn't know why she asked. She already knew he was.

'Yes.'

'I didn't think you were that keen on Ferraris. You used to be a Jaguar fan.'

'I've always liked these.' He touched the Jaguar at last, gently stroking the shining metal below the open window. 'They're mean and fast and yet they've got real class.'

She shouldn't be talking to him. She shouldn't be feeling as if he was touching her, not the car. And she certainly should not let him get any closer.

'Do you want to come for a ride?'

'Depends.'

'On what?' She held her breath, suddenly aware that if he said no, her heart would break.

'Do you know how to drive a car like this? I mean really drive it?'

'Why don't you hop in and find out . . .'

*

'Why aren't you driving a Jag?' It wasn't what she wanted to ask. But she would never, never ask him the question that she had asked herself a million times during the long dark nights.

'I'm doing this as a charity fund-raiser,' he said. 'The sponsor has donated the car. It's going to be raffled off after the race. That's why I need to win. If I do, it's more money for the kids.'

'And your navigator?' She was proud of the fact that she didn't sound jealous. Of course she wasn't jealous of that supermodel. Not one bit.

'Lyn's got sponsors too.'

The conversation stopped. Kier's eyes turned back towards the Lotus. They moved over the car, and then came back to Alex.

'You look great,' he said.

She didn't. She looked like someone who had just spent the day lying under a car fixing the exhaust. He, on the other hand, really did look great – handsome, confident and far more in control of himself than she was. Obviously, she was the only one finding this encounter difficult.

'Alex, I was wondering—'

'Alex!' an excited voice called from a few metres away.

She turned gratefully towards the interruption. Mick and Sarah were approaching, arm in arm.

'Alex!' Mick was almost bouncing as he joined the two of them. 'Alex, it's—' He stopped as if realising for the first time that they weren't alone.

'Mick. Sarah. This is Kier Thomas,' Alex said, her voice admirably free of any quiver. 'He's racing a Ferrari Dino.' It was as good an introduction as she was likely to manage.

'Hi.' Mick shook Kier's hand as if he was going to pull his arm off. Even in her current state of confusion, Alex knew something was up.

'Mick, what's wrong?'

'Ah . . .' Mick looked pointedly at Kier.

'I should go.' Kier took the hint. 'I've got a few things to do.' He smiled down at Alex again. 'It was . . . good to see you, Alex. I'm sure we'll be running into each other over the next few days.'

'I guess we will.'

'And good luck in the race.' He nodded to Mick and Sarah, turned on his heel and walked away.

Alex watched him go. She had always loved to watch him move. He had an easy grace about him that was totally masculine.

'I hope we didn't interrupt—' Sarah began, looking at Kier's departing back with one raised eyebrow.

'You didn't,' Alex said shortly. Kier had vanished into the crowd.

'We just have to tell you our news.' Mick threw an arm around Sarah's shoulders and pulled her close to him.

'News?' Alex forced her mind back to the conversation. 'What did the doctor say? Are you all right?'

'Oh yes, better than all right.' The answer bubbled out of Mick and he and Sarah exchanged a meaningful look. 'We're pregnant!' he announced, his face glowing with excitement and pride.

'Pregnant?' Alex blinked.

'Pregnant,' Mick almost shouted.

'Mick,' Sarah pleaded. 'You don't have to shout.'

'Oh yes I do,' Mick bounced a little more. 'I want to shout it from the rooftops.'

Sarah blushed a little and smiled up at him. For a few

seconds, the two of them were enveloped in a cloud of happiness that excluded Alex. That excluded the whole world. Alex had known that sort of happiness once. She managed not to look across at the spot where Kier had disappeared.

'That's good news,' she said. 'I'm really happy for you.'

She was too. This pregnancy might have come a little earlier than Mick and Sarah had expected, but she knew they both wanted a large family.

'Thanks,' Sarah said.

'But there is a bit of a problem.' Mick's face became more serious. 'Sarah can't race.'

'Can't race?'

'Alex, the doctor was very firm on this,' Mick said. 'Everything is all right, but he's worried that her blood pressure is too high. He said she can't race.'

Alex opened her mouth, but the words wouldn't come.

'Oh Alex, I am so sorry.' Sarah looked crestfallen.

'No. No. Don't be,' Alex hastened to assure her. This was an important day for Sarah and Mick, and she wasn't going to be the one to spoil their happiness. 'It's fine. This is more important than the race.'

'I feel like I've let you down.' Sarah still looked subdued.

'Don't.' Alex gave her friend a hug. 'I'm happy for you. I'm just sorry that you'll miss out on the prize money. It would be even more useful now.'

'That doesn't matter.' Mick was standing about ten feet tall. 'We'll work something out.'

Alex remembered that feeling. When you were in love, the whole world was at your feet and anything was possible. She just hoped that Sarah and Mick would hold that feeling for longer than she had.

'We'll stay with you,' Mick added. 'I can still help you with the race. You might be able to find another navigator. Maybe I can . . .'

'No. You are a great mechanic, Mick, but we both know you're not a navigator.' She smiled to soften the words, knowing they were both thinking the same thing – that rally driving was dangerous and it wouldn't do Sarah any good to worry about Mick out on the course.

'You go home. Tell your families. Enjoy the moment.' Although she meant it, every word was a death knell to her dream.

'Our families!' Sarah's face lit up. 'Mick, I want to call Mum. I can't wait to tell her.'

Mick flashed Alex an anxious look.

'It's fine,' Alex assured him. 'Go. I'll talk to you again before you leave. And by the way, congratulations.'

Left alone, her disappointment was almost a physical pain. She would never find a new navigator. One who knew this race and this course. That just wasn't going to happen three days before the start of the race. She had to withdraw. She sighed. Well, at least that solved the problem of Kier. If she went home, she wouldn't have to see him again. Wouldn't have to fight against feelings she thought she had buried a long time ago. Maybe giving up the race was the best thing she could do.

She turned back to her car, and ran her hand lovingly over the gleaming red paint. For once, she didn't feel comforted.

'Sorry,' she whispered.

The headlights tunnelled into the darkness. Kier swiftly changed down a gear and the engine roared as the Ferrari took the corner fast and tight. As he straightened the wheel, he felt the tension beginning to ease from his shoulders. This test drive was more for his benefit than the car's. The Ferrari was ready to race. He had thought he was too, until he'd found himself looking down into Alex's startled face.

Alex. Of all the car rallies in all the world . . .

The road ahead began to climb a small rise. Kier pushed harder on the accelerator, knowing as he did so that it was foolish. He shouldn't be driving this fast on roads he didn't know. But how he loved driving like this – hard and fast. Alone in the darkness.

He hadn't always been alone . . .

The white lines blurred as the Jaguar raced down the highway. Kier darted a quick look at the girl in the seat beside him. She really did know how to drive, revving the big V12 engine until it was almost screaming, before quickly and confidently changing up through the gears. Her hands gripped the steering wheel easily – firm but not too tight. Despite the fact that her feet barely reached the pedals, she was very much in control and he had a feeling she liked it that way.

'I'm impressed,' he said.

'I thought you would be.' She flashed him a sideways glance.

'The car's not bad either.'

She chuckled, a light, joyous sound that wrapped itself around his heart. 'By the way, I'm Alex.'

He knew who she was. Everyone knew the boss's daughter. But she didn't know who he was. She didn't know his name, much less where he had come from. Yet she had let him into the car. She had trusted him. That didn't happen often to someone like him. It felt pretty good.

'I'm Kier.'

He hit the button to lower the electric window, feeling the wind come rushing in. Alex did the same.

'I wish this came as a soft top,' Alex yelled over the wind noise. 'Driving at this speed with the top down would be really something.'

She was really something, he thought as he glanced at the dashboard. Little things like the speed limit obviously didn't bother her one bit. Although at the speed they were travelling, a police car was the least of their worries. If they hit a 'roo or blew a tyre, they'd be dead. He wondered if that thought had ever occurred to Alex. She seemed totally without fear. Did that come from being rich, or was it her own special gift?

He turned his face back toward the windscreen, where the towering gum trees were just momentary shapes, dark on dark, flying past at the edge of the lights. A distant glow announced an oncoming vehicle, and Alex eased back on the accelerator. He could almost feel her disappointment.

She had the car back within the speed limit by the time the oncoming car passed them, its red tail lights appearing seconds later in the rear-view mirror.

'I don't want to get busted,' she said by way of explanation.

'I take it you don't have a licence?'

'Not exactly. And Dad would ground me for life if he ever found out about this.'

'I'm betting this isn't the first time,' Kier said.

She shrugged her shoulders. 'If you want something, you should just go for it. There's not much point only doing the easy things.'

'There speaks a rich girl.' The words were out before Kier could stop them.

Alex slammed her foot down on the brake.

'Hey!' Kier grabbed for the dashboard as he was flung forward.

The tyres screeched as the big car began to slide sideways. Beside him, Alex fought to keep the car under control. Finally it came to rest, angled across the road, the headlights pointing out into the scrub.

'Don't ever call me that.' Alex turned on him. He could barely see her face in the dim light, but he could feel her anger. 'My father is rich. I'm not. And when I am, it will be my money, not his.'

'Sorry.' So, he thought, she has a temper to match her hair.

They sat in the darkness for what seemed a long time. He could hear her breathing. She was still looking at him, but in the darkness he couldn't read her expression.

'What were you doing outside my gate this late at night, Kier?'

The change of subject caught him by surprise, but it

was a reasonable question. The entrance to Tom Reilly's kingdom was well removed from the white-painted wooden houses where his workers lived.

'I was out for a walk,' Kier said. He hoped it would satisfy her, because he wasn't going to tell her the real reason.

'Well, be careful what you say or you'll have a long walk home.'

She turned her face towards the windscreen again and slipped the Jag back into gear. Just as she edged it forward, a sudden flurry of movement erupted beside the car. Three large kangaroos appeared, quickly passing through the beam of the headlights across the road back into the darkness of the bush. Kier had a sudden thought that his intemperate remark had just saved them from a nasty accident. He wondered if the same thought had occurred to Alex. She drove far more sedately as she turned back the way they had come. Of course, her idea of sedate would have caused a traffic cop to reach for his ticket book.

A flash of movement in the far corner of the headlights dragged Kier back to the present.

'Shit!'

He hit the brakes. With a squeal of tyres, the red Ferrari began to slow down. But it wasn't going to be enough. Instinct took over. Kier eased back on the brakes and flung the car to the other side of the road. He missed the first kangaroo, but his control over the vehicle was gone. The second 'roo was in mid-air, leaping away, when the Ferrari caught it a glancing blow. That was the beginning of the end. Kier didn't dare let go of the steering wheel. He could only hope the car wouldn't flip as it slid sideways off the bitumen road into the wide gravel verge.

He was sliding into a stand of young gum trees. He had just enough time to notice how thin the trunks were as he hit the first. There was the scream of tearing metal, and a sharp snap, like a gunshot, as the tree trunk shattered. He released the steering wheel and raised his arms to protect his face and head as the windscreen exploded inwards. All around him was the grinding of metal and the crashing of timber. Kier was thrown forward, his seatbelt snapping tight against his chest. The world was noise and pain for what seemed a very long time.

Then it was suddenly very, very quiet.

Instinctively Kier reached out to turn the engine off, but it wasn't necessary. The car had already stalled. His hands were shaking as he lowered them and looked about him. One headlight had miraculously remained intact, serving only to highlight the damage done. He was covered in fragments of glass from the windscreen and splinters of timber from the trees. The front of the car was twisted and torn from the impact. The bonnet was badly dented, one windscreen wiper sticking out at a crazy angle. The car had spun around as it crashed into the scrub and appeared to be facing back the way it had come. Broken gum trees showed the path it had taken. Kier felt something touch his face. Instinctively he wiped his fingers over his right cheek. They came away damp and sticky with blood. There was blood trickling down his left arm too, on to the leather seat of the Ferrari. He ignored the urge to wipe it away. Any movement brought an accompanying flash of pain. He did, however, hold both hands in front of his face. Illuminated by the glow from the dash, he wiggled his fingers. They hurt – but they worked. That small achievement seemed to steady his thoughts.

He had to get out of the car. His hands were shaking

as he reached down to release the seatbelt. The Ferrari was a race car, with a racing harness instead of a normal belt. The extra straps across his hips and chest might just have saved his life, but they were very difficult to undo with fingers that seemed to have lost all their strength. He struggled with the belt for a few seconds before it let go. Cautiously he tried to move his legs. They too were shaky, but there was no serious pain. He had a feeling that was going to change over the next few hours, as abused muscles began to stiffen and the bruises started to show. Kier grabbed the handle and tried to open the door. It moved a few inches and stopped. He guessed it was badly buckled. He'd have to use the passenger door. The seat beside him was covered with glass and broken bits of gum tree. He pushed the largest bits on to the floor, and moved cautiously toward the door. He tried the handle, willing it to open. For a few seconds, it didn't move. He pushed harder, and with a groan of tortured metal, the door swung open. He pulled himself out of the car and stepped away, then leaned against a nearby tree and took several deep breaths.

When his legs had stopped shaking, he turned to look at the Ferrari.

'Shit!'

The sports car was not going to line up at the race start in three days' time. In fact, it was entirely possible it might never be driven again. Not a single panel was intact. One wing was torn away, a jagged edge of metal revealing a tyre that must have blown as the car slid into the scrub. The front of the car had been crushed. He had no way of knowing how badly damaged the engine was. The exhaust would probably have been wrenched off. As for the suspension . . .

Kier gave up thinking about the car's injuries. His own were starting to make themselves felt. The blood on his left hand came from a long gash on his forearm. It was still bleeding. He pulled his shirt off and wrapped it around the injury. Considering what he had just been through, he seemed to have relatively few cuts, but his body felt as if he'd been run over by a bulldozer. He knew that within a few hours, he'd be so stiff he would barely be able to drive. Not that he had anything to drive, he thought with disgust, and it was his own stupid fault.

He looked up and down the dark road. Nothing. No distant lights offered hope of assistance.

For some reason he reached into the car to turn off the one remaining headlight, before he walked away. As he did, he noticed the deep gashes in the passenger seat. One of the splintered tree branches had speared though the windscreen and torn the leather to shreds. He was suddenly very thankful that his bad mood had caused him to take this test drive alone. The thought of what might have happened to Lyn had she been sitting next to him . . .

He turned away from the car and picked his way through the shattered stand of gums, back towards the road. He looked around, but saw no sign of the animal he had hit. That wasn't surprising. It was very dark. The kangaroo was probably injured and had fled into the thick scrub. There was nothing he could do to help it. His problem now was to help himself. He might not be badly hurt, but he guessed shock might start to set in soon. At this time of the year, overnight temperatures were starting to drop. The last thing he needed was a night in the open. He was reaching into his pocket for his mobile phone when he remembered leaving it back in his motel room, charging.

He turned slowly around, and looked at the road again. Still no lights. This wasn't exactly a freeway.

'Well, I guess I'd better start walking.' He said the words out loud to give himself the impetus he needed to start.

Cradling his injured hand against his chest, he set off back the way he had come.

What had he been thinking, driving that fast on a country road late at night? He'd spent enough years driving in the bush to know better than that. It was never a question of if a kangaroo would jump in front of the car – only of when it would happen. He was lucky he wasn't dead. Had it happened on a bend, he probably would be. He hadn't done anything this stupid for a long time. He wasn't a reckless kid any more. He was a man who should have more sense. Who had believed he did – until he saw Alex.

She was still the wild and beautiful girl who had captivated him all those years ago. But something in her eyes was different. She was wary. Defensive. Was that his fault? A sense of guilt crept coldly around his heart, as familiar as the voice of an old friend. He should have left that guilt behind years ago. He was a kid back then. Far too young to be forced into those decisions. The man still regretted what the boy had done, but there was no going back. They weren't kids any more. He had irreparably changed all their lives. He'd learned to live with the guilt, and made something of himself. How much, he wondered, had Alex changed in the past twelve years? How had she coped with the pain?

And speaking of pain . . . Kier was finding it very hard to stay upright. His body protested at every step he took. More than anything, he wanted to stop walking and sit down. He didn't, because once he stopped, he might not get going again. He kept his eyes fixed on the road and forced himself to take the next step . . . and the next. With each one, he was closer to help.

He pulled a handkerchief out of his pocket, to wipe the blood and sweat from his face. As he did, his wallet dropped on to the roadway. Carefully, he bent down to retrieve it and saw that it had fallen open. In the moonlight, he could see the dark-haired child smiling up at him from the photo he always carried. He touched it briefly, then realised he had left a bloody smear on the clear plastic covering of the photo. As he used a corner of his shirt to wipe it off, his hand started to shake again with the renewed realisation of what might have happened. It wasn't just his own life he had to think about. He closed the wallet and carefully put it back in his pocket. Then he took another step. And another.

He had long since given up looking for cars when a flash in the distance caught his eye.

'Thank you, God!'

He didn't think he could have walked much further.

He stopped forcing his feet forward. He stood at the side of the road and waited for the lights. The car seemed to take a very long time to reach him. When it did, it was a blue Alfa Romeo. The large number 71 displayed on the door identified it as another rally competitor. As it stopped near him, he searched his mind for the marque and year. He thought it might be an early sixties Giulia, but he wasn't sure. It suddenly became very important that he should be able to identify the car. He didn't know why.

'Are you all right?' The driver was a bearded man. He sounded concerned. Kier decided he must look as bad as he felt.

'I could use some help.'

The driver was out of the car in an instant. He put a hand on Kier's shoulder as if to steady him. Kier didn't understand why. He was fine. He really was.

'Okay, mate. Let's get you to the car.'

'Yeah. I think I should sit down.' Kier was suddenly deathly tired.

The older man guided him to the passenger door, opened it and hovered next to Kier as he slid into the passenger seat.

'Wait there a minute.'

Kier wasn't going anywhere. He heard the driver retrieve something from the boot.

'Close your eyes for a second.'

Kier complied with the instruction. Even through his closed lids, he could see the flare of bright light.

'All right, look at me.'

The Alfa driver was crouched next to the car, an open black bag at his feet. He was holding a torch. Kier blinked as his eyes adjusted.

'Follow my finger,' the other man instructed, holding his hand up in front of Kier. Kier did as he was told.

'What's your name?'

'Kier. Kier Thomas.'

'What happened?' As the man spoke, he was searching in his bag for something.

'I crashed my damn car.'

'Was there anyone with you?'

'No. I was alone,' Kier told him.

'All right. You've got a nasty cut on your forehead. I'm just going to put a dressing on it.'

'Are you a doctor?'

'I am. Paul White. Now, let me take a look at that arm.'

Kier winced as Paul replaced the bloody shirt wrapped around Kier's arm with a clean white dressing then sat back on his haunches. 'I think you'll live. I'd better get you back to town.'

'Thanks.'

Kier looked for a seatbelt. He tried to buckle it, but with only one hand, he didn't have a hope. His rescuer did it for him.

'This is a race car,' Kier said hesitantly.

'That's right. Lucky for you I came out here for a bit of a run.' Paul fastened his own belt. In a few seconds he had the car turned around and was driving back the way he had come. As they crested the next hill, Kier saw the lights of Canberra some way in the distance.

'I wouldn't have made it,' he said. 'Thanks for picking me up.'

'No worries.' Paul cast a quick sideways glance at him. 'We'll be back soon. I can take you to the hospital.'

'No. Take me back to the showgrounds,' Kier told him.

'No way. You need to get those injuries properly seen to. You might need an X-ray. You need to be in hospital, not at a car rally.'

'I'm fine,' Kier lied.

'I don't know about that.' Paul hesitated. 'All right. There's an ambulance station at the showgrounds. The doctor on duty there can stitch the cuts. But if there aren't proper dressings on those wounds next time I see you, I'm going to drag you off to get it done.'

'Okay,' Kier agreed, sensing that underneath the smile, Paul was deadly serious.

Paul seemed content with that. 'You're the guy with the red Ferrari?' he asked.

'I was.' Kier grimaced.

'Damn! How bad?'

'Put it this way, you won't be facing any competition from me this year.'

'Sorry to hear that.' Paul said. 'That was a really nice car. What happened?'

'Kangaroo.' Talking was suddenly too much of an effort. Kier leaned back into the seat and closed his eyes. Paul took the hint and fell silent, and Kier spent the last few kilometres of the journey wondering if a kangaroo really had caused the crash, or if a woman with green eyes to die for had been his undoing . . . again.

'What the hell happened to you?' Lyn's heart contracted in shock as Kier almost staggered into the empty parking slot that should have contained the Ferrari. She looked him up and down. He was shirtless, and small cuts and bloodstains covered his chest and shoulders. A dressing on his arm was dark with blood. He had a smaller dressing on his forehead, also stained dull red. He looked like hell. The crews working on the nearby cars stopped and turned their way.

'Lyn. I'm sorry. I had an accident.' Kier looked unsteady on his feet.

'Are you all right?' She raised a hand as if to help him, then realised there was nothing she could do. There wasn't even anywhere for him to sit.

'Yeah. I look worse than I am.'

'I should hope so.' She wasn't convinced. 'What happened?'

'Kangaroo.'

Lyn's heart sank. This didn't sound good. 'The car?'

Kier shook his head, wincing a little with the pain.

'Damn it!' She closed her eyes and turned her head

away, fighting back a mixture of concern, anger and disappointment.

'Thanks for the ride,' Kier said to someone she couldn't see.

'You're welcome. If there's anything I can do, just let me know,' replied a pleasant deep voice.

Lyn turned her attention to Kier's companion. He was one of the few people around not wearing overalls. He was dressed in faded blue jeans and a white cotton shirt that appeared to be stained with Kier's blood in several places. She guessed he was in his late thirties, with grey liberally scattered through his hair and full beard.

'I'm sorry,' she said. 'I didn't mean to be rude.'

'It's fine. I understand.' The man smiled at her. It was an open smile, with not a trace of subterfuge or deception. 'I'm Paul White.'

'Lyn Stanton,' she said, holding out her hand.

He shook it, without the wandering gaze that she usually met. It was as if he hadn't noticed that she was a model at least an inch taller than he was. His eyes were hazel, and were as open and friendly as his smile.

'I'm sorry you won't be racing,' he said. 'I was looking forward to going up against the Ferrari.'

Lyn shrugged. She really didn't trust herself to speak. This race was important to her, and the thought of being forced out of it was almost enough to drive her to tears.

'You should go to the ambulance station,' Paul said to Kier as he turned away.

'Thanks again.' Kier's voice didn't sound too strong.

'He's right, you know,' Lyn said. 'You need medical attention. Come on.'

'I'm sorry, Lyn,' Kier said again as he let her lead him

down the lines of parked cars. They attracted more than a few curious glances.

'Our sponsor is going to be pretty upset when he hears what happened to his car.' She didn't trust herself to say anything more. If she did, she might say something she would regret. Like tell him he was a bloody idiot.

Kier didn't say anything. Lyn cast a quick look sideways. He wasn't in any fit state for conversation. She said nothing more as they walked to the ambulance station. She deposited Kier in the capable hands of the ambulance crew and set out towards the stewards' office. She needed to advise them of what had happened. And withdraw from the race.

Damn it!

Her steps dragged. An image of a young girl in a wheelchair filled her mind. And the tired face of a mother weighed down with a burden almost too heavy to bear. Lyn fought back her regret and kept walking.

The stewards' office was in one of the showground pavilions. People were clustered about, reading notices and talking about cars, rallies and drivers. Lyn nodded to a couple of them, but walked straight past to the far corner of the room, where the chief steward resided. She would talk to him first, then speak to someone about recovering the wreckage of the Ferrari. The call to the sponsor she would leave to Kier. The last call would be the most difficult, and that one was for her alone.

Another woman was already talking to the steward. Lyn stood politely back for her to finish her business. She was so wrapped up in her own thoughts, it took a few minutes for the conversation at the desk to filter through to her.

'. . . have to withdraw.'

So, she and Kier weren't the only ones who wouldn't be making the starting line. Lyn took a closer look at the woman at the desk. It must be Alex Reilly, the only woman driver in the race. Lyn had seen her photo in the press kit. She didn't have Lyn and Kier's celebrity status, but a woman driver was always noticed.

'There is time for you to nominate another navigator,' the steward said.

That made Lyn listen more closely. Maybe she wouldn't have to make that phone call.

'I'll never find a navigator at this late stage,' Alex said. 'I'm out.'

'Wait a minute.' Lyn stepped forward.

Alex turned to look up at her with cold eyes. 'Sorry?'

'I didn't mean to eavesdrop, but I couldn't help overhearing what you were saying. Don't withdraw yet. We need to talk.'

'What about?' Alex was a good half a head shorter than Lyn, but she had a really lovely face and great eyes. As a model, Lyn knew real beauty when she saw it, even if it was hidden under a bit of grease and a lot of disappointment and anger.

'Just give me a minute, will you?' Lyn said.

The other woman nodded reluctantly.

Lyn turned to the steward. 'I've got a definite withdrawal for you. Car number forty-six. Ferrari. Thomas and Stanton. We're out.'

'Reason?' the steward said, as his eyes wandered over Lyn's figure.

'The car's damaged,' she said. 'My idiot driver managed to write it off this evening.'

A sharp intake of breath dragged her eyes back to Alex.

'What happened? Is Kier all right?'

'Do you know Kier?'

'I . . . did. It was a long time ago. Is he all right?' Alex's voice was taut with concern.

'He's a bit battered, but he's in far better shape than our car.' Lyn watched the relief spread over Alex's face. 'He was out on a test run. I don't know the details, but I gather there was a 'roo involved.'

'Oh!'

The woman's reaction told Lyn there was definitely a story there. 'He's at the ambulance station,' she said. 'A few cuts. I should imagine he's pretty bruised. His ego not the least of all.'

Lyn saw relief flash across Alex's face. 'So,' she continued before Alex could speak, 'I've got a proposal. I'm a navigator without a car or a driver. You're a driver with a car and no navigator. Why don't we join forces?'

'What?' Alex's forehead creased with surprise.

'Join forces. The two of us could make a team.'

'I don't think so . . .'

'Can't we at least talk it through? What have you got to lose?' Lyn hoped she didn't sound too desperate.

There was a few seconds' pause. 'All right.'

'Don't write her out yet,' Lyn instructed the steward. 'We'll be back.'

The far end of the pavilion was lined with eateries providing hot food and, more importantly, hot coffee for the dozens of people working through the night on the rally cars. Lyn and Alex bought some indifferent coffee and found an unoccupied plastic table and chairs.

'So?' Alex asked.

'You've lost your navigator?' Lyn asked.

'She found out today that she's pregnant,' Alex told

her. 'That's good news for her and her boyfriend. He is . . . he was my support and mechanic. But it's not such good news for me.'

'She won't race?'

'She can't. The doctor said she shouldn't. Anyway,' Alex smiled ruefully, 'I couldn't ask her to. If anything happened I would never forgive myself. They are going home tomorrow.'

'You need a new navigator, and I am a navigator,' Lyn said matter-of-factly.

'Well, yes. But . . .'

'But what? Without a navigator, you're out of the race. I'm already out. You can get us both back in. It works for both of us.'

'I don't think so.'

'Why?' Lyn demanded. 'I'm a damn good navigator.'

Alex didn't answer.

'I know what I'm doing. And I really need to race,' Lyn added.

'Why do you need to race?' Alex still sounded suspicious.

'It's a long story,' Lyn said.

'I've got nowhere to go.'

Lyn looked steadily at Alex. They were as different as it was possible for two women of similar age to be. Where Alex was short, with dark red hair, Lyn was tall and blonde. Lyn had read Alex's profile in the press kit. She was a high-powered lawyer, who probably thought a model like Lyn was just an airhead. It wouldn't be the first time Lyn had faced that sort of prejudice.

'I've been sponsored in this race,' Lyn said. 'I get so much for competing, plus the sponsors will match any prize money.'

Lyn could tell by the way Alex frowned that the woman was surprised, and just a little bit interested.

'And the money was for . . . ?' Alex asked.

Lyn took a deep breath. She could never talk about this without pain. 'It's for charity,' she said. 'I'm patron of a charity that provides care and support for children and adults with physical and mental disabilities. And for their families. My . . . my younger sister goes there.'

'Oh.'

Lyn could see the sympathy in Alex's eyes. 'Being a model helps me to raise money for them. The car was a donation. It was going to be raffled after the race.' She smiled ruefully. 'I guess that's not going to happen now.' As she said the words, Lyn felt a deep pang of regret. She felt as if she had let her little sister down. Damn it, she wasn't going to do that. She loved Lorna far too much to give up without a fight.

'The race is only three days away.' Alex might be sympathetic, but that obviously wasn't going to be enough. 'We need to get used to each other. To develop language and course notes. To drive the course together. There just isn't time.'

'We can make time,' Lyn said. 'I've driven the course. My notes are ready. We can make this work.'

'That's still not going to be enough,' Alex said. 'We don't have any support. I can do the mechanics, but we need someone else.'

'That's where Kier comes in,' Lyn replied. 'He knows what he's doing.'

'No way!' The response was instantaneous and forceful. 'There's no way I'm going to work with Kier. He is not to lay one finger on my car!'

There it was again – that tone of voice that told Lyn

there was quite a story waiting to be told. But now wasn't the time to ask. The important thing was to get Alex to agree to join forces.

'Look,' she said firmly. 'I want to race. So do you. I don't know what's between you and Kier . . . and I don't care about that. But I do care about my little sister. I care about raising this money. I want to win this race. Don't you?' She looked the other woman squarely in the face as she issued the challenge.

Alex held her gaze for a few seconds, then took a long drink from her coffee. 'I still don't think we'll have enough time to prepare. To get used to each other's way of racing.'

'We'll make time. We can start tomorrow.'

Alex shook her head. 'Tomorrow I have to present the car for inspection.'

Lyn spotted Kier. He was walking towards them, a puzzled frown on his face as he looked from one to the other. 'Kier can look after that.'

'Look after what?' Kier asked as he lowered himself gingerly into a seat next to them.

Alex jumped as if she had been stung. She turned to look at Kier, and her face froze with shock. Lyn understood why. The bruises were starting to show on Kier's face. Instead of stitches, the cut on his forehead had been treated with butterfly dressings. His face was still pale, despite his tan. Someone had loaned him a T-shirt, but that didn't hide the cuts on his hands or the new thick dressing on his left arm. He looked terrible, but that wasn't enough to account for the sudden pallor on Alex's face.

'What did the doctor say? Are you all right?' Lyn asked.

'He says I'll live. The painkillers help.' Kier started to smile, then winced. 'So tell me, what am I supposed to be looking after?'

'Alex needs a navigator, so we're going to join forces for the race,' Lyn said, ignoring the tension that was growing around her. 'We need you to act as support and mechanic,' she continued quickly, before Alex could say anything.

Kier raised an eyebrow and looked at Alex.

'I don't know,' Alex said softly. 'I still don't think we'll have time. It's not that easy to become a team.'

Kier gave Alex a long appraising look. 'There's not much point in only doing the easy things, is there?' he said.

'Left five. One hundred metres downhill. Then right seven and go. You've got two hundred straight uphill after that.'

Lyn's voice was firm and confident as she called instructions.

'There's a bridge?' Alex asked.

'Not yet. Leave the navigating to me. You drive.'

Alex tightened her grip on the wheel. Lyn was right. If they were going to be real competitors in this race, she had to learn to trust her navigator. The problem was – trust wasn't one of her strong points. She steered the car around the gentle right turn, then pushed the accelerator to the floor. The Holden Commodore lacked the power and speed of her Lotus, but it was good enough for this trial run, and competitors' cars were not permitted on the course this close to race day. They'd take the Lotus for a fast run later over different roads.

'Brake now. Left three and on to the bridge in fifty.'

Alex slammed her foot on the brake. The tail wobbled a bit as the car turned into a sharp left-hand bend. Lyn's calls were spot on. The curve was definitely a three. The smaller the number, the tighter the turn.

The bridge was old, its surface rough and broken. At

the far edge, one wheel dropped into a jagged pothole and the car bounced sharply. The tyre held.

'Eighty metres, then right five.'

Alex pushed down on the accelerator again. It was time to find out just how well this partnership was going to work.

'Brake now for a right five, easing to a four. Then go for it. You've got one-eighty straight.'

Alex heard the words, but she barely touched the brake. She took the corner far too fast. The tail of the car broke out. She fought to hold it on the road, trying to ignore the roaring engine and the squeal of the tyres. Instead, she was listening to the woman sitting next to her. Lyn's breathing never altered.

'Go. Go. Go,' Lyn said in the same firm tone she had been using all along.

Alex did.

'I should point out that you are twenty k over the limit,' Lyn said. 'If you're caught, you'll be disqualified.'

'I know.'

'In that case, there's a right two with a dip, but you can take it at this speed.'

'Done.'

All four wheels of the Holden left the ground as the car hurtled over the lip out of the dip.

Alex and Lyn exchanged swift looks. Both were grinning.

Alex eased back on the pedal and the car began to slow down. She'd learned everything she needed to know.

'I think this might just work,' she said. 'You're a pretty good navigator.'

'Kier is a pretty good teacher.'

'I know.' The words were out before Alex had time to think about all they implied. 'All right,' she hurried on before Lyn could speak. 'I want to take another look at the road out towards the tracking station. I think there are a couple of places where we might be able to shave a few extra seconds off our time.'

'Okay.'

Alex drove slowly. Next time she drove these roads, she'd be moving very fast. Fast enough to . . . She bit back that thought. She was not going to be freaked out by Kier's accident. They were race drivers. That sort of thing happened. Just because it was him . . . That didn't matter. There was nothing between them now. All that had died a long, long time ago.

'So, how do you know Kier?'

Had Lyn read her mind? Alex paused for a moment before replying. 'We grew up in the same town.'

'Really? Were you at school together?'

Alex grinned inwardly. That was a joke. Jacqueline Reilly would not have allowed her precious daughter to go to school with the abattoir workers' and stockmen's kids. Not Alexandra Reilly.

'No,' she answered shortly. 'Can you make a note about the loose edge there?'

'Already done,' said Lyn. 'So, I guess you haven't seen each other for a while.'

Damn the woman, Alex thought. Couldn't she take a hint? The last thing Alex wanted was to talk about Kier.

'No. Not for a long time.'

'We only met last year,' Lyn volunteered.

Alex said nothing. She didn't want to know. She really didn't. But she guessed Lyn was going to tell her anyway.

'Yes, it was at a racetrack.'

'Another classic car race?' Alex asked before she could stop herself.

'No.' Lyn chuckled as if Alex had said something funny. 'Randwick. One of his horses was racing.'

'Kier has racehorses?'

Lyn looked at her sharply. 'Didn't you know? He's a trainer. Very successful, too. He had a runner in the Melbourne Cup last year.'

Alex suddenly understood the joke about horsepower that Lyn had shared with the reporters the day before. 'Did he win?'

'Second.'

Alex let that sink in. Kier was a racehorse trainer? It made sense. He had always been as good with horses as he was with cars. Maybe better. She remembered the black colt her father had bought. No one could handle it. Most of the stockmen were afraid of it. She hadn't been afraid of it. Nor had Kier. They had . . .

'You really haven't seen him in a long time, have you?' Lyn's voice dragged her back.

Why did the woman insist on going on about Kier? Couldn't she see that he was the last thing Alex wanted to talk about? It was only going to make it harder for them to work together. 'No. I haven't,' Alex said shortly, hoping her tone would discourage Lyn from further conversation on this particular topic.

The pause that followed seemed to last for a very long time.

'Kier and I are just friends,' Lyn explained. 'Well, we're friends of friends, if you know what I mean. We'd only met a couple of times when I decided I wanted to have a go at a major fund-raiser. When he heard, Kier suggested the rally – and helped me find a sponsor. It was really generous of him, but we're not—'

'It doesn't matter,' Alex interrupted her. 'All I care about is the race.'

'All right.' Lyn didn't sound as if she thought everything was all right.

They drove in silence a bit longer. Ahead of them the light caught a brilliant white satellite dish looking up into the clear blue sky.

'Tidbinbilla tracking station,' Lyn said. 'Did you know it took part in the first moon landing?'

Alex raised an eyebrow, genuinely surprised and diverted. 'Really?'

'Yes. They built a special wing on the main building to house the equipment.'

'How do you know that?'

'I read it somewhere. I do read more than fashion magazines,' Lyn said a bit testily.

'I guess you do,' Alex said. 'Me, it's law books and car magazines. If she saw my coffee table, my mother would be horrified. She'd immediately go out and buy a truckload of *Vogue* for me to read.'

'That's mothers for you.'

'Yes. I guess it is.' They laughed together.

The sun was low when they turned the dusty hire car back through the gates of Canberra showgrounds. They'd driven hundreds of kilometres during the day, covering large sections of the race course. Both women stretched their cramped limbs as they got out of the car.

'I'm going to check the Lotus,' Alex said. 'Make sure there wasn't a problem with scrutineering.'

'Do you need me?'

'No.'

'In that case, I'm heading back to the hotel. I could use a shower.'

'You mean you don't want to get covered in grease? Are you going all girlie on me?' Alex teased.

'You bet I am.' Lyn raised a hand in salute as she turned away.

Driving with Lyn might not be such a bad thing after all, Alex thought as she walked towards the big machinery pavilion where the race cars were assembled. She was beginning to think she had misjudged her. The model was certainly beautiful, but she wasn't an airhead. As for her IQ, Alex had a sneaking feeling that Lyn was just as smart as she was – maybe smarter. And there was no doubting her determination to win.

The hubbub inside the pavilion hadn't died down during the day. If anything, it was busier and more frantic than earlier. All the cars were being inspected today – and those that failed would be out of the race. All around her, drivers and mechanics were working to make sure they weren't left behind. Alex felt a small smug glow of satisfaction. While there were always a few last-minute tweaks, her car was ready. She didn't believe in good or bad luck. She believed in hard work and success; or laziness and failure.

The Lotus looked lovely. A rare and precious thing even among the dozens of other magnificent machines. Her heart lifted as she looked at it. But . . . the bonnet was up. That wasn't right. There were people clustered around it, looking under the bonnet. It couldn't be the scrutineers. They had been scheduled to look at her car this morning. There was no way they were running that late.

What the hell was going on?

She didn't run, but she was at the car in seconds. Kier was the first to see her.

'Alex—'

'What's going on?' She didn't give him time to finish. 'Where's Mick?' There was no sign of her mechanic.

'He and Sarah are getting their stuff together. They are leaving tonight,' Kier answered. 'I told them I could take care of this.'

'Take care of what?' Alex almost shouted.

'The second inspection.'

'Second inspection?' Alex's heart dropped. That could only mean one thing. The Lotus had failed the first. She turned as if to speak to the men who were peering under her bonnet. Kier put a hand on her arm to restrain her.

'Alex, it'll be fine. It's just the throttle return spring.'

'There was nothing wrong with it,' Alex protested.

'No, there wasn't.' One of the race officials emerged from beneath the car's bonnet. 'The trouble was that you only had one.'

Alex felt her jaw drop open. How could she have missed that? The rules required a second spring, to stop the accelerator being jammed open if the first broke. It was a simple, basic mistake. She didn't make basic mistakes.

'It's fine now. Good work.' The scrutineer made a notation on his clipboard and walked away.

As soon as he was gone, Alex turned back to the car, ready to see for herself that the new spring was fine. 'I guess we were lucky the spare parts people had one.'

'They didn't.'

'Then where did you get a new spring?'

Kier smiled. 'I didn't. That's the spring out of an old toaster.'

'It's what?'

Kier chuckled. 'Paul White gave me the idea. He was at the parts truck when I went looking for the spring they didn't have. He said the door spring off an old-style toaster would do the job just fine. I remembered that one of the coffee huts had the right sort of toaster. They thought it was a great joke, and gave it to me.'

Alex didn't think it was funny. 'You've put a spare part from an old toaster in my one-hundred-and-twenty-thousand-dollar sports car? And I'm supposed to race with that?'

'It'll be fine,' Kier said with a smile. 'Trust me.'

'Trust *you*?'

Kier's face froze as if she'd hit him. For what seemed a very long time, they stood looking at each other, the air between them quivering with unsaid words. Kier shook his head slowly. Then he turned and walked away.

Alex would not watch him leave. Instead she turned back to her beloved car. She looked under the bonnet. For a long time, she had trouble focusing on the offending spring. It wasn't that she was crying. Her eyes were watering because she was tired after a long hard day staring at the road. It was the dust. And the petrol fumes. She shook her head to clear both her eyes and her mind. The spring looked and felt fine. In fact, she wasn't sure she could tell for certain which was the official car part and which had been toasting bread a few hours earlier. Slowly she stood up and gently lowered the bonnet. The car was fine. Maybe she could trust Kier, but she had trusted him once before, and been horribly wrong.

Deep in thought, she locked the car and turned towards the exit. She needed a support man, and Kier was her only option. That didn't mean she had to totally trust him. He wouldn't deliberately sabotage her, because he'd be doing it to his friend Lyn as well. But just in case, she'd make damn certain she didn't give him the chance. Not to hurt her car. And not to hurt her. She would win this race and walk away. That would show Kier Thomas what she was really made of!

Every race had to have its show day. A day for public viewing of the cars, VIP tours and speeches. It wasn't Kier's favourite part of the race, but he had to admit that the two hundred rally cars made a spectacular display on the broad green lawns in front of the Parliament House. A rainbow of colours and chrome glinted in the sun as a sea of people flowed past. Men and boys pored over their dream cars, but there were women too, enjoying the bustle and excitement under the blue arch of cloudless sky. Kier looked towards the speaker's podium and the huge building behind it. To him, it appeared as though some giant had cut the top off the hill, built the ultra-modern Parliament House, then put the hill back on top of it. The green lawns sloped up beside the curved marble façade and on to the building's roof. To top it all off, a flagpole taller than the building itself supported an Australian flag about the size of a tennis court. In the courtyard in front of the building, various dignitaries were making speeches about the rally, welcoming competitors and visitors alike. Kier was in no mood to join the celebrations.

He turned away from the spectacle, and began to walk down the hill. Tall gum trees ran in lines down the slope, edging the park and its colourful display and ending at the while marble gleam of the old Parliament House. It looked far more peaceful and inviting down there.

'Hey, Kier.' Paul White was walking towards him across the lawn. They shook hands, and Paul nodded as he glanced at the cuts and bruises on Kier's face and arm. 'You're still not exactly a pretty sight, but I guess those bruises will start to fade soon.'

'In the meantime, I'm doing my best not to scare small children,' Kier said. 'By the way, thanks for the tip about the spring. It worked a treat.'

'Glad to help,' Paul said. 'What did your driver think of the idea?'

'Alex is a bit fussy about that Lotus,' Kier said with a rueful smile. 'But if a toaster spring lets her race, she'll live with it.'

'Has Lyn forgiven you for crashing the Ferrari yet?' Paul asked with a grin.

'Almost,' Kier said. 'She and Alex seem to be getting on all right. I think.'

The two men talked for a few more minutes, then Kier headed further down the hill, having promised to go and take a good look at Paul's Alfa Romeo, now that he was in a better state to fully appreciate its charms. Alex and the Lotus were parked on the right-hand side of the park. Kier stayed to the left. Not that he was avoiding her, he told himself. He just wanted to check out the competition. He walked down the line of cars, stopping here and there to exchange a few words with another competitor.

The last vehicle in the line was a surprise. The white transit van was as out of place as a carthorse on a race track. There was a logo painted on the door, but he didn't have time to study it before a woman accosted him.

'Hi there.' Her voice was almost terrifyingly cheerful. 'I can tell by the overalls that you're one of the drivers.'

'Was,' he corrected her. 'I have the honour of being the first driver to crash out of the rally. Before it even started.'

'Oh, so you're the one who hit the kangaroo.' The woman's voice lost some of its cheer.

'Yes. I am.'

If Kier had expected his bruises and bandages to engender some sympathy, he was sadly mistaken. The woman standing in front of him was tiny, barely reaching his shoulder, and she was a good few years older than him. She was wearing no make-up. Her jeans were well faded with wear, as was her T-shirt. Her hair was caught into a loose ponytail. Kier wasn't one to judge people by their looks, but the woman was . . . well . . . scruffy.

'So you're out of the race now?' She didn't sound sympathetic.

'Not quite,' Kier said. 'I'm joining one of the other teams. As support crew.'

'Then I still need to talk to you.'

'What about?'

'My name is Dee Parker,' she said. 'I'll be with you on the race.'

'In that?' Kier chuckled as he indicated the transit van.

'Not racing,' Dee corrected. 'I work as a volunteer with the National Parks and Wildlife. You guys are going to be racing through the Kosciuszko National Park. My job is to make sure you don't do too much damage. To the wildlife.' She spoke the last words in an accusing tone.

'I think I was more damaged than that 'roo,' Kier said, his defences rising.

'Did you even look for it? To see if it was injured?'

'I wasn't in any fit state to go looking for it.'

'Be that as it may, you should still have reported it. Here,' she thrust a piece of paper at him, 'keep this with you. That's my phone number there. And some instructions on what to do if you hit something.'

'But—'

'No buts. If you guys want permission to race in the park again next year, you'll do the right thing now.'

There was a lot of force packed into one small woman.

'Yes, ma'am.' Kier almost saluted.

'Good.'

Kier carefully folded the paper and placed it in his breast pocket. He smiled at Dee, and turned away. That was just what he needed – another woman mad at him. This whole rally wasn't going quite the way he had planned. He'd crashed the car, and robbed Lyn of some of the sponsorship she needed so much. He'd upset some crazy wildlife woman. Then there was Alex. She was pissed off at him for using a toaster spring in her precious Lotus. Even before that, she was generically pissed at him. She certainly didn't trust him. As for his feelings towards her . . .

He kept walking. A deep cutting with a busy road at the bottom separated the new Parliament House from the old. Kier leaned on the concrete safety barrier and looked past the cutting to the elegant colonial-style building at the bottom of the hill. Past and present, separated by a gulf he couldn't cross. That was fitting. It had been different once. When they were young. When barriers were meant to be crossed and trust was so much easier. He turned to stare back up the hill at the crowded lawn. Somewhere up there was a shiny red Lotus, and a woman with a temperament to match . . .

*

The music drifted on the soft breeze that caressed the gardens of the big graceful white homestead. Weeks of watering had made the vast lawns unusually green and lush. Large flowering plants in wooden tubs were dotted among the big gum trees, adding brilliant splashes of colour. The trees themselves were draped with coloured lights, which would be illuminated as soon as the sun sank. Marquees provided seating and shade for those who wanted it. Even the marquees were draped with flowers and silks for the Big Occasion. The liberal application of money had turned the baked brown outback into a paradise.

Jacqueline Reilly was throwing a party, the likes of which none of the locals had ever seen before. A birthday party for the cattle king – Thomas Reilly. Kier supposed that when you had enough land to be your own country, and all the money in the world, this was how you celebrated a birthday. With a couple of hundred of your very closest friends. Some had flown in for the event, parking their aeroplanes in a neat line on Reilly's private airstrip. Others had come by road, driving through the huge wrought-iron gateway in sleek, shiny machines that Kier had only ever seen in the pages of magazines. Thomas Reilly was known for his collection of fine cars, and it appeared his friends had similar tastes. What would he say if he knew that Kier had dared to ride in one of those priceless cars? Kier guessed that would be nothing to what he would do if he knew Kier had dared to look at his most precious possession – his daughter.

From his vantage point halfway up the tall iron windmill near the machinery sheds, Kier scanned the crowd moving through the garden. He shouldn't be here. The stockmen and abattoir workers were having their own party for the boss, at the pub in town. Reilly was paying for that too. Kier doubted it was simply generosity. Free beer at the pub was the easiest way to ensure the stockmen and plant workers didn't come anywhere near this fancy do. His own father was there. His brother Rob too. Kier had no desire to join them. They were family, but their brand of beer and whisky-soaked good times was not for him. He didn't belong here, at the big house, either. His kind wasn't good enough for these people. Not that it really mattered. He was only here to take a look at the cars.

Then Alex walked out of the house, and everything changed.

The flowers and the lights and the fancy people faded into the background as she walked down the wide front stairs. Her dress was a blue so pale it was almost white. The wide full skirt floated above her knees, revealing tanned legs. She walked with the easy grace of a wild young thing. This was a very different Alex to the one he'd shared that late-night ride with just a few days before. There was little sign of the tomboy sneaking her dad's car for a joyride. This beautiful young woman moved through the crowd with confidence and ease. But as he looked at her face, Kier realised that her smile was as false as the garden her mother had created.

She walked through the crowd, spoke when spoken to, and took her place at her father's side. Thomas put an arm around her shoulders, claiming her as his own. Kier thought that was wrong. Alex belonged to no one but herself. After a few minutes, duty done, she turned away. Kier watched her walk towards him, her face changing with every step she took. Her mood was lifting as she left the party behind. Suddenly she stopped. Her face creased in a frown as she looked around. Then she glanced up at the tall windmill and saw him clinging to the metal structure.

She looked back over her shoulder to the party. He knew what she was thinking. If her father saw him – or even worse, if her mother saw him – he could well lose his job. That suddenly didn't seem very important. She indicated with a nod of her head that he should join her behind the machinery shed.

Kier slid down the ladder and darted around the back of the big shed. His steps slowed as he saw her waiting for him. She looked like an angel – beautiful and untouchable. Unconsciously Kier wiped his hands on his jeans. Then she grinned at him.

'If my mother catches us, we're dead.'

In the bright sunlight, her eyes sparkled, the most beautiful green he had ever seen. This wasn't the grey-green of gum leaves or the burnt green of the grass. Nor was it the dull green that lined dark clouds when a storm threatened. This was the brilliant clear green of some rare and precious gem. Her smile was a gift – and she was smiling at him.

'She won't catch us.' Not even Jacqueline Reilly could spoil this moment.

'I was going to look at the cars.'

'So was I.'

Kier held out his hand, and without hesitation, she took it. Her hand was soft, but she held his as if she meant never to let go. They walked quickly along the back of the shed, then darted through the gate into the small paddock that had been turned into a car park. Together they walked down the lines of cars, admiring them. A couple of drivers were polishing their charges, as they waited to take their *employers home. Alex seemed far more at ease here than she had among her parents' friends. She belonged here, and Kier belonged at her side.*

'If you could have any car in the world, what would it be?' he asked her.

'A Lotus,' she replied without hesitation. 'The 26 R.'

'Nice,' he said, thinking how much the long, sleek lines of the sports car would suit Alex. It was a free-spirited car – like the girl beside him.

'And you?'

'Well, just recently, I've become a bit of a Jaguar fan.' He smiled down at her and she smiled back, sharing the joke.

'Alex . . . what are you doing?'

They turned to see a tall man in a suit standing behind them. Kier recognised him immediately. It was Jim Cassidy, Thomas Reilly's right-hand man and foreman.

'Just looking at the cars.' All the joy was gone from her voice.

'And this is . . . ?' The man glanced at Kier as if he was a stray dog that had wandered in from the road.

'I'm Kier Thomas.' He didn't hold out his hand. He knew the man would not take it.

'Shouldn't you be at the pub? I hear there's free beer for the stockmen.'

Kier didn't answer.

'As for you, young lady, your mother is looking for you.' Cassidy's lips curled into a smile as he spoke, but there was no warmth in it.

'All right.'

Alex's fingers closed so tightly around Kier's hand, it almost hurt. Then she let go and walked away without turning back.

Cassidy gave Kier one long, menacing look. 'I think it's time for you to go.'

He jumped as Lyn touched his shoulder.

'What did you say?'

'I said, Alex and I going back to the showgrounds,' Lyn said, frowning. 'Are you all right?'

'Yeah.' Kier felt a twinge of disappointment that Lyn was alone. He assumed Alex was still with her car. 'I was just . . . thinking.'

Lyn didn't look convinced. 'We didn't see you at the welcome ceremony.'

'I've never been much for ceremony,' Kier said.

On the grassy slope, cars were starting to move. The competitors were to parade through the city's heart as they wound their way back to the showgrounds.

'You go and join Alex,' Kier said to Lyn. 'I've got the hire car. I'll give the parade a miss and see you back at the showgrounds.'

As Lyn moved away, Kier took a deep breath, trying to shake the feelings that were so much a part of his memories. Back then he hadn't belonged at Thomas Reilly's party, yet Alex had made him feel welcome. Things were so different now. He had earned his place amid the competitors and celebrities. Now it was Alex who made him feel unworthy. She had every right to distrust him. Hate him even. But he wasn't about to let that get to him. He'd lived with guilt long enough. He wasn't going to do it again. He would do everything in his power to help Alex – and when the race was over, he would try to forget her. Again.

Lyn closed her eyes, and visualised the course. In the next five days they would climb the slopes of the country's highest mountains, and race across the vast brown plains. But today, on day one of the race, they had to deal with the suburbs. This first leg was through the streets of a residential neighbourhood that had been closed off for the morning. There would be no other traffic; no dogs to run into the street or children on bicycles to avoid. The danger was in the corners, most of which were very tight. The course notes she was clutching had everything she needed to know. How long each stretch of road was. What landmarks preceded each corner and how fast Alex could take each one. The two of them had driven the course the night before in the hire car, but that wasn't enough. Now that the race was actually upon her, Lyn was nervous. She had never done anything like this before. By comparison, strutting down a slippery catwalk while wearing six-inch heels and not much else was a piece of cake.

The Lotus was parked by the side of the road, about a hundred metres from the actual starting line. All around her, stewards were calling cars into an orderly procession. There was just one minute between each car's start time, and drivers had to be in the right place at exactly the right time. Anyone who was even a few seconds late would incur a penalty in their race time. The Lotus would be called soon – but Alex wasn't here. She had vanished in the direction of the portaloos on the footpath a few minutes ago, leaving Lyn in charge. If something went wrong, Alex would kill her. Not only that, there were other people relying on her to do well – her sister Lorna, her parents, and all the other families who needed the money her sponsorship would raise. They'd all be watching the race on television, in the newspapers and on the web. The mere thought of letting them down was enough to make her gut twist.

A pale blue car pulled to the side of the road behind the Lotus. Lyn paid little attention to it until the driver got out.

'Hi, Lyn.'

It was Paul White, the man who had rescued Kier after his accident and then saved his bacon again at the scrutineering.

'Hi, Paul.' She was pleased to see him. She had checked his profile in the race press kit. He'd done dozens of rallies, and won a few of them. If he was relaxed and smiling, then maybe she didn't have to panic. At least, not just yet.

'You ready?' he asked.

'I think so. Thanks to you and your idea about using a toaster spring on the throttle.'

'It was nothing. Did you know that in 1942, the great Juan Fangio used part of a frying pan to repair his sump during the Gran Premio Rally in Argentina?'

Lyn blinked. 'Umm . . .'

His eyes crinkled as he smiled. 'It's quite a story. I'll

tell you about it some time. Until then, believe me when I say a toaster spring is far from the silliest repair I've ever seen on a race car.'

'Did the guy with the frying pan win?'

'No – but he did finish the race. Isn't that what matters?'

Lyn guessed that it was.

'You'll do just fine,' Paul said. 'That Lotus is a beautiful machine. She won't let you down.'

'I just hope I don't let it . . . her . . . down.'

'You won't.' He said the words as if he had not the slightest doubt in her ability. 'You'll be great.'

Lyn had thought she was beyond blushing. For years she'd been getting undressed at crowded fashion shows. She had walked down runways wearing bikinis the size of postage stamps; been photographed in nothing but designer underwear. Dealing with leering men and temperamental designers had toughened her. But suddenly she felt her cheeks glow, just a little.

'All right. Number fifty-three. The Lotus. I need you next!' The steward was waving his arms.

'Oh God. Where's Alex?' Lyn spun around and spotted her driver running towards the line of cars from the Portaloos. 'Come on,' she yelled. 'We're next.'

'Good luck,' Paul called as he returned to his own car.

Alex pulled on her helmet, flung herself into her seat and started the engine. Lyn was still doing up her seatbelt when the Lotus began moving towards the starting line. There were three cars ahead of them. That meant three minutes to go.

'All right,' Alex said. 'Are you ready for this?'

'You bet!' Lyn pulled her race helmet over her head and tightened the strap. She really was as ready as she was ever going to be. 'From the go, you've got two hundred metres straight, then a tight five right-hand turn. Stay wide on the corner, there's a pothole.'

'I've got it.' Alex pulled forward. There were two cars ahead of them.

'Base time for this leg is twenty-three minutes and thirty seconds,' Lyn warned, as she closed her hand around her stopwatch. Base time was the expected time from the fastest car in the class. The Lotus was one of the fastest cars in her class, if not the fastest. They had to get close to base time if they were to have any chance of winning.

'We'll ace it.' Alex flexed her gloved fingers on the wheel as they pulled into the second spot.

The car in front of them was a silver Porsche. It roared away and the steward waved the Lotus forward to the starting line. Alex slipped the car into gear, and inched forward. A few metres in front of them, to either side of the car, the starting lights glowed orange. Lyn could clearly see the big countdown clock.

'Thirty seconds.' There was nothing else she could do now except try to keep the fear and uncertainty out of her voice.

'Ten seconds. Nine . . . eight . . .' Beside the car, the steward joined the countdown.

'Three . . . two . . . one . . .' The light turned green. 'Go!'

Lyn's shout was drowned by the roar of the engine as Alex thrust down on the accelerator. The little car shot away like a bullet from a gun. The leather seat slammed Lyn in the back. Her fingers clenched on the course notes in her lap, and her eyes turned to the speedo. It was her job to call the speed. Alex had eyes only for the road.

'Thirty ... fifty ... Next is a right five. Stay wide. Then in forty another right five ...'

'Got it,' Alex called back.

Lyn's eyes began a ceaseless movement. From the dashboard to the windscreen to the course notes in her hand, then back to the dashboard again via the remorseless hands of the stopwatch. All her nervousness was gone. She was racing! She was vaguely aware of things flashing past outside the car. Houses and trees. Groups of people watching from the safety of their verandas and balconies. There were street lights and road signs, but she ignored them. They didn't matter. All she had eyes for was the race.

'We're on time,' she told Alex. 'Ahead eighty metres to a five right that opens out. You can take it at this speed.'

Alex did exactly as Lyn told her. She kept her speed up. The tail of the Lotus broke out and they slid around the next corner, the tyres howling in protest. Then the car darted forward as Alex put her foot down hard.

'Lyn, talk to me,' Alex yelled above the engine noise.

'There's another five right coming up.'

'Another right ...'

'No,' Lyn screamed. 'Left. Five left.'

'Left?'

'Left,' Lyn screamed again, her heart in her mouth. 'Sorry!'

Alex took the corner hard. 'Come on, Lyn. Get it together. What's next?'

'One hundred. Then right.'

'Right. Are you sure this time?'

'Yes, damn it. Right!'

It was the busiest twenty-three minutes of Lyn's life. She watched every second on the stopwatch; every metre of road; every twitch of the speedo and the oil pressure gauge on the dashboard. It seemed no time at all before she saw a yellow flag ahead.

'One hundred metres to go,' she shouted.

They roared across the line. Lyn hit the lap timer on her stopwatch as Alex jammed her foot on the brake.

'How did we do?' Alex was breathing heavily, as if she had run the course rather than driven it.

'Twenty-three fifty,' Lyn said, elated. They were off to a good start.

'Move up!' A steward was beside them.

Alex eased the car up beside a stewards' table where two men were conferring over a clipboard.

'Car number fifty-three,' Lyn called.

'Twenty-three forty-six,' the steward called back.

'Right,' Lyn agreed with a smile, and made an amendment to her notes. Four seconds didn't seem like much of a difference, but when it came to the final legs, those seconds might be important.

'You're off at nine fifty-six,' the steward said, still not looking up from his clipboard.

Lyn glanced at the big digital timer behind the stewards' desk. They had a little over three minutes to get to the start of the next leg. 'This is a transport leg,' she reminded Alex. 'It takes us out of town and into the hills.'

Transport legs were a little less harrowing. They were simply a method of getting competitors to the next designated race stage. Held on open roads, with other traffic, the transport legs were not a race, and drivers caught speeding risked disqualification. But they were still timed. They had to reach the next checkpoint in advance of their designated start time for the next high-speed section.

They pulled away from the stewards' table, following the car in front as they formed another starting line. Lyn briefly considered taking off her race helmet while they waited. She could use some wind in her face and maybe some air that didn't reek of petrol fumes and oil. But there just wasn't time.

A powder-blue Alfa Romeo pulled up next to the Lotus. Lyn looked across into the smiling face of Paul White. His mouth moved, but between the muffling of the helmet and the roar of engines, she couldn't hear a word. She could however see the huge grin on Paul's face. She grinned back, and gave him the thumbs-up before they took their place on the starting line for the next stage.

The first break in the relentless pressure of the race came two hours later, when Alex steered the Lotus into the parking area beside a factory outlet shopping centre. The centre's huge car park had been taken over by the rally. Two hundred race cars would pass through it in the next couple of hours. Although the competitors' lunch breaks were staggered according to their start times, the whole place was havoc. There were officials and competitors, support teams and media, all tripping over each other as they fought their way to the food area for lunch. As Alex drove up the ramp into the car park, stewards waved the Lotus to a parking position. She turned the engine off, and for the first time that morning, the two women slid out of the car.

'Bloody hell,' Lyn exclaimed as she removed her helmet, 'that was a lot tougher than I thought it would be.'

'And this is only the first leg.' Alex grinned. 'We've got five days of this. More than one thousand kilometres to go.'

'You're loving it, aren't you?' Lyn chuckled.

'You bet! How's our time?' Alex asked as she ran her fingers through her sweat-damp hair, flattened against her head by the weight of the crash helmet.

'Good.' Lyn did some maths in her head. 'I would be really surprised if we're not pretty close to the lead in our class.'

'My guess is, top two or maybe three.' Kier emerged from behind a nearby Porsche, holding a cardboard box in his hand. 'Here you go.'

The box contained sandwiches, coffee and bottles of water. Lyn twisted the top off one of the bottles and gulped down the cool, clear liquid.

'That helps,' she said.

'Thanks,' Alex said as she tossed her leather gloves on to her car seat, and began unwrapping a sandwich.

Lyn took the last sandwich. She didn't look too closely at it as she wolfed it down. As a model, she spent a lot of time watching her weight. But for the next few days, that was the least of her concerns. As she washed the sandwich down with some coffee, she had a good look around. There were dozens of cars nearby, each with a small group of people huddled around it. But she couldn't see anything that looked like a powder-blue Alfa Romeo. She told herself that she wasn't disappointed.

Thanks to Kier's sandwich delivery, the lunch part of the break was over in a few minutes, and suddenly Lyn found she had absolutely nothing to do. Alex was already digging around under the bonnet of the car. Kier was standing by to help her. All around, people were working frantically – except for Lyn. She had no mechanical skills. As for her course notes – she was as ready for the next stage as she would ever be. She could stand around and feel useless for the next forty minutes. She could spend it looking for a little blue car. Or she could do something useful. Having asked Kier where the support car was parked, she set off to do the latter.

Her expensive laptop computer was on the back seat of the support car. She pulled it out of its bag, and perched on the bonnet as she switched it on. Technology was a wonderful thing. Just yesterday she'd been taking photographs with her phone; now she was connecting to the internet from a car park. She didn't really understand how it all worked, but she was so very grateful that it did. Duty dictated her first port of call. She nodded as the screen in front of her slowly filled with words and photographs. The blog and photos she'd sent the day before looked good on her sponsor's website. There were a few comments that she quickly answered. It was important to keep the sponsor happy. Then she called up her e-mail. The one from her mother was right on top. She scanned it quickly, then read it more slowly a second time.

Lorna was fine. That was the most important thing. When Lorna was fine, the pressure on their mother was less. Lyn always worried when she was away, and not just about Lorna. Her mother was the strongest woman Lyn had ever met, but sometimes . . . She pushed that thought away. She had learned long ago to enjoy the good news when it came, because bad news wasn't going to be that far behind.

The race blog, it seemed, was a huge hit with everyone at the Sydney Hills Care Centre. The carers had printed out the photographs to pin to the huge map on the wall on which they were tracking the race. Not that Lorna could read a map. She probably didn't even understand what was going on. But the bright colours and the sound of voices were all she needed to make her happy. Lyn noticed an attachment on her mother's e-mail, and quickly double-clicked.

The wheelchairs had balloons tied to them. The patients were mostly children, and a few young adults, like Lorna. Their carers were smiling into the camera and on the wall behind them was a huge sign that read 'Good Luck Lyn'. Lyn felt tears prick her eyes as she looked at her little sister's face. Lorna was eighteen years old, but her mind was that of a small child. She suffered from Angelman syndrome, a rare genetic disorder that left her considerably handicapped. But Lyn believed she was comfortable and happy. At least, she seemed happy in her protected little world. The carers called her their angel. She was Lyn's angel too, and Lyn wasn't about to let her down. She would wring every cent she could from her participation in this race. The centre needed it.

'Lyn!'

Kier's voice pulled her back to the present. She glanced down at her watch, synchronised this morning to the race clock. 'Shit!'

'You've got less than five minutes,' Kier called after her as she started running in the direction of the Lotus.

'Come on,' Alex yelled as Lyn approached the Lotus. 'Where have you been?'

'Sorry.' Lyn slid into the car.

'Lyn, you've got to focus this afternoon,' Alex said. 'Three times this morning you changed your call.'

'I know.' Lyn was contrite. 'It won't happen again.'

'I hope not. If we miss just one, we're out of contention. It's up to you to keep us on course.'

Lyn bit her lip. Alex was being harsh – but she was also right. Lyn determined that she would do better. As she buckled her harness, she also suddenly became aware that what she should have done during the break was find a ladies' bathroom. Well, it was too late now. The engine was revving as Alex drove to the starting line. Alex would have a fit if Lyn said anything now. She'd just have to cross her legs until the next break.

The day had not been a total disaster. As she drove slowly towards Queanbeyan showgrounds, Alex guessed that they could be no more than a few seconds behind the leaders. It was late afternoon, and today's racing had been quite short; just a little over two hundred kilometres. The country had been hilly, but not as tough as it was going to be in the mountains. She had managed to refuel ready for the next day's racing, and the car seemed to be in perfect order. She followed the stewards' directions into the parc fermé, where the cars would be kept overnight, under the watchful eyes of the security guards. She turned the engine off and let herself relax for the first time, resting her head on the steering wheel.

'Well,' Lyn sighed, 'that was hard work, but I think I kind of enjoyed it.'

Alex looked sideways to meet Lyn's grin.

'I did too,' she said, realising that it was true. 'I owe you an apology. I'm sorry I bit you. At lunchtime. You didn't deserve that.'

'You were a tad snappy,' Lyn said, her smile taking any sting out of the words.

'This is my first race too. I guess I was nervous.'

'That made two of us, but I think we did all right.'

Alex had to agree. Maybe teaming up with Lyn hadn't been such a bad idea.

'Lyn. Alex. Can you step out of the car, please? Just for a couple of quick shots.'

Alex looked up. She recognised the man standing in front of the car as the rally's official photographer.

'Can't this wait?' she asked.

'If we get it done, then we're free for the rest of the evening,' Lyn suggested as she got out of the car.

Alex sighed. Lyn was right. Slowly she climbed out of the car and removed her gloves and race helmet. Her hair was glued to the top of her head with sweat. Her face, she was sure, was equally sweaty. Lyn, though, looked perfectly poised. She shook her head and her hair seemed to spring back into life. How did she do that?

'Both of you, on the bonnet, please. Holding your helmets,' the photographer directed.

'No one sits on my bonnet—' Alex began.

'So we'll lean against it,' Lyn whispered furiously in her ear, 'or pretend to if you prefer. We have to do this.'

'Why?'

'I've got a sponsor, remember. The more often my picture appears, the more money I raise. And it's for a good cause.'

'Do you really enjoy this sort of thing?' Alex asked, genuinely curious as she joined Lyn leaning against the dust-covered bonnet.

'It pays well.' Lyn tossed her head and adopted another pose.

It would want to pay very well, Alex thought, to make the intrusion bearable. She smiled at the camera, trying not to feel too self-conscious. Attracted by the photographer's flash, more of the media contingent was converging on their position. The single flashbulb was joined by half a dozen more. Reporters shouted questions and waved microphones. Alex let Lyn do most of the talking, until a deep voice joined the clamour.

'Hey guys, I think you should expect to see the ladies in the top three when times are posted.'

The media scrum parted a little to make way for Kier. Alex noted that he appeared not at all tired by the day's activities. In fact, he looked annoyingly fresh and far too handsome.

'Kier – you're crewing for them now, aren't you?' a reporter asked.

'I am indeed,' Kier stepped closer to Alex and Lyn, 'and proud of it.'

His presence initiated another round of camera flashes. Alex couldn't help but wonder who would see the photos. She hadn't told her parents she was racing. She spoke to them rarely and told them very little about her day-to-day life. Her father, however, with his love of old cars, might chance to read about the rally in one of his car magazines. One small part of her hoped that he might feel just a twinge of pride in his daughter, but experience told her that was unlikely. Very little she had ever done had won approval in her father's eyes. As for her mother . . . Alex doubted Jacqueline read anything other than fashion magazines and the society pages of newspapers. Although with Lyn as her navigator, the team photos might end up in just such a place. Would her mother recognise the man next to Alex as the boy she had despised all those years ago? Would she care?

'Put your arms around the girls,' one of the photographers called.

Alex stiffened. She didn't want Kier's arm around her. She didn't want him to touch her. She knew how his hands would feel. Strong and gentle at the same time.

Full of promise. Full of lies! She felt Kier turn towards her. Felt his glance, almost as if he was asking permission. She wanted to scream a denial. But she couldn't. She tensed herself, as if to withstand a blow.

Kier hesitated, as if sensing her withdrawal.

Just then, a purple Datsun purred past. The driver was one of the race celebrities, a well-known television soap star. The media scrum vanished as quickly as it had formed.

'I'm heading over to look for times,' Alex said, trying not to feel relieved, as if she had just escaped some dreadful fate.

'They're not up yet,' Kier told her. 'I checked just before I came over.'

'In that case,' Lyn said with a smile, 'I'm going to have a shower, then I guess I'd better get blogging.'

'Here.' Kier held out his hand.

Alex was startled to see Lyn take a hotel room key from his fingers. Her surprise must have shown on her face.

'I checked Lyn and me in to our hotel rooms.' Kier looked directly at Alex as he put a noticeable emphasis on the plural. 'I would have done the same for you, but I didn't know which hotel you were in.'

Alex felt a touch of chagrin. Kier and Lyn had started this venture as a team, so of course they'd be at the same hotel. As her team would have been, had Mick and Sarah still been with her. Lyn had already told her there was nothing going on between her and Kier. And it wasn't as if Alex had any call to feel jealous.

'Don't worry,' she said. 'I suppose I have to cancel the rooms I had booked for Mick and Sarah. I meant to do it earlier, and forgot.'

'I'll look after it,' Kier said. 'That's my job.'

They parted company then, agreeing to meet in an hour to wait for the first day's results to be posted, Alex found her hotel, and checked in. A long, hot shower eased some of the tension from her shoulders. Comfortably dressed in blue jeans and a T-shirt, she shook out her race suit. The pale blue overalls were already showing signs of sweat, and smelled ever so slightly of petrol fumes. She hung them near the open window, then combed out her wet hair, but didn't bother drying it. Another day inside that helmet, and it would simply need washing again.

When she left the hotel, she decided to walk back to the showgrounds. It wasn't far, and after a day sitting behind the wheel of a car, she appreciated the chance to stretch her legs. Most of the kinks had worked out of her muscles by the time she arrived and flashed her race ID. This site was much smaller than the Canberra base. The cars had been gathered in what would normally be the farm machinery exhibition space. The mobile food stalls and spare parts retailers who were following the race had established themselves nearby, and were already doing a roaring trade. As was the bar.

Alex wasn't yet ready to give up her few minutes' solitude, so she took the long route towards the stewards' office, via the stables. Surprisingly, there were still some horses in residence. A shaggy chestnut pony thrust his head over his stable door as she approached, no doubt hoping that she might be carrying food. Alex stopped to give him a pat behind the ear. The chestnut immediately thrust his head up against her, searching her pockets for a treat.

'Sorry, old boy,' she said. 'If I'd known you were here . . .'

He was no thoroughbred. He was far from handsome,

but he was well cared for, and extremely friendly. Everything about him told Alex that somewhere there was a girl who loved this shaggy pony as much as she had ever loved anything in her young life . . .

Alex buried her face in the mare's neck, enjoying the warm, earthy scent of her. The mare kept her nose deep in her feed bin, munching steadily through her breakfast. Alex felt more at home here in the stables than she did in her parents' house. Ever since she'd been a little girl, the stables had been her sanctuary. Her mother never came here. When her father visited, he was always too busy to notice Alex. This was the one place where she could be herself; alone except for the one creature who loved her unconditionally. Alex had been given the pony for her eighth birthday. For both of them, it had been love at first sight. The mare was getting old now. Alex had outgrown her, and now rode bigger and better mounts. But Tash was her first and greatest love.

'Alex.'

With a sigh, Alex turned to face the speaker. She had never liked Jim Cassidy. He was arrogant and rude. He liked to order her around. She had a feeling she knew what he was about to say.

'What do you want?'

'I just wanted to tell you that I don't think you should be hanging around with that Thomas kid. The whole family is bad news.'

'What do you mean, bad news?'

'Well, his brother is a thug. He's in with a bad crowd and is always looking for a fight. His father is a drunk. Comes to work reeking of beer. The whole family is like that. They're trash.'

'Kier's different!' Alex leaped to her friend's defence.

'They are all tarred with the same brush. You stay away from him.'

'Who are you to tell me what to do?' Alex demanded. 'You are not my father.'

'No, but I am concerned about you. That boy is just using you. Don't forget who your father is.'

Alex spun on her heel and walked out of the stables. She had to get out of there. Cassidy was wrong about Kier. He wasn't using her. Kier didn't care about her father's money. He liked her. She just knew that he did.

Her footsteps took her through the stables, towards the small spelling paddocks on the far side of the complex. She was planning to walk down to the creek, to spend some time alone, but she stopped at the last fence. This paddock contained her father's newest purchase: a two-year-old black thoroughbred colt of impeccable breeding. The colt was unbroken, and proving to be quite a handful. Even Jim Cassidy couldn't control this one. But someone could. Someone was in the paddock with his hands gently smoothing the colt's long, wild mane.

Alex slipped quietly over to the gate and looked between the wooden rails. It was Kier. He was turned away from her, and his face was hidden against the horse's neck, but she would know him anywhere. She could hear him speaking softly to reassure the nervous animal as he stroked its glossy coat. She couldn't hear the words, but his voice was like a gentle caress. His head was bowed, his cheek resting against the colt's arched neck. Alex was entranced. The colt was wearing no halter. There was nothing to stop him walking away. Running away more like it. That was his usual reaction to any man who tried to get close to him. But he appeared to think that Kier was different.

'Why don't you come in?'

It took a few seconds for Alex to realise he was talking to her. The tempo and tone of his voice hadn't changed and he hadn't looked up, but he had known she was there. She hesitated for a second, Jim Cassidy's words ringing in her ears. She ignored them, and slipped through the gate, closing it carefully behind her.

The colt caught the movement out of the corner of his eye. He flung his head up in alarm and snorted wildly. His eyes rolled as he fixed his gaze upon her. For every step she took forward, the colt took one back. His muscles were quivering, poised for flight. Only one thing kept him there. Kier's voice.

'Come on, a big strong colt like you. Why are you afraid? It's only Alex. She won't hurt you.'

'That's right. I won't.' Alex took her cue from Kier and spoke softly to the wild-eyed colt. 'You're a bit of a wuss if you're frightened of me.'

It was all too much for the colt, and he suddenly leaped away. Kier didn't move. He waited for Alex to join him.

'Stand very still,' he said in the same soothing tone. 'He'll be back.'

'Are you sure?' Alex asked.

'He's lonely out here by himself,' Kier said. 'He won't be able to resist coming to talk to us.'

Alex knew what he meant. She stood motionless beside him. Out of the corner of her eye, she saw the colt edge a little closer to them.

'Jim Cassidy says that he needs to learn who's boss,' Kier said softly. 'But that's not right, is it, fellow?'

The colt's ears flickered and he took a hesitant step forward.

'My dad says the most important thing is not to be afraid of him,' Alex offered.

'That's important,' Kier said, 'but there's something even more important.'

The colt took another step towards them, his ears flicking constantly as he listened to their voices.

'He needs to know that there's no reason to fear you,' Kier said.

He stretched one hand out, palm upwards and fingers slightly curled. The colt took one more step and reached out to nuzzle it. Alex held her breath. The colt took another half-step, his neck extended so that his soft muzzle brushed against her hair. She felt his warm breath on her cheek. Slowly she reached up and stroked the colt's soft coat. The animal relaxed, and rubbed his cheek against her. Alex looked at Kier. He was smiling, his dark eyes shining as he nodded his approval. He was right, Alex thought. Fear went both ways, and trust had to go both ways too.

Alex took a slow, deep breath and shrugged off the memories. That was a long time ago. She gave the shaggy pony one last pat and headed towards the riot of colour and sound that was the staging area. She could tell from the noise around the stewards' office that the day's results were up. As she approached, she saw Kier standing near the crowd, talking to Paul White. He looked so much at ease, and confident among the other drivers. He wasn't the boy from the wrong side of the tracks any more. The misfit who didn't belong in his world or hers. He'd found his place. As she had. Maybe it was time to let the past go. If she could do that, maybe she could look at him without feeling the pain of his betrayal.

'Well?' she asked as she drew closer.

'I haven't looked,' Kier said. 'I was waiting for you.'

'Well?' Lyn echoed as she joined them.

'I guess we'd better look.' Alex pushed her way through to the noticeboard, Lyn close behind her. She ran an anxious eye down the list. The rally was divided into several different classes. Somewhere there would be a listing for—

'There!' Lyn cried, stabbing a finger at the notice.

Alex's eyes seemed to take several seconds to focus on the numbers written in an untidy scrawl. That couldn't be right . . .

'Third.' She read the page twice, just to make sure that she wasn't seeing things. 'There's just eight seconds in it!' Her voice rose with elation. Only eight seconds! In her first race.

'Wow!' Lyn threw her arms around her in a joyful hug. 'Third! That's great.'

Alex hugged her back, elation bubbling through her.

'Kier – we're third.' Lyn pushed her way back through the crowd. She practically bounced up to Kier, and before Alex knew quite what was happening, she was enveloped in a group hug.

His arm was around her too fast for her to avoid. His face was so close she could feel his breath on her skin. Lyn was still jumping up and down, oblivious to the sudden stillness that had come over the other two. Kier's eyes sought Alex's, and she felt her world shift slightly, as if some force was drawing her into a vortex of forgotten emotions. The feel of his arm around her was as familiar as his face. And as strange. He had always been taller than her, and he still managed to make her feel quite small. Vulnerable. Yet deep inside, she felt an old familiar stirring of emotion, and something more . . .

She broke away from the others and stepped quickly back.

'It seems celebrations are in order.' A deep voice dragged her back to the present.

'Did you see, Paul? We're third,' Lyn said, her voice happy but suddenly almost shy.

'Yes, you are, but I'm right behind you.' Paul grinned as he spoke. 'It looks like it's going to be a pretty close race.'

'That's the best kind,' Alex said, forcing a smile on to her face as Kier's arm dropped from around her.

'We should celebrate,' Lyn said.

'I want to work on the car,' Alex replied quickly.

Lyn frowned. 'You said everything was fine when we pulled up.'

She was right. It wasn't the car Alex was thinking about, so much as her own need for time alone. The Lotus was her excuse and her sanctuary. A place to hide until the turmoil inside her was gone. 'I just need to, you know, clean the windscreen. That sort of thing.'

'Just one quick drink. We have to eat anyway,' Lyn pleaded. 'Then you can work on the car to your heart's content.'

Alex couldn't say no, and if she was honest with herself, she didn't want to. She was thrilled with the result and wanted to celebrate. The problem was Kier. Or rather, the way she felt when he was around. She had to get control of her emotions. To get to a place where she could deal with Kier, or the next few days were going to be a nightmare. After that, he'd be gone again. She pretended she hadn't felt the tiny twinge of regret that accompanied that thought.

Acting as support and logistics was not as much fun as driving the Ferrari would have been, but it did have its compensations. Kier steered his hired car down a rough dirt track, the dust billowing out behind. He took a corner at speed, feeling the tail of the car start to drift out. He steered into the slide, enjoying the sensation of gradually bringing the car back under his control, then accelerated again, telling himself he was only driving like this because he had to get to the lunch staging area quickly. He was lying. He was driving like this because he was still a bit of a boy racer at heart. Or maybe it was just a way to forget about the women he was working for, and his ability to let them down totally.

Well, not totally. Lyn seemed to have recovered her good humour and forgiven him for crashing the Ferrari. She was, after all, still in the race. The crash and her decision to join forces with Alex in an all-girl team had attracted a bit of media attention and given her fund-raising a boost. And Paul's new friendship with their group didn't seem to bother her one little bit. They'd chatted away last night over a burger and beer, with Paul telling tales of legendary car rallies and drivers.

Alex, however, had been a different matter. She had

been subdued and distant. A couple of times Kier had caught her glancing at him, but she'd looked away rather than meet his eyes. He had a feeling that her behaviour was nothing to do with the race and everything to do with him.

It was Lyn's fault. He had never intended to take Alex in his arms, but Lyn's exuberance and that group hug had come too fast for him to avoid. He wouldn't do it again. It was like putting his arms around a storm. Exhilarating and dangerous and just a little bit frightening. He had thought those feelings were long gone, worn down by time and guilt and regret. He was wrong. She had felt something too, something that had unsettled her as much as it had him. She had barely touched her burger, and left the group with her beer only half finished. He guessed she had gone to work on the car, but everything in her manner had warned him to stay away. He had, for his own sake as much as for hers. They couldn't afford emotional entanglement. The last time had almost destroyed him. He would do whatever it took to help her win the race. Then they'd both go their separate ways.

He would start by being on time to the lunch break and standing by with food, tools and anything else she needed. While the race cars had set off on a long three-leg cross-country loop, Kier and the other support drivers were taking short cuts around back roads to get to the next staging area ahead of their drivers. Kier seemed to have chosen a route no one else was taking. The support teams vied with each other in friendly competition over who knew the fastest back routes.

As he took another corner at speed, a white van suddenly loomed in front of him. It was stopped in the middle of the road. He hit the brakes and pulled up, his bonnet just inches from the van, then turned the engine off and got out of his car. He walked around to the van driver's door, which was slightly open. He immediately recognised the National Parks and Wildlife badge on the side.

'Hello!' he called.

'Just a second.'

The voice came from the side of the road. He turned towards it. He could see movement behind the trunk of a large gum tree. A flash of colour as someone ... Embarrassed, Kier quickly looked away from the woman adjusting her long tie-dyed skirt as she emerged from behind the tree. That one quick glance was enough for him to recognise Dee Parker, the volunteer he'd met in Canberra two days before, who had a thing for kangaroos and was yet another woman totally pissed off at him.

'You know, you shouldn't leave your van in the middle of the road while you do that,' he couldn't stop himself saying. 'You could cause an accident.'

Dee Parker stopped in front of him and looked up, a disgusted frown on her face. She obviously recognised him too. 'Do I look that stupid?'

Whatever answer he gave, he was in trouble, so he decided it was a rhetorical question.

'Do you need some help?' he asked.

'Yes, I do,' Dee answered. 'My van has broken down.'

Damn it! Kier didn't have time for this. But neither could he just drive away and leave the poor woman stranded.

'I could have a look at it,' he said doubtfully.

'Thanks, but it wouldn't do much good. It's the ignition switch. It'll need to be towed.'

'Are you sure?' He didn't think Dee looked like the mechanical type.

'It's been giving me trouble for a little while. My mechanic has got a new switch on order – but it hasn't arrived yet.'

'Maybe I could jury-rig something?' He didn't have the time to waste, but he felt he should at least offer.

'Wouldn't do any good if you did. The battery was on its last legs – and while I was trying to get the van started again, it died altogether.'

Problem solved. 'Well, I can give you a lift to the next staging area.' He would still be there before Alex.

'That would be very helpful. Thank you.' Dee walked back to her van and stood by the open door.

'We need to get going,' Kier prompted.

'But first we have to push the van to the side of the road. We wouldn't want to cause an accident.' Her smile was saccharine sweet.

She was right. 'Okay.' Kier gave in. 'I'll push. You steer.'

'I can steer and push,' Dee said, hitching up her voluminous skirt. 'It'll take both of us to get this thing moving.'

She was right. The van was heavy and the road was as flat as a billiard table. Kier put his shoulder and back into it, and slowly they pushed the van far enough to clear the roadway.

'Right, let's go.' Kier strode purposefully towards his car, the clock in his head ticking loudly.

'Wait a minute. We can't leave the animals.'

'Animals?' That didn't sound good.

'Yes. It'll get too hot inside the van. They'll die. I'll take them with me.' Dee vanished through the side door of the van.

Curiosity got the better of Kier, and knowing he would probably regret it, he walked back to peer into the van's interior. It was set up as a mobile vet clinic, with space for someone to sleep, if they didn't mind getting up close and personal with the patients. Hanging from one wall was a series of woolly . . . pouches, he guessed was the best description. A long tail protruding from one suggested a young kangaroo was in residence. A baby koala was blinking short-sightedly at him from another. Dee was holding a third pouch in her hands.

'Here, take him.' She thrust the soft, slightly smelly bundle at him.

Kier took it gingerly and looked down. Something bald and stub-nosed and whiskered peered up at him through eyes that looked newly opened. 'What is that?' he asked.

'It's a southern hairy-nosed wombat,' Dee replied. 'Quite rare. That one is about four months old. Isn't she lovely?'

It was possibly the ugliest thing Kier had ever seen. And didn't all wombats have hairy noses? 'You're nursing it?'

'Yes. I've been nursing her for about three months. Her mother was killed on a road in South Australia.'

'Oh. I'm sorry.'

'Yes.' Dee glared at him from the darkened interior of the van. 'Driver hit her. Some flashy sports car.'

Despite his incident with the 'roo, Kier could hardly be held responsible for every driver to hit an animal in the road. He was tempted to ask if the driver had been hurt in the accident, but figured it was better not to.

'Can we get going now?'

'Yes. I've got them all.'

When Dee climbed down from the van, she had a big wicker basket in one hand, with at least three of the woolly pouches carefully placed inside it. She had another pouch strapped to her front, like a baby, and yet another hung over her shoulder like a bag.

'How many of these have you got?' Kier asked in astonishment.

'Two joeys, two koalas and two wombats,' Dee replied.

Kier gave up trying to make sense of the whole thing, and walked swiftly back to his car, hoping that would encourage Dee to follow. She did, then seemed to spend an age trying to find suitable safe places to put the animals amid the car parts, tools and rucksacks that filled the back of his car. She finally gave up, and Kier realised the animals were coming in the front with her. He looked at his watch. He didn't care what Dee did with her charges, just as long as they could get under way right now. He could still make the lunch staging area ahead of Alex, if he put his foot down.

They had barely covered a kilometre when Kier heard a phone ring. Dee produced a mobile from somewhere within her skirts.

'Yes?' She listened for a long time. 'I know where that is. It won't take me long to get there.'

'Get where?' Kier asked as she put the phone down.

'There's a report of an injured wedgie. It's not far from here. We need to go and get it.'

'A wedgie?'

'A wedge-tailed eagle.' Dee sniffed in exasperation.

'I know what it is,' Kier said, 'but why do we have to go and get it? I've got to get to the lunch staging post. My driver will be expecting me.'

'What for?'

'For support. That's my job. I have to be there in case there's something wrong. In case she needs me.'

'In *case* she does? I definitely do. Come on. We can't just leave it to die on the side of the road.'

'Isn't there someone else?' Kier asked desperately.

'No. It's not far. Turn around. There is a track just near the van. We have to go down that.'

For a minute Kier was tempted to say no. He glanced at Dee. She was glaring at him, her determination showing in every line of her face.

'I hear you're a racehorse trainer.' She studied him carefully. 'What if it was one of your horses?'

He turned the car around.

Dee seemed to know exactly where to go. She directed him down a couple of narrow dirt roads and through a farm gate into a paddock dotted with gum trees and grazing cows.

'You're kidding,' Kier said. 'This car isn't a four-wheel drive.'

'We can't use the road. It's closed for the race,' Dee said accusingly. 'This will be fine. There's a farm track. I can drive if you like.'

Kier put the car into gear and eased through the gate. Dee was right. There was a farm track, and it was perfectly serviceable. At last he stopped just near a fence. As he got out of the car, he heard the unmistakable roar of a race car at high speed. On the other side of the fence was a road. A second later, a car flashed past. Barely had its engine note faded into silence than Kier heard another car approaching.

'Over here. I need your help.'

Dee had found her injured wedgie. The big eagle was caught up in the barbed-wire fence, its clawed feet just able to touch the ground. One huge wing had become entangled in loose wires. The other trailed on the ground. As she approached, the bird started to struggle, flinging itself wildly about in an effort to break free. The struggle lasted for just a few seconds, and then it stopped and glared at its would-be rescuer with fierce yellow eyes. Its savage beak was open as it panted in distress.

'Some bastard has shot it.' Dee's voice was taut with anger.

'Why?' Kier asked.

'The graziers think they take the newborn lambs.'

'And do they?' To Kier's eyes the thing looked big and dangerous enough to tackle anything.

'Sometimes,' Dee admitted. 'But only if the lamb is very small or hurt or separated from its mother. But they are just doing it to survive. There's no need to do this to it.'

Kier could see a gaping wound in the bird's wing. Blood spattered the grass around it. He understood then that if Dee didn't do something, the bird would die.

'How can I help?'

'I don't suppose you've got a blanket in the car?'

Kier thought for a few seconds. 'I've got a car cover. It's heavy cotton. It's pretty big.'

'It'll have to do.'

Kier fetched the cover. Dee shook it out and nodded her approval. She took one end and told Kier to take the other. With the sheet stretched between them, they approached the bird. Dee's aim was to cover it.

'If he can't see, he won't struggle,' she told Kier. 'When he calms down, you can cut the fence wires and free him.'

They were less than two metres from the fence, when

the bird began to panic, flinging itself about wildly, its beak open.

'Quick, now, before he hurts himself more.'

It wasn't the bird Kier was worried about. The razor-sharp beak missed his fingers by centimetres as he dropped the car cover over the wedgie. He already had enough injuries. The bird, however, stopped thrashing immediately.

'Let's get to it,' Dee ordered.

It wasn't easy. The bird was hopelessly entangled. The barbed wire bit into Kier's flesh as he worked with a pair of pliers. Fresh spots of blood now stained the dressing on his arm. It took even longer than he'd expected.

The red Lotus flew past just as Kier cut the last wire. He caught the flash of colour out of the corner of his eyes. The car was unmistakable. His shoulders sagged. There was no possibility now that he'd get to the lunch station ahead of Alex. She would be furious with him, and rightly so. He'd let her down once again. He was never going to get her trust back if he kept on like this. He glanced over at Dee, who had wrapped the big bird carefully, tucking its wings safely against its body, and was now trying to decide how best to load it into his car. It wasn't his fault. He couldn't have just abandoned Dee and the injured bird. But Alex wouldn't see it that way.

He could only hope that nothing went wrong with the Lotus – and Alex didn't need him.

'Shit. There it goes again,' Alex shouted.

Lyn felt it too. There was definitely something wrong.

'Any idea what it is?' she yelled back over an engine that was sounding more like an old farm truck than a race car.

'Carbie,' Alex said. 'I'll bet the needle valve is jammed.'

Lyn had a vague idea what a carburettor was, but as for a needle valve and why it might be jammed . . .

'We've got about ten kilometres to the checkpoint and lunch break.' She stuck to what she knew. 'Will we make it?'

'I don't think so. How are we for time?'

Lyn glanced at her stopwatch. She could already feel the car slowing down. 'Not too bad.'

'All right. I think I can fix this . . . hang on.'

Alex braked hard. The road they were on ran parallel to an old stock route. There was a wide area of brown earth with a few patchy tufts of grass where she could get the car safely off the road. The Lotus had barely stopped moving when she leaped out.

'Get me something out of the boot. A wrench. Anything,' she yelled as she dashed to the front of the car.

Lyn followed her instructions. She opened the boot and grabbed the first heavy tool she saw – a shifting spanner. For once Alex didn't yell at her for slamming the boot lid.

'That'll do it.' Alex gave something under the bonnet two hard, swift bangs with the spanner. 'Get back in the car,' she yelled as she slammed the bonnet.

Lyn was still buckling her harness when Alex jammed her foot back on the accelerator. The engine roared, a familiar powerful sound.

'Got it,' Alex yelled triumphantly.

The car's tyres kicked up a cloud of dust as Alex threw it back towards the road. 'Did anyone overtake us?' she asked.

'I don't think so,' Lyn said. She glanced at the

stopwatch again. The pit stop had taken less than a minute.

'Good. When we get to the checkpoint, find Kier. We'll have to get this fixed – or else we could be in real trouble this afternoon.'

'All right. Eighty metres ahead, there's a dip. You can take it at about one-ten.'

The car was airborne when they cleared the dip.

Lyn guessed they were about twenty seconds over base time when they pulled into the lunch checkpoint. They reported to the stewards, and Alex parked the Lotus in a convenient place for working on it.

'We have to find Kier,' she said as soon as she was out of the car.

'What do we need?'

'He's got the tools,' Alex said. 'You find him. Tell him it's the needle valve. He'll know what I need. I'm going to the parts truck. They'll have a new valve.'

She vanished into the crowd. Lyn looked about, expecting to see Kier materialise as he had done yesterday, clutching food and exuding an aura of calm confidence.

Nothing.

Lyn stood on her toes, but even she wasn't tall enough to spot Kier in the crowd. She opened the Lotus door and stepped up on to the door frame. Those extra few centimetres helped, but there was still no sign of Kier. Where was he? Maybe he was buying them lunch, like yesterday. She got down from her perch and shut the door. The Lotus wasn't locked, but she guessed that was the least of their problems right now. She set off at a trot towards the food stalls. The crowd was thick, but several minutes of pushing and generally making herself unpopular with the people in the queues convinced her that Kier wasn't there. She turned back to the Lotus.

Alex had the bonnet up. A small collection of tools lay at her feet. She looked up as Lyn approached.

'Where is he?'

'I don't know.'

'Damn him!'

'Did you get the part you needed?' Lyn asked.

'Yes, but I haven't got enough tools to do the job. They are all in Kier's car. And there's just not enough time to do this by myself.'

Lyn looked wildly around. For the first time in her life, she wished she knew something about what went on under the bonnet of a car. There was nothing she could do. Or was there?

'I'll be right back,' she yelled as she broke into a run.

She reached the blue Alfa in seconds. Paul was leaning against the door, talking to someone whom Lyn assumed was his navigator.

'Hi, Lyn,' Paul said. 'Have you met Jack—'

'Paul, we need your help,' Lyn interrupted.

'What's wrong?'

Lyn explained.

Before she had even finished speaking, Paul was moving towards his boot. 'Your carbie is a Weber? Then I've got what you need. Jack, I'll be back soon.'

'Do you need me too?' his navigator asked genially.

'No. You get some lunch, and check the Alfa.'

'Okay.'

'Sorry about this,' Lyn said to Jack as she turned to follow Paul. The navigator just smiled and nodded.

Alex looked up as they approached her car, clearly

expecting to see Kier. For a fraction of a second, Lyn thought she saw Alex's face start to crumple, as if she was hurt. Or about to burst into tears. It was gone so fast she could have imagined it, to be replaced by hard anger.

'Where is he?'

'I don't know, but Paul offered to help.'

Paul was already opening his tool kit. Without another word, Alex turned back to the job at hand, and within a few moments they were both engrossed in their work.

Lyn stood by the Lotus in an agony of indecision. Should she go looking for Kier? He must be here somewhere. He wasn't the sort of person to let them down.

'How much time have we got?' Alex called from under the bonnet.

Lyn looked at her watch. 'About fifty minutes.'

'That won't be enough.'

'It will be,' Paul's deep, calm voice assured her. 'Now, can you hold this while I . . .'

Lyn didn't understand what they were talking about. She felt totally useless. There was nothing she could do but watch the clock ticking, and all that would do was make things worse.

'Lyn,' Paul's head emerged from under the bonnet, 'is there any chance you could get us all a sandwich and a coffee? Maybe a bottle of water. I think we're going to need it.'

Glad of something to do, Lyn headed in the direction of the food stalls. The crowds were still fairly thick, and she had to join a queue. As she waited, she kept searching the crowd. Where was Kier? By the time she returned to the car, there were metal parts carefully lined up on a rag draped across the wing, and the odour of petrol fumes was strong enough to drown out the inviting smell of the coffee she was carrying. Paul and Alex were still bent over the engine, their heads buried under the bonnet as they worked on the . . . whatever it was, their bums stuck up in the air like ducks on a pond.

Mind you, there was nothing duck-like about Paul's bum. The overalls that had so effectively hidden it until now were pulled quite tight across his hips and lower back. The body underneath the dark blue fireproof suit was fit and well put together. As he worked on the engine, Lyn could see his muscular shoulders moving. He looked very strong.

As if sensing her gaze, Paul half turned to look at her, smiling as he recognised her.

He's really quite handsome, Lyn thought, and immediately recognised how incongruous that thought was. She spent her working life surrounded by male models who were handsome enough to draw a woman's eyes to a billboard or an ad in a magazine. She regularly saw them stripped to their underwear, their carefully toned bodies tanned and glossy. She worked with them wearing the briefest of swimsuits. Not once had she felt the sudden low tingle that suffused her now, as a grease-covered, slightly greying and bearded man grinned cheekily at her.

Why was that?

Her mind drifted back to the previous night. The four of them had set out to eat at one of the many food stalls that seemed to appear like magic each time the rally stopped for the night. A burger and a beer at a plastic table. It hardly counted as dinner. Alex had left quickly to work on the car. Kier went in a different direction soon afterwards, leaving Lyn and Paul to chat over a second beer. She couldn't remember when she'd last felt so relaxed. So happy. For once in her life she was with a man who was as interested in what she had to say as in what she looked like. Paul's conversation tended to leap from topic to topic with an almost breathtaking agility. He was smart and amusing. He seemed to think she was too . . .

'Lyn?'

'What?' Lyn suddenly realised she was staring at Paul, who was now standing in front of her, one hand extended for a sandwich. For the second time in as many days, she found herself at the point of blushing.

'How are the repairs?' she asked quickly.

'We're getting there,' Paul said.

'There's not enough time to eat,' Alex called from under the bonnet.

Lyn could hear the tension in her voice. She looked at Paul. One corner of his mouth lifted in a wry grin as he demolished his sandwich in a few seconds, then washed it down with a swig from a bottle of water. He handed the bottle back to Lyn and turned back to the job.

'You eat something,' he said to Alex. 'I've got this.'

'I'm fine,' came the reply.

'No you're not,' Paul argued, possibly unaware that he was risking life and limb with Alex in a temper. 'If you don't eat something, you'll never make it through the afternoon. I said I've got this.' The tone of his voice brooked no further argument.

Alex emerged from under the bonnet and took the sandwich Lyn offered. Her face was murderous as she spun around, searching the crowd. Lyn didn't have to guess who she was looking for. She found herself hoping that Kier wouldn't turn up. Not until after they had left.

'How are we for time?' Alex asked.

'Five minutes.' Lyn didn't have to look at her watch.

She'd been keeping close track of time from the moment they'd driven into the lunch area.

'I'm almost done,' Paul called from under the bonnet. 'I just need to tighten this . . .'

'Car number fifty-three! Where are you? I need you right now!' The steward's call came just as Paul emerged from under the bonnet, wiping the last of the grease and oil off his hands.

'Good luck,' he said as he marched swiftly back to the blue Alfa Romeo, where his navigator would be waiting.

'Thanks,' Lyn called after him.

'My pleasure!' The reply drifted back over his shoulder. It really was, Lyn thought. Maybe that was what it was about Paul. He seemed to take such pleasure from life.

'Come on.' Alex was back in the car, and revving the engine to test it.

'How does it sound?' Lyn asked as she strapped herself in.

'It sounds good.' Alex slipped the car into gear and edged into place in the starting line-up.

'That was nice of Paul to help,' Lyn said thoughtfully.

'Yes. But when I see Kier, I am going to kill him.'

'**W**here were you?'
     Kier didn't turn around. He didn't want to see her face.

'I'm sorry.' The words were hopelessly inadequate. Nothing he could say would excuse him.

At this hour of the early morning, the sunlight was soft and gentle, turning the harsh outback landscape into something incredibly beautiful. Before the heat of the day, the riverbank was a peaceful place. A haven away from prying eyes and the pressures of work and family. But not today. The blanket that lay in the grass was rumpled and dirty and damp with morning dew. Plastic food containers lay scattered about, left by the animals who had come scavenging for the contents. The drinks esky had been overturned, the ice long since melted. The animals hadn't been interested in the wine bottle. It lay on its side, accusing him.

It would have been their first real date. A late-night picnic by the river. Alex had suggested it, and by the look of the ruined picnic site, she had gone to a lot of trouble to make it nice. There were even a couple of candles, burned down to mere nubs. Their first date. And he hadn't shown up.

'Why?' Her voice quivered as she spoke.

Slowly he bent down and picked up a stone. He turned it over in his hands, feeling the rough texture hard against his skin. There was no excuse – but there was a reason. With a slow underhand throw, he tossed the stone into the river. The splash as it hit the water sounded unnaturally loud in the still morning air. He turned around.

She was sitting on a fallen tree, her arms wrapped around her knees. Her hair hung loose, framing a tear-stained face. Her eyes were bright, with more tears or with anger, he wasn't sure which. She was wearing a dress instead of jeans. Her feet were bare. In the dust in front of her lay a pair of strappy shoes, the exact opposite of the riding boots she normally wore. The load of guilt and remorse on Kier's shoulders grew just a bit heavier.

'You've been here all night.' It wasn't a question.

'I've been waiting for you.'

They were right. Jim Cassidy. Her family. Her mother's friends. Everyone who thought he wasn't good enough for her. He wasn't. He knew that now. He was from the wrong part of town. The wrong family. It was the wrong time and place for them. He should just walk away. But he owed her an explanation.

'I was at the police station.'

'What?'

'I spent most of last night at the police station.' He hesitated, then decided she should hear it all. 'I was in a cell. Under arrest.'

He braced himself for the anger and accusations. He'd had one lot already from his parents. It would be much harder to take coming from Alex.

He heard her sharp intake of breath. 'What happened?'

'My brother Rob, that's what happened.'

She must have heard the bitterness in his voice. She was beside him, her fingers grasped his hand and she pulled him back to sit next to her on the fallen tree.

'Tell me.'

'He and a couple of his mates were planning to sneak into the pub. Lift some booze. I was just coming down here when I saw them meeting up. Heard them talking about it. I . . . I hid in the back of his ute. I thought I could talk him out of it. I was wrong.'

'He didn't listen to you?'

'No.' That wasn't even part of it. Kier still felt the shame of Rob's words when he realised his younger brother had followed him. He had done a lot more than yell at Kier. He had taken some cheap shots, to embarrass him in front of his rowdy mates. Then they'd gone ahead with the plan and dragged him into it with them. He could be lookout, they said. He hadn't even been able to get that right.

'You got caught?'

'There was someone staying overnight at the pub. They heard one of the guys forcing the lock on the back door. They called the cops.'

'And where were you?'

'I was outside. I didn't know what to do. I was the first one they arrested.'

'Didn't you tell the cops you were trying to stop them?'

'No.'

'But—'

'Alex, he's my brother. I couldn't just lay the blame on him. What about my mother? What would she think if I tried to save myself by dumping Rob in it? Anyway, the cops wouldn't have believed me.'

Her silence told him she agreed.

'Dad came and bailed us out.' Kier hurried on, just wanting to get the moment over. 'He's pretty pissed at us right now.' He rubbed his arm, where the bruises were just starting to show. His father wasn't one for gentleness when it came to his troublesome sons.

'Did he hit you?'

'Not really.'

She said nothing, but the way her fingers tightened around his told him she understood.

'So what happens now?'

'I don't know. I don't think we'll go to jail. We didn't actually steal anything.' He tried to sound confident, but he wasn't. This was his first brush with the law, but his brother had been in this sort of trouble before. He'd had more than one warning.

'They won't send you to jail. You're only seventeen. They can't!' The last words were a cry of protest.

Alex had her own definition of right and wrong. It was one of the reasons he liked her so much. Her judgement of people – her judgement of him – was not defined by someone else's rules. Unfortunately, other people's rules did apply in the rest of the world.

'I'm sorry I wasn't here,' he said. 'I wanted to be. I was coming, but I had to try to stop my brother.'

'It's all right.' Alex squeezed his hand again. 'I understand. Family should come first.'

He looked at her as she spoke, hearing his own anguish reflected in her voice. He knew that wasn't the way it worked in her family. Her father's business came first. Or her mother's friends. Never Alex. She was never first, and she should be.

'We'll have a picnic some other time,' she went on. 'It'll be just the same.'

But it wouldn't be the same. It couldn't be. He had taken something from her. The joy of that first real date. That was something she would never get back – because of him. He squeezed her hand, not able to speak, as he vowed that he would never, ever let her down again.

'Parking or working?' the gate steward asked.

'Working,' Kier said automatically, although he really had no idea if Alex would need his help this evening. Or want it.

'All right – to your left. There's space for support vehicles behind the sheep pens.' The steward waved him through.

Tonight's race headquarters were at the Cooma showgrounds. It looked pretty much the same as Queanbeyan the night before: a collection of wooden buildings and machinery sheds. It was already starting to fill with support teams, media, caterers and stewards, but of the race cars there was no sign. He checked his watch, found a parking spot, and settled down to wait. There was nothing else he could do. The first car wasn't due for at least an hour yet.

The little red Lotus drove into the showgrounds just as the sun was starting to sink. Kier heaved a small sigh of relief as he watched Alex steer into her place in the parc fermé. The race rules didn't allow mechanical work there, which meant she wasn't having any trouble with the car. His failure to show up at lunchtime hadn't been a problem. He was eager to hear how the day had gone – and whether Alex had improved on her good times of yesterday.

'Where the hell were you?' She had removed her racing helmet and was holding it in her gloved hands. She looked as if she wanted to hurl it at him. 'At lunchtime. Where were you?'

'I got held up,' Kier said, feeling his defences rising. 'Why? Did you have a problem?'

'Yes. I had a problem. You were my problem. I had to install a new needle valve. You were supposed to be there to help.' Her eyes were bright, not with tears but with pure unadulterated rage.

'God, I'm sorry.' Kier felt his stomach lurch with guilt. 'That wildlife woman, Dee Parker, broke down. Then there were all the animals. And there was an eagle she wanted to rescue. I had to take her . . .' He stopped talking. It wasn't doing any good. He could tell by the look on Alex's face that she wasn't listening. She turned on her heel and stormed away.

Kier wanted to follow her. He wanted to explain. Needed to explain that this time was different. Except it wasn't. He'd let her down, as he had in the past. No wonder she held such a low opinion of him. She had every reason to.

'Don't worry. She'll get over it.' Lyn put a comforting hand on his arm. He hadn't even noticed her get out of the car. 'Paul was there to help us out. They got it fixed and it didn't miss a beat all afternoon.'

'I should have been there,' Kier said, watching Alex's back vanish into the crowd.

'In some ways you did us a favour,' Lyn added. 'She was so pissed off at you that she drove like a demon. Nearly killed us a couple of times, but I guess we're probably in the lead now.'

Kier shook his head. That didn't make it all right. Not even close to all right.

'I'd just stay clear of her for a while. Maybe once the

times go up she'll calm down a bit.'

'Thanks, Lyn,' Kier said. 'But I think it's going to take a bit longer than that.'

Lyn patted his arm sympathetically and headed in search of her hotel and a hot shower.

Kier decided to wait around for the day's results. There was nothing else he could do. In the meantime, he would clean the windscreen and lights of the Lotus. It wasn't much, but it was something useful, and it might stop him feeling like he was slipping back through time, becoming the teenager who always seemed to do the wrong thing – especially around those people he cared about the most.

The phone in his pocket rang. He pulled it out and looked at the caller ID. Katie. He flicked the top open.

'Hello, sweetheart.'

'Hi, Dad. How did it go today?'

'Not too bad,' he told her.

Yesterday, Katie had been on the list of women who were mad at him. In her case, it was because he'd crashed the Ferrari. Not that she was overly concerned about the car or the kangaroo, but having a father racing with a supermodel had apparently catapulted her up her school's social ladder. Having him as support crew was nowhere near as exciting.

'Are the girls winning?' she asked.

'We don't know yet. The results aren't up. Maybe.'

'Cool! The boys in my class would really, really hate that.'

As he listened to Katie's voice bubbling down the phone, Kier's mood lifted. He had made a lot of mistakes in his life. To be sure, Katie was the result of one of those mistakes, but in this case, he had no regrets. She was his beautiful daughter, and he loved her unreservedly.

'You'll never guess what I did today,' he said when she paused for breath. 'I rescued an eagle!'

Her excited reply left him in no doubt that his Good Samaritan act had scored him more points with Katie than with Alex.

Ten minutes under a refreshing shower had eased the kinks from Alex's shoulders, but not the anger from her heart. The day's results wouldn't be posted for at least another hour – and she had nothing to do. She almost wished there was something wrong with the car. At least that would take her mind off Kier. It might give her a chance to work out some of her anger. She slipped on a pair of jeans and a T-shirt, and as she did, she realised she was starting to feel hungry. She decided to head back to the showgrounds. She was sure Lyn would come back to check their official time. Maybe the two of them should get dinner together. Alex knew she'd been pretty impossible all afternoon. She had been short-tempered and had scared even herself a couple of times by driving like a maniac. They might be looking pretty good on the leaderboard now, but she should still find Lyn and apologise. Lyn was proving to be a good navigator – and Alex had a feeling they might even become friends, if she gave it a chance. That was the answer. She should stop fretting about Kier and relax a bit. She and Lyn might even have a drink. One couldn't hurt.

She left the hotel and crossed the road to the show-grounds. As she walked through the gate, she spotted the white van with the wildlife service logo on the door. The bonnet was up and someone was working underneath it. But that wasn't what attracted her attention. Two people were standing near the van's side door. One was a woman who looked like an ageing hippie. That must be the Parker woman she'd heard so much about. The other was a man wearing blue jeans, and heavy-duty leather gloves that came most of the way up to his elbows. As Alex watched, he reached into the van and pulled out a bundle wrapped in what looked like a green blanket.

The bundle moved and a clawed foot slashed the air. Long, vicious talons closed around the man's gloved fist, digging deep into the thick, rough leather.

'Careful,' Dee Parker warned the man. 'That wing's pretty bad. He's in a lot of pain. It's a good thing I was with that rally guy when I got the call. There's no way I could have done this on my own.'

With that rally guy? She heard Kier's words again – understanding them properly for the first time. *There was an eagle she wanted to rescue*. Alex hadn't been in the mood to listen, but he'd been telling the truth.

'Can I have that blanket back,' Dee called to the man with the bird. 'It's some sort of car cover. I want to give it back to the guy who helped me.'

'Sure, Dee. Just hang on.' The man carried the eagle to a nearby car that had the words Veterinary Clinic painted on the side. A large wooden box sat on the ground next to it. In a manoeuvre too fast and smooth for Alex to follow, he somehow transferred the injured bird from the bundle to the box, without any fuss or injury to either the bird or himself. Alex was impressed. After looking at the clawed foot, she wouldn't have wanted to get that close to the bird.

'Excuse me.' Alex approached Dee. 'I'm sorry. The man who helped you with the eagle was Kier Thomas, wasn't it?'

'That's him,' Dee said. 'The guy who hit the 'roo just before the start of the race.'

Alex nodded in what she hoped was a sympathetic fashion. 'I know him. I'm going to see him now. Do you want me to deliver that for you?' She pointed to the rumpled car cover, now eagle-free.

'Well, yes. That would be great,' Dee said. 'Please thank him for me. He was really terrific. He was worried about not being late to the lunch stage. Something about helping his driver.'

'Oh . . .'

'I guess I just bludgeoned him into helping me. He was pretty good, too. Didn't frighten the bird any more than it was already. Tell him that I hope everything was all right, and he didn't get into trouble.'

'I will.'

'Great. Thanks. I'd better get on. I've got babies to feed.'

Babies? Alex decided she didn't want to know. Murmuring something she hoped was appropriate, she bundled up the car cover and made her retreat.

Kier wasn't at the stewards' station, where people were already waiting for the day's official results. Alex nodded a greeting to a couple of the other drivers, then turned away. She found Kier's hire car behind the sheep pens, where all the support vehicles were parked. She had a spare key in her pocket, and decided to put the car cover in the boot. She shook it out as she did, and a few feathers floated to the ground. She bent and picked one up. It was golden brown, black-tipped and elegantly curved. She stroked it softly. It was really quite lovely. She hoped the bird would survive whatever injuries it had received.

She found Kier in the only other place she looked. With the Lotus. He had a bucket of soapy water, and was washing the windscreen. She watched him for a few moments, before he knew she was there. Perhaps he felt her eyes on him, because he looked up and smiled tentatively.

'Hi.'

'Hi.'

The silence that followed was awkward, but not as bad as she had expected.

'I wanted to say I'm sorry,' Kier said. 'I should have been—'

'No. I'm sorry,' Alex cut him off. 'I didn't listen to you. You did exactly what you should have done.' She held the feather out.

He took it gently and studied it.

'He's gone to the vet,' Alex said. 'I hope he's going to be all right.'

'So do I,' Kier said, nodding. He looked at her, his dark eyes asking for her understanding. 'I couldn't leave it to die.'

'I know.'

They both fell silent. Alex was remembering Kier's affection for the black colt, all those years ago. Perhaps he was too.

'By the way,' she said, 'I put the car cover back in the boot of the Holden.'

'Thanks.'

'Kier . . .' Alex hesitated, reluctant to speak of what was foremost in her mind. She was afraid of where it might lead. But she was equally afraid of what would happen if she didn't put the ghosts to rest. 'I think . . . Do we need to talk? About us?'

Kier's eyes were unreadable as he studied her face. 'What about us?'

'Well,' Alex's courage failed her, 'I just wanted to say that, whatever happened in the past, we shouldn't let it get in the way now.'

Those weren't the words she'd wanted to say, and she could tell by the look on his face that they were not the words he'd expected to hear. But it was the best she could do. She was too afraid to reach deeper inside herself, and awaken a whole world of pain.

'No. We shouldn't. That was a long time ago.' Kier spoke softly. 'I never meant to—'

'I know.' She interrupted him before he could venture into dangerous waters. 'We were very young. Very foolish. Shall we just let the past rest?'

'I guess so.' He sounded hesitant.

'We can work together. Can't we?' Alex hated the almost pleading tone of her own voice.

'Of course we can.'

'Then let's just forget all about then – and focus on the here and now,' she said, hoping that would put an end to the subject.

The ongoing silence was only marginally less awkward, and it seemed as if it would last for ever. The sudden clamour of voices from near the stewards' room was a very welcome interruption.

'The times must have been posted,' Alex said.

'Shall we?'

She nodded.

Lyn was already there when they arrived. She had somehow wormed her way to the front of the crowd and was running her finger down the leaderboard.

'Yes!' She punched the air, earning a little cheer from the men around her.

'Lyn?' called Alex, her hopes rising.

'We're in front!' Lyn called as she pushed her way through the crowd towards them. 'A fifteen-second lead.'

'Fifteen seconds?' Kier raised an eyebrow in mock astonishment. 'You must have been really flying this afternoon.'

'We were,' Alex said briefly, remembering why.

'You'll have to get pissed at Kier a bit more often,' Lyn said, 'if that's what it's going to do to our times.'

'I think not,' Kier said hurriedly. 'Instead, why don't I buy us dinner and a drink to celebrate? There's nothing we have to do to the car tonight, is there, Alex?'

There wasn't. There was no reason at all for her to say no. There didn't have to be a reason for everything, did there?

'All right,' she said.

The three of them made their way to one corner of the showgrounds, where a barbecue and bar had been set up. The bar was crowded with racers and supporters, officials, photographers and the other assorted hangers-on who are always to be found in the vicinity of any car race . . . or any bar.

'Beer?' Kier asked.

From the makeshift look of the place, Alex doubted that there would be anything other than beer. But it would be cold and wet, and right now, that sounded pretty good. She nodded. While she and Lyn waited for Kier to return, she noticed that her navigator's attention was elsewhere.

'Who are you looking for?' she asked.

Lyn almost blushed. 'I was just wondering if Paul was here.'

'Paul White?'

Lyn nodded sheepishly. 'I was just . . .' Her voice trailed off.

Alex smiled to see Lyn, the gorgeous model, looking so discomforted. 'I can see that. When did this happen?'

'When did what happen?' Lyn asked defensively.

'You know what I mean.'

'Nothing's happened,' Lyn said firmly.

'But you wish it would?' Alex teased.

'No . . . but . . . it might be nice . . .'

'What might be nice?' Kier's voice interrupted them.

'A steak from the barbecue,' Alex said quickly, coming to Lyn's rescue.

'Good idea,' Kier agreed. 'By the way, look who I found at the bar.'

He stepped to one side, and Paul appeared at his shoulder.

'Hello, ladies,' he said, giving a mock bow.

'Hi, Paul,' Alex said.

Lyn just smiled.

'I see from the results that everything went well for you after our lunchtime repairs,' Paul said. 'You have great times for this afternoon's stages. Well done.'

'Thanks. And thank you for your help,' Alex said.

'It was my pleasure.' Paul took a deep drink of his beer. 'Now, did someone mention steak? I could eat half a cow, the way I feel right now.'

The four of them made their way to the barbecue. As they walked, they seemed to naturally form into two couples, Paul and Lyn in the lead, with Alex and Kier following on behind. It didn't mean anything, Alex thought. Well, it might for Lyn and Paul, but it certainly didn't for her and Kier. They had been this route once before, and were not likely to make the same mistake again.

At the barbecue, they joined an excited crowd, jostling for food as they talked about cars and times, roads and races. Alex watched the ease with which Kier talked to the men and women around him. He'd changed a lot over the years. There was little sign of the youth who'd been so out of place in her world. She could still remember the time he'd appeared in court. It wasn't his fault. His brother Rob had gotten into trouble and dragged Kier along with him. But that day, Kier had been an outsider in so many ways. The judge had been lenient with him, because of his youth, and set him loose with a warning. Alex could remember her father's manager talking about it. Jim Cassidy had seen Rob and Kier's arrest as nothing more or less than they deserved and predicted a bad end for both of them. Well, in Kier's case, he had been wrong. Not that it had mattered, the way things turned out.

'A penny for them.'

Kier's voice interrupted her reverie.

'What?'

'A penny for your thoughts.'

'They're not worth that much,' Alex said. 'Anyway, shouldn't it be a cent?'

'Maybe.' Kier grinned. 'But somehow that doesn't have the same ring to it. Can I get you another?' He indicated the empty beer glass in her hand.

'No. Thanks. I'm racing tomorrow, remember?'

'You take it seriously, don't you?'

'There's not much point doing it if you don't take it seriously.'

Kier didn't answer. All around them, racegoers were starting to really let their hair down. The beer was flowing freely.

'Some of them will be in trouble if they get tested tomorrow,' Alex said.

'But not you.' Kier smiled. 'I was always the one getting into trouble. Never you.'

'Not always,' Alex pointed out. 'I wasn't quite the good girl that people seemed to think.'

'No. You weren't.'

His voice was soft with memory as he spoke. Alex looked up into his face. He was standing so close to her she could almost hear his heartbeat. For so many years, she had wondered what sort of a man Kier had become. How different from the boy who had shared her youth. Now she knew. He was strong and confident. More handsome now than then. He still cared – about his horses. About the eagle. About her? Alex found herself wanting to run her hand up the soft cotton of his shirt, to feel the solid flesh that until now had only been a dream. Her fingers tingled with memory that longed to be renewed.

'I'm sorry I let you down.' His voice was as soft as the caress of a feather.

Alex searched his face. Did he mean today? Or did he mean all those years ago? Today's lapse was already forgiven. But as for the past . . . could she possibly forgive that?

'Kier . . . I . . .'

'I think you should just go and talk to your mates now. All right?' The voice was loud enough to be heard above the general buzz of the conversation all around them. Kier and Alex turned towards the sound.

Lyn and Paul had been standing a little apart from the rest of the crowd, chatting to each other. Another man had joined them, and had moved very close to Lyn. From the tension on Lyn's face, Alex could see that his attention was unwanted.

'Come on, man.' The stranger addressed Paul. 'I just want to talk to her.'

'Well she doesn't want to talk to you.' Paul kept his body between Lyn and the speaker.

'You don't think you're in there, do you?' the stranger spat at Paul. 'A bird like that is well out of your league, mate.'

Paul ignored the comment. 'Why don't you just head back to the bar and leave the lady alone?' His voice hardened on the last words, and Alex had a sudden glimpse of the tough man under the very affable exterior that Paul maintained.

'Yeah. All right.' Perhaps the drunk had seen that toughness too. He walked none too steadily towards the bar.

'Are you all right?' Alex asked, moving quickly to Lyn's side.

'I'm fine,' Lyn hastened to assure her. 'Thanks to Paul.'

'It's not a problem.' Paul smiled down at her.

Watching them, Alex suddenly wondered if perhaps there was more to this than met the eye.

'I think I'll head back now,' Lyn said. 'I'm not really in the mood any more.'

'And we've got to race tomorrow,' Alex added. Calling an end to the evening now was probably the safest thing – for all of them.

7

The third day of the inaugural Snowy Mountains Classic Race dawned bright and clear. The town of Cooma was well supplied with trees and the birds to go with them. Lyn heard their early-morning calls as she lay in bed, waiting for the alarm that was supposed to wake her. She'd spent a restless night, and she knew it had a lot to do with the incident at the bar. And even more to do with Paul. She could still hear the stranger's challenge to him. *Do you think you're in there?* The expression was crude, but the thought behind the question had set her tossing and turning well after she had changed into an oversize T-shirt and slipped into bed.

Was Paul attracted to her? No, that was the wrong question. She was a model, and had no pretensions about her looks. She was physically attractive to almost any straight man with eyesight and a pulse. That wasn't what she was looking for, but most men couldn't see past the face and figure. Paul seemed different. He seemed to genuinely like her. For herself. He didn't treat her like a blonde bimbo. Maybe there could be something . . .

Lyn slid out of bed. As was her habit, she turned on both the electric kettle and her laptop before heading for the shower. By the time she emerged from the bathroom in a cloud of steam, the kettle had boiled and the computer had connected itself to the internet. She made herself a cup of instant coffee and looked at her e-mail.

There were two from her mother and one from her agent. Lyn felt a twinge of guilt. Each day, as soon as she was free, she fulfilled her obligations to her sponsor, uploading a blog and any photos she'd taken. That left the evenings to check in with her mother. But last night, she'd been at the bar. After that, her thoughts had been on Paul. She hadn't spared a moment for her mother. Or, more importantly, her sister.

The first e-mail had been posted late yesterday afternoon. Her sister had had a bad day. The doctor was advising changing her medication again. Lyn fought down a mild feeling of panic and opened the second mail. It had been sent last night. Lorna had finally fallen asleep. Her mother was planning to take her back to the doctor and Lyn shouldn't worry. Lyn's lips twitched. Her mother was a fine one to say don't worry. She glanced at the clock beside the bed, then reached for her mobile phone.

'Hi, Mum.'

'Lyn. What are you doing calling me this early? Aren't you busy with race things?'

'Not yet, Mum. Soon. I wanted to see how Lorna was doing.'

'She's just awake now. She's all right. The doctor says we'll have to keep trying until we get the new medication right.'

'She didn't have an episode, did she?' Lorna's occasional seizures were not life-threatening, but they were terrifying. It was hard to watch her suffer, and be unable to do anything to help her.

'No. Nothing like that. Don't you worry.'

Lyn was certain that her mother was lying, trying to shield her. She sounded tired. Very tired. Lyn could almost see her face – the deep lines around her eyes and the grey hair cut short because there wasn't the time or money for luxuries. Caring for a severely handicapped daughter wasn't an easy task. Things had become a lot better since Lyn had started earning good money as a model. But it was a pretty tough life for a woman alone. Lyn had some memories of her father. She supposed they had been happy once. That must have been before her sister was born. By the time Lorna was two years old, her disability was obvious, and her father walked out the door, never to return. Lyn hated him for that. It wasn't just the money, although making ends meet had been very hard back then. She hated her father because he took away the support and love her mother needed.

Which was why Lyn was where she was right now – sitting in a hotel room looking at a set of blue overalls hanging near the window. She was doing this to help her mother, and the other families who needed support.

'I'm sorry I wasn't there, Mum,' she said softly.

'Don't be silly. What you are doing will help us more than I can say. The centre needs that sponsorship money. We'll all benefit. How is the race going?'

'Well, we are winning.'

The news seemed to cheer her mother.

Lyn ended the call, then checked the mail from her agent. She had been offered work in the forthcoming European fashion shows. The money was very, very good. She sent back an immediate acceptance. She hated being away from home for long periods, but she couldn't refuse. She had only a few years to earn that sort of fee. By the time her face and figure were no longer saleable, she needed to have everything Lorna would need for the future, and enough money set aside for emergencies.

What had she been doing – thinking about Paul and the possibility of a relationship? For the next few years, her priority had to be earning money to care for Lorna in the years ahead. The time would come when the full responsibility for Lorna's care would fall on Lyn's shoulders, and she couldn't ask any man to take that on. If their father couldn't love them enough to stay, how could she expect any other man to be different? Not only that, most men wanted a family, and Lyn couldn't even offer that. Angelman's syndrome was hereditary, passed down through the female line. She was never going to have children. She couldn't take that risk.

With a loud sigh, she closed her laptop. For a short while, it had been nice to dream. But that was all it was – a dream. Reality was knocking on her door. It was time to answer.

Alex wasn't sure why she was awake and restless so early. It couldn't be the row with Kier that was bothering her. They'd worked that through and were back on an even keel – ready to work together to win this race. There was nothing about Kier that should be keeping her awake at night. She showered and slipped into her racing clothes. Her helmet and leather gloves were sitting on the chair. She quickly tossed her things into her bag and left it just inside the door. By agreement, Kier was now in charge of logistics. He would collect the bag after he had seen her off on the first leg of the race. After she had given him the key to her room. She decided she didn't want to think about Kier and room keys. She forced him out of her mind, and hunger found its way in.

As she left the motel, she paused to take a long, deep breath. The mountains were still a distance away, but she felt as if she could smell the clean air. Almost feel its cool tang. Racing through the mountains would be such fun. The roads would be steep, the corners sharp. A challenge for any car and any driver, and she so loved a challenge.

Her step quickened as she approached the gate to the parking compound. She flashed her pass at the security man on the gate and went inside. It was far from deserted. Some of the mechanics would have been up all night, working. Keeping a classic race car fettled was hard work. The engine needed constant attention. The brakes had to be checked and tightened, the clutch nursed and the suspension maintained. Racing was demanding and a little dangerous. Very different from the meticulous detail of her career as a lawyer, but she was beginning to realise that she rather liked it!

The food stalls were up and running and she stopped for coffee. Someone had already paid a visit to the town's bakery – there were muffins and fruit Danish on sale. A blueberry muffin was just what she needed to prepare for the race ahead. Munching happily, she walked along the line of cars, nodding a greeting to those who lifted their heads from their work as she passed.

There it was. Her little car. Red and sleek and shiny. It looked lovely just waiting for her. She felt such a glow of satisfaction when she looked at it. It had taken a long time to find the right Lotus. Eight years ago, she had tracked it down in an old farm shed, a million kilometres from anywhere. Its owner had forgotten it and left it buried for years beneath bird droppings, dust and decay. Alex had almost wept at the neglect of such a beautiful car. She'd bought it and set about returning it to its former glory. The Lotus had filled many empty hours in her life, and she felt a thrill of pride every time she looked at it.

She finished her coffee, and tossed the empty paper cup and the muffin wrapper into a nearby rubbish bin. Before touching the car, she wiped her fingers clean on the legs of her overalls. The racing suit was starting to look a bit rumpled and stained after two days of competition, but she only had one, and the rules wouldn't allow her to wear anything else. Her mother would be horrified, and not just at the state of the overalls. Jacqueline Reilly had never understood Alex's passions. Not for the car. Not for anything.

'Alex, surely you're not going down to the stables now?' Her mother's querulous voice greeted her as she opened the back door.

'Just for a bit, Mother,' Alex called. It wasn't a lie. Alex's definition of *'a bit'* was simply different to her mother's.

'Why don't you change out of those dreadful old clothes? Put on something nice. We could have some iced tea and talk.'

Alex grimaced. Her mother spent most afternoons reading in what she called her conservatory. It was really just an enclosed part of the huge veranda that surrounded the homestead on all sides. The conservatory was a room of pastels and frills. In this sanctuary, her mother would arrange flowers, brought at great cost from the city, and read novels of a bygone era. There was very little they could talk about.

'Dad is going to be in the stables this afternoon. I've got something to show him.'

Alex couldn't hear her mother's sigh, but she didn't have to. She knew what she was thinking.

'*What about your homework?*' *Jacqueline Reilly wasn't a big believer in higher education for girls, but Alex knew she preferred her daughter to study than spend her time in the stables. At least study involved sitting down with books.*

'*I did it in the car.*'

Alex's education had been the source of many an argument between mother and daughter. A tutor had home-schooled her through her early years, but eventually she had been sent to an expensive and exclusive boarding school. Alex had hated every second of it, finally threatening to run away. The infamy of expulsion was more than her mother could face – so a compromise had been reached. Jacqueline would not contemplate Alex attending the local state school with the children of her father's workers. Instead, each day a driver took her fifty kilometres to the nearest private school. It was a Catholic school, but Protestant Jacqueline coped with that fact by simply ignoring it. The deal suited Alex, who still had some freedom. Not enough, but some. University beckoned in her future, but that was freedom too, of a different type.

'*Well, if you must go to the stables . . .*' *Jacqueline's voice was thick with pained resignation.*

Alex was out the door before her mother could change her mind. The woman acted as if this was the last century. Jacqueline might think she lived in a Jane Austen novel, but Alex knew better.

She dashed across the house yard, with its carefully watered and groomed gardens, and through the gate into the working part of the homestead, where the brown earth was dry and the grass sparse. She darted around the back of the stables, and in through a narrow door. Her saddle and bridle were where she had left them that morning. She grabbed them and walked outside.

The colt was in a small yard immediately behind the stables. He looked around and nickered softly when he heard her approach.

'Hi there,' she said as she slipped through the gate. 'Are you ready for this?'

The colt nuzzled her hand and found the expected treat. Then he stood rock steady as she slipped the bridle and saddle into place.

'This has to be good,' she told him as she strained to tighten the girth. 'We've really got to impress him. Then maybe he'll agree to let me have you.'

When the colt was ready, Alex led him around to the front of the stables. As she did, she heard the gentle purr of an engine. Her father's Jaguar was halfway down the long driveway, heading towards her.

'Damn.' She had hoped to greet him near the gate. The time it took him to drive to the stables was her time to impress him with the training she and Kier had given the colt.

Quickly she swung into the saddle. It might not be too late. The colt seemed to sense her tension and started to prance, tossing his head.

'Easy, boy,' Alex crooned, stroking his neck, trying to calm her own nerves as much as those of the horse. 'Come on now. We need to make a good impression.'

Quickly she turned the colt's head and rode him through the open gate into the schooling arena. The colt suddenly shied violently, as he spotted some brightly coloured buckets and rags left near the fence. Alex fought to retain her seat, gripping the saddle with her knees as she attempted to bring the unruly colt back under control. She tried too hard, jagging his mouth with a sharp tug on the reins. Hurt and frightened, the colt reared, pawing the air with his front hooves.

'Alex, what are you doing?' Her father was out of the car and striding towards her.

She couldn't answer him. His loud voice and sudden movements were the last straw for the nervous colt, who dropped his head and bucked. Hard. Already unseated, Alex had no chance of staying in the saddle. She landed with a thump on the soft sand of the arena. She sat for a second, hearing the thud of hooves as the frightened colt fled to the far corner of the enclosure. Slowly she got to her feet, bruised but otherwise unhurt. She dusted down her jeans and looked up into her father's furious eyes.

'What do you think you're doing?' he asked in a low, angry voice. His eyes were the same green as her own. His hair the same dark red. His temper even worse than hers.

'I've . . . We . . .' Why did he always make her feel like this? Tongue-tied and hopelessly foolish. 'I've been riding him. Training him . . .'

'Training him to do what, exactly?'

Alex dropped her gaze to the ground.

'And today, of all days. When I've got a buyer here to look at him.'

Alex started. 'A buyer? Dad, you can't sell him. Please!' She did something she rarely did, and reached out to put her hand on his arm.

Her father said nothing. His face was set in that too familiar look that told her nothing she said or did would change his mind. Just as nothing she could say or do ever seemed to please him. She let her hand fall and turned *away. Jim Cassidy passed her without a word, heading across the arena to catch the colt. As Alex walked through the gate, she paid no attention to the man standing there. He was the one who would be taking the colt away from her. No, she corrected herself. It was her father who was taking the colt away. She broke into a run.*

Kier met her an hour later, after his shift at the feed lot. She was waiting in her usual spot by the river.

'How did it go?' he asked as he slithered down the bank towards her.

'I blew it. And now Dad's selling the colt.' Alex's face was stained with tears, but her eyes were dry. She felt empty inside.

'Tell me.' He dropped to the ground next to her.

She shook her head. She couldn't talk about it. The shame of her failure was too much. She couldn't even look at Kier. He'd put as much work into training the colt as she had.

'I hate him.'

Kier put his arm around her shoulders, and Alex was surprised to discover that she had more tears yet to shed. She buried her face in Kier's cotton shirt and sobbed. He wrapped his arms around her and held her tightly. When her tears finally subsided, she became aware that he was gently stroking her hair. She pulled away from him, just a little, and lifted her head to look into his face.

His slow, soft smile seemed to fill the emptiness inside her. He raised one hand to brush her hair off her face, and then wipe away the last tears. His fingers were toughened by hard work, but his touch was velvet. He leaned towards her and pressed his lips to hers. He held her for just a few seconds, but in that time her whole world changed. He lifted his lips from hers and looked at her with such wonder in his face that she knew he felt the same. She stopped breathing as her heart and soul yearned for him to kiss her again.

'Alex, you're here early.'

Lyn had appeared by the side of the car, coffee cup in hand.

'I was feeling restless. Couldn't sleep,' Alex told her.

'Me too.'

They stood in silence for a few seconds. Then they looked at each other with recognition and both laughed.

'Men!' Alex said.

'Who needs them?' Lyn agreed.

'Well, are you ready to race?' Alex asked as she pulled the car keys from her pocket.

'You bet!' Lyn replied.

'Where's car twenty-eight? Come on. Get a move on!'

The steward's voice, made tinny and harsh by the megaphone he held, barely rose above the roar of engines and the hubbub of excited voices. The air reeked of petrol and oil, burning rubber and flaring tempers.

'Class three starts next. Anyone misses their start – tough!'

Lyn checked the course notes on her clipboard for the tenth time. They were ready. She was ready.

'How long have we got?' Alex was standing by the driver's door, Kier at her side.

'About ten minutes.'

Lyn looked around, searching for a flash of powder-blue paint. At first she didn't see it. Paul was supposed to start just two cars behind their Lotus. If he was late . . .

A steward was waving someone forward. A silver Porsche pulled into line just behind them. The driver stepped out and Lyn recognised him instantly. *You don't think you're in there, do you?* It was the man who had been bothering her at the bar. He saw her looking at him, and smiled. Well, perhaps leered would be a better word.

A phrase she'd heard someone utter earlier in the rally sprang into her mind. 'Prick in a Porsche,' she whispered, and immediately felt better.

A few seconds later, the blue Alfa pulled in to line behind the Porsche. A gloved hand emerged from the driver's window, as Paul gave her the thumbs-up, and Lyn smiled in return.

'I'm really not sure we've got enough fuel.' Alex's voice from the other side of the car was taut with tension.

'You'll be fine,' Kier told her in a soothing tone. 'There are some very fast legs out there. You're in the lead. By keeping your weight down, you've got the chance to open the gap a bit more.'

'I know, but if I run out . . .'

'We won't,' Lyn jumped in. 'Alex, it was your idea in the first place to run with a light fuel load.'

'I know. But if—'

'It's too late now to change your mind,' Lyn said. 'Kier will be at the last refuelling point if we need to stop – won't you?'

'Yes.'

'Just concentrate on the driving,' Lyn said. Alex nodded, and Lyn felt a touch of relief. Her conversation with her mother had only served to reinforce the importance of the race. She just had to win. Those kids were relying on her. Lorna was relying on her. And in her turn, Lyn was relying on Alex. And Kier. Whatever history those two shared, she was not going to let it interfere with the race.

'Number fifty-three. The red Lotus!' A steward was approaching, a sheaf of papers in his hand.

'What is it?' Alex intercepted him.

'I need to check for an oil leak.'

'What? You've got to be kidding. I'm about to be called in to line. There isn't time.'

'Tough,' the steward said. 'You've been reported for an oil leak. You're not going out on that course until I've had a look. Safety issue.'

Something made Lyn glance over at the Porsche. The driver was back behind the wheel, and wearing his helmet, but Lyn imagined she could see a smile on his face. No prizes for guessing who had reported them. Alex was moving towards the steward, holding her race helmet in her hands as if she wanted to hit him with it. Lyn stepped between them.

'Look,' she smiled at the steward, 'are you absolutely certain you have to do that now?'

'Absolutely certain!' The man folded his arms. He was about fifty years old, with a paunch and a lot of grey in what remained of his hair. He was also enjoying his little bit of power.

Lyn pulled off one of her leather racing gloves, and placed her hand on the man's arm. 'Because it's really important that we be on the starting line on time.' She smiled up at him, giving him the full power of the blue eyes that had sold a million tubes of mascara.

'I'd like to help.' The steward shrugged his shoulders, but she could see a spark of interest in his eyes. 'Still, I don't see how I can. You've been reported as leaking oil at the parc fermé. Rules are rules.'

'Of course they are,' Lyn purred, glad she hadn't yet caught her hair up in its customary ponytail. She shook her head a little, and watched the steward's eyes follow a long blond lock as it curled over her shoulder and on to her breasts. She let her hand slide down his arm in an inviting caress. The man blinked and grinned. He had no defence against weapons honed to a fine edge in the cut-throat world of modelling.

'Yeah. Well . . .'

'It's not really that important, is it?' Lyn leaned forward a little to speak softly into his ear. 'I mean, you didn't see any oil, did you?'

'Well . . . no. But someone did report it, and I'm still supposed to check.'

Lyn stepped closer to the steward. 'You might easily have just missed us this morning,' she said. 'If you'd been held up a little with one of the other cars.'

'Well, possibly.'

'Then you'd have to check us tonight. At the parc fermé.'

'Yes. I'll probably have to check quite a few cars then.' The man puffed up his chest like a bantam rooster.

'Because if you checked me . . . I mean us now, you'd have to hurry. But this evening, there'd be all the time you needed to have a good look at everything.'

Behind her she heard an explosion of sound from Alex. She ran her fingers along the man's arm again.

She had him. She could see it in his eyes.

'Number fifty-three. The Lotus. Move up.'

'We've got to go now,' Lyn said, with one final brilliant smile. 'You'll have to catch me tonight. All right?'

'All right.'

Lyn slid into her seat. Alex was already strapped in behind the wheel. 'Move!' Lyn said. 'Quickly. Before he changes his mind.'

Alex didn't have to be told twice. She jammed her foot down on the accelerator. Lyn buckled her harness, and slipped her helmet over her head, very glad they were on their way.

'That was amazing,' Alex said as they waited at the start line. 'I can't believe you did that.'

'It works every time,' Lyn said. 'You should try it.'

'It works for you because you're blonde with legs that go on for ever,' Alex said. 'Me. Short. Red hair and a temper to match. I wouldn't stand a chance.'

'You'd be surprised.'

'Are you going to be there when he checks for oil leaks this evening?' Alex asked.

'No way,' Lyn said. 'That's Kier's job. I don't want to see that steward ever again.'

Lyn glanced in the side mirror. She could see the powder-blue Alfa pulling into line two cars behind them. Had Paul been watching as she flirted her way through the rules? It was a pretty low thing to do. Would he think she was just a tart? Would he think that she would actually—

'Thirty seconds.' The call from the starting steward forced her attention back to the job in hand.

'Five. Four. Three . . .' Lyn took up the countdown, while fumbling with the papers in her lap.

With a roar, the Lotus surged forward.

'What's first?' Alex yelled.

'Ah . . .' Lyn cursed herself for not being prepared. That was how races were lost.

'Lyn. Talk to me!' There was a touch of panic in Alex's voice.

'Left.' She had it now. 'Left five, then down to another left five. Don't swing too wide on the corner. The edge is rough.'

Knowing as she did it that she was too late, Lyn clicked the start button on her stopwatch.

*

The refuelling station was in a picnic area beside the Snowy River. Kier imagined that under normal circumstances it would be a very pleasant spot. The river was quite wide and fast-flowing, the water reflecting the clear blue of the sky. Willow trees lined the banks. Someone – he assumed it was the local council – had put picnic tables under the trees, paved a wide parking area and built a toilet block. It was very different from the narrow brown creek where he and Alex had spent so much time during their youth, yet he could see them together in a place as peaceful as this.

Today, however, the peace and quiet had been shattered by the arrival of the car rally. Stewards wearing fluorescent yellow safety vests had set up a one-way system through the car park, marked out with flags and orange witches' hats. The support vehicles, like Kier's own, had been allotted parking spaces on a nearby section of rough mowed grass. The race drivers would enter the refuelling area at the southern end, and be directed to one of three fuelling lanes. Once there, each driver had to turn off their engine before refuelling could begin. The support crews carried big metal jerrycans, each holding about twenty litres of fuel. Fire safety was paramount, and bright red extinguishers were everywhere.

Kier had a jerrycan at his feet. This wasn't what he'd planned. He had been looking forward to racing the Ferrari. He sighed, flexing his shoulders, which were still stiff from the accident. That crash might have done a whole lot more than wreck his car. He was lucky to have escaped unscathed. And maybe it wasn't all bad. Without the crash, he wouldn't have been teamed with Alex. He glanced at his watch. She wasn't due for another fifteen minutes. He wasn't sure if she would stop for fuel. She might have enough to carry on to the end of the race leg. But if she needed him, he would be here, ready to refuel as quickly as possible. There was no way he'd let her down this time.

The roar of an engine caught his attention. He looked towards the entry lane. A pale green BMW was just turning into the parking area. The car had a wide scratch down one side. Kier guessed that the driver had taken a corner just a bit too fast, and side-swiped a fence post, or possibly a tree. He was lucky he hadn't been put out of the race. The BMW pulled up at the first available refuelling point. In seconds, his support team was there. Two of them hefted a jerrycan, and the smell of petrol wafted across the park. Kier could almost hear the watching support crews counting off the time lost as the refuelling team reached for the second can. The driver hadn't even got out of the car. The refuelling was over, and the crew stepped back, giving the driver the thumbs-up.

'Wait!' The steward's loud cry stopped everyone in their tracks. The steward leaped in front of the BMW, waving his hands to signal engine off.

The support crew started forward to protest.

'Out of the car. Now!' yelled the steward in a voice that brooked no disobedience. The driver obeyed, raising his arms in question as he stepped away from his vehicle.

The steward simply pointed.

Kier followed the man's hand and saw with horror a dark stain spreading across the car park. Fuel spill. When the car had spun off the road, something must have torn a gash in the tank. His race was over. Around him, people were reaching for fire extinguishers, just in case the unthinkable happened.

'This station is closed!' the steward called to his colleagues near the entrance. They responded immediately. As Kier watched, his heart sinking, two stewards began fixing yellow warning tape across the entrance. Another had moved towards the roadway, ready to flag away any driver who tried to turn in to the picnic area. Until the spill was dealt with, no one was going to be refuelling there.

Damn it!

Kier looked at his watch again. By now, Alex would have passed the last checkpoint. She'd get no warning that the refuelling station was closed until she arrived and was flagged away. His only hope was that the spill would be cleared quickly. He glanced over at the BMW. There was no chance of the refuelling area reopening. Petrol was still pouring from the ruptured fuel tank. The support crew had been too efficient. There was too much fuel in the tank now. They might try to siphon it out, but whatever they did, the refuelling station would still be closed when Alex arrived.

Kier shook his head in disgust and sprinted for his car. The race maps and course notes were on the back seat. He spread them across his bonnet and started measuring. Alex would have two options. The previous refuelling point was quite some distance back the way she had come. Doubling back would take time and fuel. The lunch staging area was much further away, but it was in the right direction. The big question was – would she have enough fuel? She would have to choose to go forward or backward. And that meant Kier had to choose. If she went back, he had to be there waiting for her. If she went forward, she'd need him there. He had to make the right decision. He wasn't going to let her down again.

Kier took a deep breath and turned his face to the clear blue sky. His indecision lasted for just a few seconds. Forward. The Alex he knew never went back. She had fought her father. Tamed a wild colt. Befriended a youth from the wrong side of the tracks. She would never go back.

He bent over the map again. As support crew, he wasn't allowed on the race course, but there were back roads. He could use those to go directly to the next staging area. The rally leg twisted due south before turning back towards the checkpoint. If he left now, and went due west, he'd get there ahead of her. If they let him leave.

Most of the stewards were clustered around the BMW, but there were still some officials monitoring the rest of the site. He ran to the nearest.

'I need to leave. Now.'

'Jeez, mate. I dunno. We can't have engines starting while there's a fuel spill.'

'But I'm not in the staging area,' Kier insisted. 'That's me. At the back of the support car park. I'm nowhere near the BMW. And I've got to go.'

'Well . . .'

Kier wanted to scream with frustration. Or hit someone. 'Come on, mate. Give me a break.'

'All right. Stay on the fence line. You're out the gate in two minutes, or not at all.'

Kier didn't even stay to thank him. He ran back to the car, and turned the ignition key, then edged carefully forward, his heart hammering as the sound of his engine attracted the notice of the other stewards. Any one of them could stop him if they wanted. He couldn't ignore their instructions. They'd penalise Alex if he did.

By some miracle, no one tried to stop him. He pulled the Holden on to a dirt road, and turned west. The lunch staging area wasn't that far.

'Shit!' Alex saw the flash of the steward's safety vest.

'That's the refuelling area,' Lyn said.

'Not any more,' Alex shouted as the steward waved the Lotus on. She had reduced speed to turn in to the fuelling point, but now she jammed her foot down on the accelerator and the car surged ahead.

'We could go back to the last refuelling area,' Lyn offered.

'There's no point,' Alex said with utmost certainty. 'Kier won't be there. He never goes back.'

'Do we have enough fuel to get to the lunch area?' Lyn asked.

'We have to. How's our time?'

The morning stage had been hard and fast.

'Good. I guess we're almost a minute ahead of base time.'

'All right. I'm going to have to conserve fuel. Keep calling times for me.'

Running out of fuel would destroy any chance she had of winning. Drive too hard and she wouldn't make the checkpoint. She could conserve her fuel by driving cautiously. She could coast down the hills and keep the revs low. But cautious meant slow and her time would bleed away. That was almost as bad as running out of petrol. It was going to be a close thing.

'How far?' she asked Lyn.

'About twenty-five k.'

It was going to be very close. Alex gritted her teeth and turned her mind to her fuel supply.

*

It was too close.

They still hadn't sighted the finish flag when the engine coughed for the first time.

'Shit!' Alex eased back on the accelerator. 'How far?'

'Less than a kilometre,' Lyn said. 'Any second now we should see . . . There it is!'

Alex could see the checkpoint now. She felt a glimmer of hope, then the car coughed again. She took a deep breath and made a decision. She planted her foot and the car gathered speed. But there just wasn't any petrol left. They were running on fumes. The engine coughed again. She depressed the clutch, and with the engine disengaged, the car's dwindling speed carried it forward. They were down to about ten kilometres an hour when they passed the finish line.

'We made it.' Lyn sounded relieved.

Alex wasn't so sure. They weren't out of the woods yet. She steered the car towards the stewards' desk. The engine was still running, but roughly. Every few seconds it sucked air, and coughed like a sick dog.

At her side, Lyn was speaking through the window to the stewards, checking their time. Come on, Lyn, Alex thought. They didn't have time for this.

'Go!' Lyn said.

She hadn't wasted any time; it just felt that way to Alex.

Alex dropped the Lotus into gear. As she released the clutch, the car jumped forward a metre or more, then stalled.

'Shit. Damn it!' She cursed as she reached for the ignition. Slipping the car back into neutral, she hit the starter. The engine sputtered, coughed and failed. There was simply nothing left for it to burn.

She tried again. The starter motor howled, but the engine just couldn't catch.

'Now what?' Lyn asked.

Alex had no idea. They were still inside the stewards' control zone. If they got out of the car, they'd be penalised. If anyone gave them a push, they'd be penalised. She let her forehead drop on to her hands, where they still gripped the steering wheel. They had to be at the lunch area in thirty minutes, or yet another penalty would be marked against them. There was no way out.

'Use the starter motor!'

A voice calling from beyond the pedestrian barrier forced its way into her consciousness. She looked up. Kier was standing at the barrier, unable to cross. He saw her glance his way.

'Use the starter motor!' he called again.

What was he on about? Alex had enough on her plate.

'Put it in first gear. Then use the starter motor!' He was leaning over the barrier, his arms held out as if to help her.

The starter motor? If she tried that, the car would just . . .

'Yes!' She understood.

'What?' Lyn asked.

Alex slipped the car until first gear and released the clutch. Silently apologising to the Lotus for what she was about to do, she hit the ignition. With a whirr, the car kangaroo-hopped a few metres and stalled.

'What are you doing?' Lyn asked, but Alex ignored her and hit the ignition once more.

The car jerked forward again. They had gained another couple of metres.

'Yeah!' Lyn understood now.

Alex did it again. And again.

'You're getting there,' Kier yelled from the sidelines. 'Again.'

Hoping the starter motor wouldn't break under the strain, Alex hit it again. They were now about halfway to the end of the control zone. Again.

A cheer outside the car caught her attention. The crowd had realised what was going on, and each time the Lotus hopped forward, they roared their encouragement.

Twenty metres, and Alex silently begged the Lotus to forgive her for the cruel treatment. Kier was keeping pace with them along the barrier, waiting for the moment he could step across without penalty. The crowd was moving with him.

Ten.

This time the starter was slower to respond. Please God, Alex prayed silently. Let the battery hold out just a bit longer.

Five metres.

The cheer that sounded as they crossed the line could have been heard back in Canberra.

Alex barely had time to realise they'd made it when Kier was at the open window.

'Stay there,' he ordered. 'The petrol station is about a kilometre away.'

Her heart sank. A kilometre? They couldn't refuel here. It was against the rules. That meant pushing the Lotus to the petrol station. With just the three of them.

'All right, guys, let's get to it.' Kier was still standing by her door.

He was answered by another cheer, and suddenly the car was surrounded by race spectators.

'Take it out of gear,' Kier instructed.

Within a fraction of a second, the car was moving. At least a dozen men were leaning into the job. The Lotus picked up speed, and Alex realised that the crowd intended to push her all the way.

'This is just amazing,' Lyn said, twisting her head to smile at the men who were so happily coming to their aid.

Overwhelmed by surprise and gratitude, Alex could only nod and fight back the tears that were suddenly not very far away. She blinked rapidly and saw up ahead the coloured flags of the petrol station. Spectators had gathered there to watch the race cars refuel, and they were now all looking her way. They started to cheer as she turned on to the driveway. She braked next to a pump, and let her hands fall from the wheel.

She didn't move as the petrol cap was removed and someone started pumping petrol into her tank. Finally she removed her helmet and looked at Lyn.

'Time?'

'We should make it to the next staging area pretty much on time. Maybe a few seconds late at most.' Lyn was grinning widely. She wound down her window and started thanking the men who were still crowded around the car.

Alex reached for the door handle. She got out of the car to find Kier standing right next to her, directing operations.

'It's like having a real pit crew,' he said, and grinned.

Alex was too astonished to speak.

'Will you need me at the lunch area?' Kier asked.

She shook her head.

'I'd like to stay and thank the guys.'

'Say thanks for me too,' Alex finally said.

'I will.'

A call from the rear of the car told her the tank was full and she was ready to go. She searched for the right thing to say, and couldn't find it. Kier had saved the race for her. She didn't know how to thank him, or the others who had literally thrown their weight behind her. Instead, she stood on her toes and kissed Kier on the cheek. A cheer of approval from their helpers enveloped her as she slid back behind the wheel, donned her helmet and started the engine.

Refuelled, the Lotus responded eagerly the moment she touched the accelerator. As she turned out on to the roadway, she glanced in the rear-view mirror. Kier was standing by the pump, looking after her, while laughing men slapped him on the back.

She directed her eyes back to the road.

The police were waiting at the entrance to the national park. Kier saw them as he joined the queue of support vehicles waiting to be allowed in. The racers were driving a long loop south through Berridale and Dalgety, giving the support crews time to get into the mountains ahead of them. The Perisher Valley ski resort, empty now for the summer, was to be their overnight stop. It had all the right facilities – accommodation lodges, restaurants and a huge car park.

A steward waved him forward.

'Credentials, please.' It was the policeman who asked, not the steward. He was standing back a little from the car, watching Kier with steady eyes.

Kier wasn't edgy around police any more. He had no need to be. He met the officer's unsmiling gaze and held it for a few seconds before reaching into the glove box for his papers.

The policeman looked briefly at the papers, then handed them to the steward and began to walk slowly around the car.

'Is there a problem?' Kier asked the steward.

'Protesters,' the steward said. 'We've been told that wildlife activists are going to try to stop the race.'

'Wildlife activists?' Kier frowned. 'I thought we had that woman with us. From the park authority.' He wasn't likely to forget Dee Parker and her eagle.

'Oh, the National Parks Service isn't the problem,' the steward said as he handed back Kier's papers. 'This is some other group.'

'It's all right, sir. You can continue.' The policeman waved Kier on.

As he drove away, Kier looked in the rear-view mirror. The policeman was checking the next car. A grim smile twitched the corner of his lips. He thought he had lost his dislike of police, but apparently not. He'd thought his old life was well behind him – until a few days ago, when Alex Reilly suddenly appeared beside him, with her haunting green eyes, and a smile that put the sun to shame.

The road climbed steeply into the high country. This time of year, it was green and dotted with wild flowers. Kier wound his window down to enjoy the crisp, clean air. The tall gums of the previous day's route gave way to short, stunted alpine shrubs and grassy bogs. The edge of the road was lined with thin, bright red posts taller than Kier. It took him a few minutes to realise they were for marking the roadway when the snow buried it. The Perisher Valley opened in front of him, wide and flat, with a cluster of buildings at its centre. This was the ski resort. He could see the flags and signs put up by the rally stewards. He drove towards the visitor centre and the skeletal ski lift towers that marched steadily up the hill. The ski lodges were not exactly architectural wonders. Plain and functional, many of them did at least boast windows looking out across the slopes. He guessed there wouldn't be room for all the racers at Perisher. Some would no doubt be staying further up the road at another resort.

He pulled into the support vehicle zone and got out to stretch his legs. It was still fairly quiet. The first of the race cars wasn't due for at least another forty or fifty minutes. He walked towards the visitor centre, where he hoped to find coffee. As he crossed the car park, he realised that tonight the race cars would not be held inside a fenced car park. They were going to have to rely on guards doing foot patrols for security – which explained the number of police. That and whatever threats had been made by the protesters. He felt a twinge of concern. The race cars were valuable. He didn't expect anyone to even attempt to steal one from under the noses of the police, not to mention the drivers, who fussed over the vehicles like precious children. But sabotage? Maybe.

He was still feeling disquieted as he returned to the car with his coffee. He sat on the bonnet and watched the police checking the new arrivals. All he could do was keep his eyes open, and if he saw anything suspicious he would report it. He wouldn't make the same mistake again . . .

The voices stopped the minute Kier arrived home from work. The front yard of the house had become a parking lot for his brother's friends. Several utes sat on the dry brown patches of dying grass that were the closest they ever got to a lawn. Rob and his mates were sitting on the bonnets of the cars, drinking cans of beer. They had been talking and laughing until they realised Kier was there. He felt their eyes on him as he walked past without a word. Since the night they were all arrested at the pub, he'd said very little to his brother, and nothing at all to the blokes Rob hung around with. The judge had let him off with a warning. The others had each been sentenced to community service and had spent several Saturdays cleaning up litter around the town. That hadn't improved relations between them one bit.

The house was dark inside after the harsh glare of the sun. Kier paused briefly in the kitchen to kiss his mother's cheek, then headed for the shower to wash off the sweat and the dust and the smell of cattle. The water was clean and cool, and for a long time Kier just stood there, allowing the tiredness of a long hard day to wash away.

Tonight was special. Their town wasn't big enough for a proper movie theatre, but once a year, an outdoor cinema would roll in and set up in the school sports oval for a week of entertainment. It was a fund-raiser for the local ambulance service, but that wasn't the point. The movies they featured weren't the latest Hollywood blockbusters. But that also was of no account. What mattered was sitting under the stars, watching films. Eating and drinking and having fun in a town where day-to-day life was, at best, humdrum.

And tonight – he had a date!

Somehow Alex had convinced her mother to let her attend the showing. She had brought a girlfriend from school to stay the night – and the two girls had permission to go together. With a driver, of course, to escort them safely home the minute the film was done. Alex hadn't lied to her mother; she had simply not mentioned she was meeting Kier. They'd still have to be careful. Small towns had big eyes, big ears and loose tongues.

Back in his room, getting dressed, Kier was happily lost in contemplation of the evening's promise when a conversation outside his open window intruded.

'. . . will be at the movie. The cops too. The rest of the town will be deserted.'

Kier recognised his brother's voice.

'Not the pub, though,' a rough voice interrupted. 'Not after last time.'

'No. I think we'll do the shop.'

Kier froze. They were going to do it again! They'd learned nothing. He stood listening as his brother discussed how to break into the shop, taking the money from the cash register.

'And fags too,' one of his friends insisted.

It wasn't just criminal. It was stupid. In a small town, it wouldn't take the police long to figure out who'd done it. There was only one gang of twenty-year-old idiots, and his brother was a founding member.

Kier buttoned his shirt and thought about what he should do. He should tell his mother. Better still, his father. His father wouldn't hesitate to deal with Rob. With his fists, if that was what it took. Kier rubbed his arm, remembering the last time, and the mistakes he'd made. Not only the arrest and his father's beating, but even worse, he'd let Alex down. It had taken a long time for him to forgive himself for that. He wouldn't do it again. Let his stupid brother do what he would. Kier was not responsible for him.

The decision made, Kier left the house by the back door to avoid seeing Rob, and made his way towards the temporary movie theatre. He'd be early, but he didn't mind waiting for Alex. She was worth it.

The moment he saw her, all other thoughts left him. She walked towards him, her face wreathed in smiles. Dressed in faded blue jeans and a white T-shirt, she looked no different to all the other kids, but to Kier, she was the most beautiful thing he had ever seen. She put her hand in his, and stood on her toes to kiss his cheek, announcing their *relationship to anyone who cared to look. For the first time in his life, Kier knew what pride felt like. They found their seats, and Kier draped his arm around Alex's shoulders. As the lights dimmed and images appeared on the screen in front of them, she moved closer to him, resting her head against his shoulder. Kier decided that tonight was just perfect.*

An hour later, it all fell apart.

They heard the police sirens first. Initially they were just a faint background wail, an unwelcome interruption to the movie soundtrack. But they got louder, and soon people were turning their heads, trying to understand what was happening. When the flashing lights raced past at the end of the sports oval, a few people stood up. Kier was one of them. His feeling of dread hardened into certainty a few moments later, when an ambulance followed the police car. He squeezed Alex's hand, left her and began to run.

The police were already at his house when he arrived. He flung himself up the front stairs. His mother's face was tear-stained and fearful, but his father was nowhere to be seen. No doubt the police would find him at the pub. His mother gripped his hand as if she would never let it go. She clung to him all through the ride in the police car, and as they walked through the sterile and frightening hospital corridors. She only let go of him when she reached out to clasp Rob's hand, where it lay on the starched white sheet, amid the tubes running into his veins. When he looked at his brother lying unconscious on the bed, his face swathed in bandages and both legs encased in plaster, a whole world of guilt crashed down upon Kier's shoulders. He could have prevented this. He should have . . .

*

'Can you see him?' Alex asked as she turned off the engine.

'Give me a chance,' Lyn chuckled as she slowly opened the car door and stepped out.

Alex also stepped out of the car. She pulled the crash helmet off her head and shook out her hair as she looked at the madness around them. Race cars were pulling up for the night. Mechanics, stewards and the media were flocking about like demented pigeons. There were also a lot of police very much in evidence. The one person she could not see was Kier.

'He can't be far away,' Lyn offered.

'I just want to tell him—' Alex was interrupted by a loud yell as the silver Porsche eased past. The driver was leaning out the window.

'We gotcha, girls,' the driver yelled triumphantly.

'Not a chance,' Alex called after the departing car.

'I wouldn't be so sure about that,' a voice said behind them.

'What do you mean?' Lyn asked as Paul joined them.

'I've been watching that Porsche. It's fast. Maybe too fast.'

'How can it be too fast?' Lyn said, stepping to Paul's side.

'I . . .' Paul hesitated. 'Don't worry about it. It's probably just my imagination working overtime.'

'You don't think they are cheating?' Alex asked.

'Probably not.' Paul didn't sound certain. 'There's just something . . .'

'It's the way the car sounds,' Lyn said slowly.

'What do you mean?' Paul asked.

'I don't know.' Lyn shook her head. 'I'm a mechanical idiot, remember. It just sounds – funny. More like a motorcycle than a car. Sort of rough. No. That's the wrong word. It's . . . lumpy?'

Alex wasn't paying any attention to the conversation. She was still looking for Kier. She hadn't seen him since lunchtime, and she wanted to thank him for saving her. Even if their afternoon times had been a bit slow, they were still in the race – thanks to Kier's brilliant idea about using the starter motor to get them across the line. She stood on her toes, then, shaking her head in frustration, stepped up on to the door frame of the Lotus. At last! He was sitting on the bonnet of his support car, staring down into a coffee cup. Alex felt her heart lift at the sight of him. She didn't stop to analyse her feelings; she tossed her helmet and leather gloves on to the seat of the Lotus and turned the key in the lock. Lyn and Paul were too busy talking to even notice as she set off, not quite running.

'Kier!' she called as she drew closer.

He didn't hear her. Whatever he was seeing in the bottom of that coffee cup, it must have been pretty important.

'Kier.' She literally ran the last few metres. 'You are a genius.' She grabbed him by the shoulders. 'Thank you. Thank you. Thank you!' Unable to contain her excitement, she planted a kiss on his lips.

'What on earth . . . ?'

'The starter motor. It was genius. I would never have thought if it.'

'Oh. Well, I'm glad it worked.'

Alex felt almost as if someone had dashed cold water in her face. She took a step back. 'What's wrong?'

Kier looked at her, frowning. 'Nothing. Why?'

'You . . . you're just . . .' What could she say? You're not happy? You're not sharing my joy? You don't care?

'Sorry.' The smile on his face looked forced, but at least it was a smile. 'I was a million miles away. How was the afternoon?'

'Great. We got a good run down through Dalgety. The Datsun spun out at a corner. They're fine, but it cost them time.'

'So . . . ?' Kier didn't have to put it into words.

'I think the silver Porsche is just in front of us,' Alex said.

'Pricks in Porsches!' They pronounced the time-honoured curse in unison. This time, Kier's smile looked real.

'So, how's the Lotus?'

'Not good,' Alex said. 'I'm getting a bit of vibration at high speeds.'

'Any problems with the clutch?'

'Yeah,' Alex said. 'I'm thinking it's the universal.'

'Sounds like it,' Kier agreed. 'Have you got a spare?'

'I do. It's in one of the boxes Mick left with you. I'll change it this evening.'

'Do you need a hand?'

Alex nodded.

'I guess that means me, not Lyn,' Kier joked.

'I was wrong about Lyn,' Alex said as they walked together back towards the car. 'She's turned out to be a great navigator.'

'I always thought she would,' Kier said.

Ahead, Alex could see Lyn and Paul still deep in conversation. They probably hadn't even noticed that she had left. 'You know, I think those two might be . . .'

The words froze on her tongue. She didn't want to go there. Not with Kier standing so close. Not with the memories and the feelings his presence had been stirring. There was nothing but pain down that road. Painful memories. And maybe new chances to be hurt again. She would not go there.

She took a quick sideways glance at Kier. He didn't seem to have noticed. His attention was on the police who were walking among the cars. There seemed to be a lot of them.

'Did you hear?' Lyn and Paul were approaching, and Lyn looked quite concerned.

'Hear what?' Alex asked.

'There are protesters,' Lyn said. 'The police think they are going to try to stop the race.'

'Protesters? What have they got against us?' Alex was genuinely puzzled.

'They are some radical animal rights group,' Kier told her. 'The police were checking everyone entering the park. Hopefully they've stopped them.'

Alex frowned, but then decided she had enough to worry about with her suspect universal joint. There was nothing to be gained by worrying about protesters. That was a job for the police.

After a few more minutes, Lyn and Paul left, promising to return with the day's results as soon as they were posted. That left Alex with the Lotus, a drive shaft to fix . . . and Kier. There was a moment of awkward silence. Alex guessed Kier was waiting for her to take the lead. After all, it was her car, and the incident with the toaster spring was no doubt as fresh in his mind as it was in hers. Suddenly Alex felt a little embarrassed. She had overreacted on that one. Kier had saved her bacon and all she'd done was yell at him.

'Do you want to make a start, while I get out of my

race suit?' she said, hoping Kier would recognise the olive branch she was offering.

'Sure.' He looked a little sheepish as he handed her the key to his car. 'I haven't checked us in yet, but I think it's that lodge over there.' He pointed to one of the nearby buildings.

'No problems. I'll be right back.'

Alex grabbed her bag from the car and set off in search of her room. The lodge keeper soon had her installed in a small but perfectly reasonable room. It didn't take long to replace the race suit with the worn and stained overalls that were standard work gear for all the rally teams. Just before she left the room, she glanced in the mirror. She looked a fright. Her face was grimy, and she had the worse case of helmet hair the world had ever seen. She dashed into the bathroom for soap and cold water, running her wet fingers through her hair. Some of the curl sprang back, but it wasn't much of an improvement. She hesitated for a moment, wondering if she should have a shower. Wash her hair. Or at least brush it. She shook her head. What was she thinking? This wasn't a date. She was on her way to work on the car with Kier. What she looked like was irrelevant. And besides, he'd know that she'd tried to make herself look better. He might think she . . . No way! She turned her back on the mirror and walked out the door.

By the time she got back to the car park, Kier had assembled the parts and tools they would need, and already had the trolley jack waiting by the back of the car. He was sitting on a big toolbox, a cup of coffee in one hand and what looked like a kebab in the other. A second kebab wrapped in silver foil and a cup of coffee, still with its lid on, sat in a box beside him. Alex's heart gave a tiny jump as she saw him. He looked so at ease sitting there. So much at home in his surroundings. With himself and what he was doing. And he was still the most handsome man she had ever seen. As a teenager, his smile had been enough to set her pulse racing. She was sure the same thing would happen here and now – if she let it.

'You like it black with lots of sugar, if I remember,' Kier said, holding out the coffee cup.

'Thanks.' She took it, taking great care that her fingers didn't touch his.

Kier didn't seem to notice. 'I got some food too. I figured this would take us a while, and you might be hungry. We can always get something a bit more substantial when we are done, if you prefer.'

'Thanks.'

He downed the last of his own coffee. 'I wasn't sure – left or right drive shaft?' he asked.

'Left.'

'Okay.'

He grabbed the handle of the trolley jack and dragged it towards the back of the car. He slid it into place, bending down to check it was correctly seated under the axle. Then he began to pump the handle, working smoothly and easily as the car started to rise. His hands were even more sun-browned and work-hardened than when he was young. His shoulders were stronger. His body more solid and controlled. Alex realised that in her mind, she had been seeing the boy. The boy she had loved so desperately all those years ago. This wasn't him. This was a man. She had survived when the boy broke her heart. Could she survive if the man did the same thing? Could she even risk that he might?

'Alex?'

'Oh . . .' She dragged her thoughts back. 'Let's get going.'

'Finish your coffee. Eat the kebab while it's still warm.' Kier opened the lid of the toolbox and reached for a wrench. 'I've got this bit.'

He crouched and looked under the car. Then he lowered himself to the ground and slid under the Lotus from the side, leaving only his legs and boots showing. Alex sipped the strong black liquid and tried not to think about him. Tried to think about how easy it was to fall back into old ways. Just look at her now, letting him take the lead. Trusting him, as if all those tears had never been shed.

'Alex,' Kier called from under the car. 'I think this next bit would be easier if there were two of us.'

'Sure.'

She drank the last of the coffee and crumpled the paper cup, before tossing it into a convenient waste bin. Then she dropped to the bitumen surface, and wriggled under the back of the car next to Kier. There wasn't a lot of room. The whole underside of the car was black with grease and road grime, and so were Kier's hands. He had already loosened the bolts on the suspect universal joint. The next job was to get it all the way out.

Kier gave the first of the bolts a final twist and Alex reached past him to slip the bolt free. She slid it into the pocket of her overalls. The second one soon followed. Then the third.

'We'll need to support the drive shaft when I take out the last bolts,' Kier said.

'We can tie it up,' Alex offered.

'Fine. Use my belt,' Kier said matter-of-factly.

'What?' Alex thought she must have misheard.

'It'll take both of us to get the new doughnut in place, and the drive shaft needs to be supported. Use my belt to tie the shaft to the chassis.'

He was right about the drive shaft, and he was also right about his belt. Unlike most of the mechanics, Kier never wore overalls. He always wore a T-shirt and faded blue jeans, held up with a leather belt. There was nothing else around she could use to secure the drive shaft, and she could hardly suggest that she go and get something. Not now, with the repairs at a critical point. His belt it would have to be.

They were lying at right angles under the car, so that both of them could reach the universal joint. She was going to have to move if she was going to get her hands anywhere near his jeans. She began to wriggle her way down Kier's body, wincing as her shoulder struck the chassis. This wasn't going to be easy. She moved again, so that her shoulder was pressed against his side – and in some ways that was even more painful. She stretched out one hand, feeling for the silver buckle. Her fingers brushed the taut fabric of his T-shirt, where it stretched against his stomach. She snatched them away as if she had been burned.

'Just a second, let me move.' Kier shifted his arm, and suddenly her head was cradled on his shoulder. Now she could see what she was doing. Not only that, she could hear his heart beating. Feel his chest rise and fall as he breathed. If she closed her eyes, it would be almost like it had been when they were young and just learning about— No! That wouldn't do at all. She dragged her thoughts back to the present. If she didn't keep going, he'd start to wonder what was wrong. She reached out again. This time, her hand came to rest on his belt buckle.

Trying not to think about what she was doing, she fumbled at the leather. After a couple of tries, she managed to undo the buckle and slide the end of the belt free. She gave it a couple of experimental tugs. The belt didn't move. Kier's weight was holding it firmly in place.

'You need to . . .' What could she say? Move your hips? Lift your groin? Suddenly it all seemed faintly ridiculous. Alex had to bite back a giggle.

Kier seemed to understand what was needed. He lifted his hips slightly, and Alex tugged the belt free. Clutching the strip of leather with a sense of relief, she wriggled away from Kier, and set about fastening the drive shaft in place.

Replacing a rubber universal wasn't easy, but to Alex it seemed a breeze. Much easier than taking Kier's belt off. There were no haunting memories. No sudden heat in her face . . . or anywhere else. Only the occasional brush of his arms against hers. The feel of his muscles bunching as he pushed the recalcitrant part into place. She could watch his strong fingers as they manipulated the bolts. It was all about repairing the car now. Wasn't it?

'Alex. Kier! Are you both under there?'

It was Lyn. Alex turned her head. From her position jammed between Kier and the wheel of the car, all she could see were two pairs of boots. The others would no doubt belong to Paul.

'Have you got the times?' she called.

'Yes. Come on out.'

Kier finished tightening one more bolt. 'That should hold it for a few minutes,' he said. 'I guess you can give me back my belt now.' He began to wriggle out from under the car.

Alex undid the belt that was no longer needed to hold

the drive shaft, and slid out after him. As she ducked her head under the back bumper, she saw Kier standing over her, reaching down. She placed her hand in his, and felt his immense strength as he effortlessly pulled her to her feet.

'Thanks,' she said and handed him back his belt. She turned to see Lyn's eyes widen with interest.

'Well? What about the times?' Alex spoke quickly, before Lyn could do more than raise an eyebrow.

'Third,' Lyn said. 'By a bit over a minute.'

'Damn,' Alex cursed. A minute was the world in rally racing. 'Who?'

'The silver Porsche.'

Alex felt her heart sink. The Porsche was very, very fast. The driver and navigator were brothers. She couldn't remember their names. Everyone just referred to them as the Porsche brothers. They were pretty good. Unless luck was with her, she'd never catch them.

'The red Mini is second, and Paul is fourth,' Lyn said, beaming up at her companion.

Paul grinned, his hazel eyes sparkling with pleasure. 'I'll never catch you girls,' he said, 'but my old Alfa isn't doing too badly at all.'

'We're just heading down to the bar. We've earned a beer,' Lyn said. 'Are you going to join us?'

Alex couldn't help but notice that they were doing it again. Becoming two couples. Paul with Lyn . . . and Kier with her. That wasn't going to happen. Not again. She'd learned that lesson the hard way. Things between her and Kier had changed – but not that much.

'I don't think so,' she said slowly. 'I need to finish working on this doughnut.'

'Doughnut?' Lyn grinned, cheerfully oblivious of any

of the undercurrents that were swirling around her. 'I take it you are not referring to the dough and cinnamon sugar kind of doughnut.'

Paul chuckled. 'Come on, Lyn, let's leave them to it.'

After they had gone, Alex and Kier stood for a few seconds of awkward silence.

'I'm sure that universal is fine,' Kier finally said. He raised one hand to slowly wipe a smear of grease from the side of Alex's face. 'You look beat. Why don't you at least go take a shower? Leave the rest to me. That's my job.'

'It'll be easier if we do it together.' Alex took a step back, away from the intimacy of his gesture. She wasn't about to leave the job unfinished. If she did, it would be because she was afraid of being alone with Kier. And that just was *not* the case. Was it? 'Let's just get it done.'

By the time they were finished, Alex was exhausted. She glanced at her watch. It was well past ten o'clock, and the last thing she felt like doing was joining anyone at the bar.

'I'm going to get some sleep,' she said to Kier.

'I'll come back with you,' he said.

He didn't look sleepy, but Alex was far too exhausted to argue as they walked in silence to their lodge. Inside, they stopped first at Alex's door.

'Thanks for your help,' she said as she turned to put her key in the lock.

'You're welcome.'

'I'll see you in the morning,' she said without turning around as she opened the door.

'Good night.'

Alex slipped slowly through her door. She resisted the urge to look back. To see if Kier had turned for a final look at her before going to his own room. She shut the door behind her.

Kier's room was next to Alex's. He ran his fingers through his hair as he fell back on the bed. What a day! And as for this evening . . . Working with Alex in the tight intimacy had been . . .

He lay with his eyes closed for a moment, seeing Alex's face so close to his. Feeling the warmth of her shoulder against his. The touch of her fingers as she worked his belt loose. He had nearly lost it then. He was surprised she hadn't felt the way his body had quivered under her hand. Would he never be rid of this power she had over him? As he dragged himself slowly back to his feet, Kier became aware of music in the room. He looked around, but his television and radio were off. The walls of the lodge were pretty thin – and he realised the music must be coming from the next room. Alex's room. The song was an old slow rock ballad, with a powerful bass beat. He could almost see Alex swaying to the music, her head arched back, as he had seen her dance before, when they were young. When they were in love.

'Damn it!' He tore his clothes off and headed for the shower. He reached for the cold tap and turned it on. Full. He stepped under the shower, and gasped for breath as the cold water sluiced down his body. He held his face upwards, letting the water run over his face and into his open mouth. As he stood there, trying to empty his mind, he heard the pipes gurgle, and for a few seconds the pressure in the shower dropped. Someone else had turned on their water. Someone in the next room. Alex. He laid his palms flat against the cold tiles of the shower cubicle. Just the other side of that wall, Alex too was showering. Was she standing under a cold stream, trying, as he was, to make her body forget the powerful pull of another? Or was she luxuriating in a warm shower, letting the tiny rivulets of water flow down her flesh, caressing it and . . .

This was doing him no good at all. A cold shower just was not going to be enough. He turned the taps off, and dug into his bag for some clean underwear and socks. Once he was dressed, he opened the door and slipped quietly into the corridor. He didn't allow himself to even pause outside Alex's room. He walked quickly to the outside door and opened it. The evening air was cool, and crisp. He took several deep breaths and looked about. The moon was high, illuminating the ski slope, covered now in autumn grasses and moss. It was a long, steep walk to the top of the slope, where the ski lifts terminated. That might leave him tired enough to sleep. He shrugged, and started walking.

The party was in full swing. Despite the fact that it was a race night, more than a few drivers and navigators were kicking up their heels – and bending their elbows – to release the tension of the past three days. The mechanics and support crews who didn't risk an alcohol test the next day were very drunk. Lyn leaned against the wall and watched the slow dance around the bar. Somewhere in the midst of that melee, Paul was trying to buy his second beer, and her second glass of wine. It would be their last drinks. Neither of them was going to risk disqualification – or even worse, an accident.

At last Paul emerged from the bar scrum, a glass in each hand. He had switched his race suit for a pair of faded blue jeans and a white cotton shirt, with the long sleeves rolled up to show his sun-browned arms. That seemed to be the only outfit he ever wore. Lyn didn't mind. On him it looked good. It suited his easy, open nature. He smiled as he walked towards her. She watched the lines form around his hazel eyes and thought how handsome he was. Not beautiful like the male models she worked with. Not pretty. Or elegant. Or stylish. Just handsome – the way only a strong, good man could be.

Lyn smiled in welcome, but as she did, Paul's eyes flickered off to the side of the room.

'I've got a good idea,' he said. 'Let's go out on to the veranda. It'll be a bit quieter there.'

Lyn felt a little leap of anticipation. Was he . . .

'All right,' she said gently and allowed him to guide her out through the sliding glass doors.

The wide veranda looked out over the car park, to the mountain beyond. The moon was full, giving a soft glow to the lines of cars parked under the watchful eyes of the security patrols. The valley stretched away on either side of the resort, the trunks of the stubby alpine gums gleaming silver. The wispy clouds scudded about the mountain's peak. Lyn felt as if she was glowing too.

'I hope you don't mind leaving the party,' Paul said.

'No.' She smiled into his face. 'Not at all.'

'I thought you might want to avoid that steward.'

Lyn's romantic fantasies came crashing down around her. 'The steward?'

'Yes. The one who wanted to check you and Alex for oil leaks. You flirted with him . . .'

'Oh.' Lyn felt a sudden flush of guilt. 'Him! I feel really bad about that. I don't normally—'

'Don't feel bad. What you did wasn't cheating,' Paul reassured her.

'But still . . .' Lyn wasn't sure how to explain.

'Compared to what some people will do to win, that was nothing. He's in the bar. I saw him watching you and I just thought you might want to avoid him. In case he . . .' Paul's face suddenly creased. 'Oh God! Unless you want him . . . I mean, you want to—'

'No. No.' Lyn jumped in before the embarrassment

level got too high for either of them to stand. 'I never want to talk to him again.'

'All right.'

They stood in silence for a few moments, gazing out across the valley.

'It's really quite beautiful,' Lyn said.

'Yes, it is,' Paul replied. 'But I imagine it gets pretty cold in winter.'

'Well, that's how it got its name.'

'What do you mean?'

'In the 1850s, a man called James Spencer grazed cattle here. There was a blizzard one year that he thought was a perisher. The name stuck.'

'Really?' Paul said. 'I'm impressed that you know that.'

'Don't be. I read it on a tourist sign at the visitors' centre earlier today.'

Paul chuckled. 'I'm still impressed.' He said it slowly this time. Lyn turned to face him. His smile was almost enough to stop her breath. 'There's a lot more to you than meets the eye, Lyn.'

She winced internally, and waited for the crass comment that was sure to follow. Something about being very easy on the eye. Something about the way she looked, or the way she walked, or some lingerie photo he'd seen. That was what they all did. Some coarse statement that she was supposed to take as a compliment.

'So – now I have to try to impress you. Would it help if I told you there were almost a hundred and fifty kilometres of tunnels through these mountains – as part of the hydro power scheme? There are sixteen main dams and seven main power stations.'

'Wow. You know all that?'

'I read the brochures in the visitors' centre.'

They both laughed.

'And, I must confess, it's also family legend. I'm distantly related to William Hudson – the engineer who headed the project back in the 1950s.'

'Okay.' Lyn grinned. 'That's done it. I am actually very impressed.'

Paul's face lit up. For a few seconds, they simply stood smiling at each other. Lyn felt something inside her start to stir. Did Paul feel it too? And if he did, would he act on it? As if drawn by some force greater than gravity, she could feel herself swaying closer to him. His eyes didn't leave hers, not for an instant, and her heart lifted. He was going—

'Excuse me?'

They both spun around.

'I'm sorry to disturb you.' The woman with the untidy hair and the cotton skirt didn't look at all sorry. 'I'm Dee Parker from National Parks. I'm handing these out to all the competitors.'

She offered them both sheets of paper. Cursing the woman's timing, Lyn took one and glanced at it.

'It's a list of phone numbers and contacts, just in case there is any sort of incident.'

'Incident?' Lyn asked.

'She means if one of the cars hits an animal,' Paul said.

'That's right.' Dee's voice was sharp.

'Have some of the drivers been giving you a hard time?' Paul asked.

'Why do you say that?' Dee snapped.

'You don't have to be on the defensive with us, you know,' Paul said.

Dee sighed heavily. 'I'm sorry. It's just that some of the competitors . . . Well, you know.'

'Yes, we do,' Lyn said. 'Don't worry about them.'

'I'll try . . .' Dee's voice trailed off as she stared across at the car park.

'What's wrong?' Lyn followed her gaze. The car park was relatively quiet, but there were still people moving around. Some would be there all night, preparing for the next day's racing. The security guards were easy to spot with their bright vests. She couldn't see anything wrong.

'Over there.' Dee pointed. 'That bloke in the overalls.'

There were several men in overalls in among the cars. Lyn wasn't sure which one Dee was referring to.

'He's probably just a mechanic working on one of the cars,' Paul said reassuringly.

'I don't think so,' Dee almost whispered. 'I know him. He's one of the activists. His group was threatening to stop the race somehow.'

'Are you sure?' Paul asked.

'Yes. Absolutely sure.'

'What is he doing?' Lyn wondered.

'I'm going down there,' Paul said. 'You two wait here.'

'Be careful,' Dee warned. 'The group he belongs to are pretty radical. They're not afraid of . . . Well, there have been some nasty incidents.'

'Don't worry. I just want to see what he's doing.' Paul smiled reassuringly at Dee.

Lyn watched him walk away, fighting back conflicting emotions.

'What sort of incidents?' she asked Dee.

'They won't allow animals to be hurt,' Dee said slowly, 'but they don't feel the same way about people.'

Lyn bit her lip. Much as she admired Paul for what he was doing, she was just a little bit frightened.

*

Kier was on his way back to the lodges when he saw Paul walking around the edge of the car park. His first reaction was to change his course to avoid meeting him. He just wasn't in the mood to talk to anyone tonight. But something about the way Paul was walking made him change his mind.

'Hey. Paul.'

Paul spun to face him.

'Is everything all right?' Kier asked.

'Not exactly.'

Kier listened with growing concern as Paul explained that one of the animal rights protesters was wandering among the cars.

'Surely security should have stopped him?'

'Apparently not.'

'What are you planning to do?' Kier asked.

'I thought I'd just go down there. As if I was going to work on my car. See what's going on.'

'Want some help?'

As they crossed the car park, Kier wondered just what the activist could be up to, with so many security men and police on patrol. The guards would see, or hear, any attempt to damage the cars.

'He's over near Alex's Lotus.' Paul indicated.

'If he touches her car . . .' Kier felt anger welling up inside him. 'Come on.'

The two of them began to wend their way through the lines of parked vehicles, talking casually as if they were just out for an evening stroll. Paul kicked something that spun away between the cars. It was an empty plastic water bottle, one of several that Kier could see lying on the ground. Understanding suddenly dawned.

'Water. He's putting water in the petrol tanks.'

'But that will . . .' Paul began.

'I think you'd better alert security,' Kier said. The nearest guard was some distance away, talking to someone who was working on their car.

'And you?'

'I'll make sure he doesn't do any more damage.'

As Paul went in search of security, Kier strolled towards Alex's Lotus, as casually as he could despite the rage that gripped him. The protester was now moving away from him, down another line of cars. Kier strained to see over the roofs. There were several empty plastic water bottles lying on the ground near the Lotus.

Damn him!

He turned towards the protester and started walking just that little bit faster. The man hesitated, and glanced over his shoulder. For an instant their eyes met. Kier knew what must be written on his face, and he started to run. The protester turned and fled. Kier ran down a line of parked cars. The protester slipped between two vehicles and into the next lane. Kier didn't hesitate. He put one hand on the bonnet of a parked car and vaulted over it. Ignoring the surprised yells from someone working nearby, he did the same again, as the protester sprinted for the edge of the car park. Kier was drawing closer to him. The protester darted out from the lines of parked cars, with Kier only a few metres behind him. Ahead of them, a car was waiting, its engine running.

Kier was not going to let the man get away. His breath starting to sound loud in his own ears, he chased after his quarry. In one last desperate move, he flung himself forward, grabbing the man around the ankles and pulling him to the gravel surface just a few metres away from the haven of his escape car.

The man kicked out, catching Kier a glancing blow across the temple, just below the partially healed wound from his crash. Fighting back the pain, Kier scrambled to his feet at the same time as his captive. The protester took a wild swing at Kier, who ducked, then returned the favour. His fist connected soundly with the man's jaw, and the protester sagged. Kier grabbed his arm.

'What the hell is going on?' The shout came from a man wearing a brilliant green security guard's vest. He was hurrying towards them. A short distance away, an engine roared. Kier glanced across at the disappearing car, quickly memorising the number plate.

'Call the cops,' he panted at the guard. 'These guys are the protesters we were warned about. They've been sabotaging the cars.'

The guard reached for the radio on his belt, passing on the details of the car, which had vanished down the road towards the park entrance.

'The police are still at the ranger station,' the guard said. 'They'll get them.'

Kier took a deep breath, and looked at the man he was still gripping firmly by the shoulder. He looked very young; probably not yet out of his teens. He was still panting from the chase, but he looked at Kier with a triumphant arrogance.

'Some of them aren't going to get to the starting line tomorrow,' the youth said between deep breaths.

'What did he do?' That was the security guard.

'Water in the petrol tanks,' Kier told him. Then he gave his captive a shake. 'How many?' he demanded. 'And which cars?'

'I'm not going to tell you,' the youth said defiantly.

For a second, the face looking up at him faded, and

Kier saw his brother Rob. This kid was another young thug about to throw his life away. 'Yes you are.' Kier grabbed him by the shirt front. 'One way or another, you are going to tell me.'

'Hey, take it easy.' The security guard put a hand on Kier's shoulder. 'It's only water in the petrol tanks. No one's been hurt.'

'Do you know what water in the petrol tank means?' Kier didn't take his eyes off the young protester. 'The cars will run fine for a while. Just long enough to get up to speed. Maybe get as far as one of the long downhill legs. Then the engine will cut out. For some of the cars, that means no brakes. No power steering. If it happens to the wrong car at the wrong time and place, someone could get killed.'

Kier watched his captive's face as he spoke, but saw no signs of remorse.

'So,' he said forcefully, 'you are bloody well going to tell me which cars you sabotaged.'

'No I'm not.'

Kier curled his fingers into a fist, and took a long, deep breath.

'Come on, mate.' Paul had returned with another security guard. 'There's nothing you can do. He's just not going to tell you. And somehow, I don't think you're the sort to beat it out of him.'

'I wouldn't be so sure of that.' Kier let his fingers relax. Paul was right. The kid wasn't going to tell. And he wasn't going to beat it out of him, although every time he thought of the danger to Alex, he wanted to pound his fist into the kid's smiling face.

A flashing blue light announced the arrival of a police car. For once, Kier was pleased to see the uniform.

'I guess we need to talk to the stewards,' Paul said as the police took custody of the protester. 'And I'd better take another look at that head of yours.'

Paul's words drew Kier's attention to the fact that his head was hurting. He touched the place. 'Ouch!' He dropped his hand, and noticed that his fingers were damp with a mix of blood and sweat. He reached into his pocket for a handkerchief, but didn't find one.

'We can't let anyone even start their engine until we figure this out,' Paul said.

Even as he spoke, from nearby came the sound of an engine turning over, as one of the mechanics tested his repairs. Kier and Paul exchanged a look.

'I'll stop him. You get the stewards,' Paul said as he turned away.

By the time Kier had explained everything at the stewards' office, a good crowd had already gathered outside.

'What happens now?' he asked.

'You're sure no one has started their engine?' the chief steward asked.

'Only the Porsche brothers,' Kier replied, smiling as the other stewards in unison whispered, 'Pricks.'

'Be that as it may,' the chief steward added, 'we have to make sure this is handled in a fair manner. Thanks, Kier.'

'No worries.' Kier left the room and went in search of Paul. He and Lyn were standing on the edge of the gathered crowd.

'What's going to happen?' Lyn wanted to know.

'My guess is they'll delay the start tomorrow.'

Lyn frowned. 'But . . .'

'Because we don't know which cars were targeted,

every single driver is going to have to check his fuel,' Paul explained.

'Can we do it now?' Lyn asked.

'No,' Kier said firmly. 'We have to wait for a couple of hours, until the water has sunk to the bottom of the petrol tanks. Then it will be a pretty simple job to drain it off.'

'Except for the Porsche brothers,' Paul added with an evil grin. 'They started their engine, even though they're not supposed to this late at night. If there was water in their tank, it's in the system now. They are going to have to pull the whole thing apart.'

'How sad!' Lyn's voice made it clear she didn't think it was at all sad.

Paul chuckled. 'You know, there are times when I think you are not a very nice person.'

Kier suddenly felt like an outsider. An intruder on a private moment. He almost stepped away.

'I guess we should tell Alex,' Lyn said at last.

'No. Don't,' Kier said firmly. 'She's probably asleep by now. Let her sleep. She's going to need all her wits about her tomorrow.'

'But the car . . .'

'I'll stay awake and check the tank in a couple of hours,' Kier said.

'He's right,' Paul added. 'You should get some sleep too, Lyn.'

'You're not going to wait up?' Lyn asked.

'Not for long. There were no bottles near the Alfa. They didn't get that far. My guess is I'm fine. I'll double-check tomorrow morning, but I'm not worried.'

'All right. Good night.' Lyn's smile lingered a little longer on Paul than it did on Kier before she turned away.

The two men watched her go.

'She's coping with this very well, for a girl who isn't into cars,' Kier said.

'Yes. She's pretty amazing.'

'Are you and Lyn . . . ?' Kier darted a questioning glance at Paul.

'God, no!' Paul answered instantly. 'Not that I wouldn't . . . I mean . . . She's gorgeous and all that, but . . .'

'But what?' Kier demanded.

'She's out of my league,' Paul said sadly. 'She's a model. She's famous. Moves in all sorts of glamorous circles. What is she going to want with a crusty old bloke like me?'

Kier wanted to tell Paul that he knew exactly how he was feeling. He had felt like that once. Not good enough. In his case, it had been true, but that didn't mean that Paul and Lyn were doomed.

'Don't sell yourself short, mate.' He slapped Paul gently on the shoulder. 'And don't sell Lyn short either. I haven't known her long, but there are depths to her that most people don't even see.'

Paul seemed to think for a moment. 'You're right,' he said at last with a rueful grin. 'They can't shoot a man for trying.'

'Why don't you get some sleep?' Kier suggested. 'You've got to drive tomorrow too.'

'Are you sure you don't need a hand?'

'I'll be fine. I can sleep tomorrow. You go.'

Paul nodded and turned towards the ski lodges. Kier watched him go, an unprepossessing man in faded jeans and a well-worn shirt, yet in some ways Kier envied him. Paul had the strength to ignore the opinions of others and live his life his own way. He would have the courage to fight for what he wanted. To give himself and Lyn a chance.

Kier ran his fingers gently over the bonnet of Alex's Lotus, once again haunted by the feeling that he just was not good enough.

'**Y**ou are not going to see that boy again!'

'You can't stop me!' Alex shouted the words in her mother's face.

Jacqueline Reilly took a long, slow breath. Alex could see that she was fighting to control her emotions. Her mother always controlled her emotions. She considered it unladylike to do otherwise. As for shouting . . . that was unthinkable. Almost as unthinkable as allowing her daughter to become involved with the son of one of her husband's employees, and one with a brother about to be sent to jail.

'Alexandra.' Jacqueline's voice was carefully modulated and without rancour. 'It is not appropriate for you to be seen with this boy. He works for your father. And his brother is in trouble with the law. I just will not allow it.'

'I love him.' The words exploded from her heart. She hadn't dared say them aloud before, not even to herself.

'That's ridiculous,' Jacqueline said evenly. 'You are just a child. You have no idea what love is.'

Yes I do, Alex wanted to shout. Love is waking up every morning barely able to breathe for wanting to be with him. Love is the pain I feel when he is hurting. Love is knowing that every day will be better if it has him in it. She felt the *tears pricking the back of her eyes, but she blinked them away. Her mother would not make her cry!*

'You can't stop me, Mother,' she said. 'I turn seventeen next week.'

'Yes, you do,' Jacqueline said. 'And it's therefore time you started thinking about the future. You'll be going to university next year. Living in the city, you'll meet the right sort of young men. Men who can offer you the future you deserve.'

'How do you know who is "right" for me?' Alex said. 'Mother, you barely know me. And you don't know Kier at all.'

Jacqueline's eyes narrowed speculatively. Alex could see what she was thinking. She was wondering if Alex and Kier had slept together.

'Enough of this,' Jacqueline said, obviously dismissing the idea as ludicrous. 'There is nothing more to be said. You will cease your involvement with this boy.'

'Or what?' Alex challenged.

Her mother said nothing. She simply turned and walked out of the room into her conservatory, where, no doubt, there were flowers waiting to be arranged and some fictional character who deserved her attention far more than her daughter did.

Alex slipped out the back door feeling as if she was escaping a prison. A glance at the sun told her it was past time for the meat-packing plant to close. She walked swiftly down to the riverbank. Kier was already there. She saw him through the trees, and her heart almost broke. He was sitting on the fallen tree trunk, staring at the slow-moving water. His shoulders were slumped, as if he carried the weight of the world on his back. She wished there was some way she could ease his burden.

'Hi,' she said as she walked the last few metres to his side.

His face changed as he turned to her. She saw him take a hold of his pain and push it to one side, creating space for her at the centre of his world. 'Hi.'

She dropped on to the tree trunk next to him.

'Tell me.'

'He was released from hospital this morning,' Kier said, taking her hand in his.

'Is he home or . . .'

'In jail? No, he's home. There's not much risk that he'll escape. He can barely walk, even on crutches.'

Alex heard the pain in his voice. When Rob and his friends were discovered breaking into the shop the night of the film show, they had tried to run. The high-speed police chase had ended when Rob's ute slid off the road, rolled and crashed through a fence into a building. One of his friends had died. Rob had survived the crash – but only just. Alex didn't like Rob, and she suspected Kier didn't like him much either. But Kier was nothing if not fiercely loyal, and that loyalty still extended to his brother, despite everything.

'So what happens now?'

'It depends what the police charge him with. If they want to, they could throw the book at him, and with his record, he'll end up in prison.' Kier's voice shook just a little on the final words.

Alex knew what he was thinking. Rob had already paid a high price for that night. His face was permanently scarred from the accident. He was likely to limp for the rest of his life. What other scars would prison leave on him? She wanted to say something. To offer Kier some sort of comfort. But nothing she could say would change *anything. Instead she simply held his hand.*

'I should have stopped him.' Kier's words were little more than a whisper.

'There's no way you could have known what was going to happen.'

'But I did.' The words were a painful cry. 'Alex, I knew what they were planning. I heard them talking. I should have stopped them.'

His grip on her hand was so tight it felt as if her fingers would break. She ignored the pain. 'They wouldn't have listened to you,' she said. 'You didn't stop them last time. You couldn't have stopped them this time. It wasn't your fault!'

'I know.'

The agony in his voice was more than she could stand, and there was nothing she could do to help him. She put her arm around him. Slowly he turned to look at her. Then he was kissing her. Holding her as if she was his salvation. As if he would lose himself in her and never let her go. As she met his kisses with equal passion, she knew in her heart how she could help him. On her seventeenth birthday, she would give him the only gift that had any real value . . .

Alex opened her eyes and stared at the dull off-white ceiling of her room. What a fool she had been. How naive. At sixteen, she really had no idea of what love was. Over the years, the relationship must have grown in her mind, been exaggerated into something it could never have been. She could not really have been in love. Not the sort of love that lasted a lifetime. Yet as she slipped from the bed, she could feel the sharp need in her body. It wasn't love. It was just unfinished business. A promise unfulfilled. Perhaps she should fix that. Then maybe Kier would stop disturbing her every waking and sleeping moment.

After a quick shower, she went in search of coffee and found the whole valley buzzing with news of the incident the previous night. After catching snatches of information from other drivers in the coffee queue, she hurried towards the car park. Was her Lotus all right? The red car was exactly as she had left it – with one notable exception. She pulled the piece of paper from underneath the windscreen wiper. It was a printed notice from the stewards, summoning all drivers to a meeting later in the morning. There was also a strict warning not to start any car's engine. Her heart sank as she read the note, but at the bottom was a ray of light. Someone had scribbled a few words.

She's fine. Don't worry. K.

Kier! She looked around, but there was no sign of him. 'Have you seen Kier?' she asked a couple of passing people, but they shook their heads.

Casting one more worried glance at her precious Lotus, she set out in search of him. It was still early, and there weren't many people about. When he wasn't to be seen at the food stalls or the stewards' office, Alex decided to try the only other possibility. She almost ran back to the ski lodge. When she reached Kier's door, she didn't just knock. She pounded on it. When she didn't get an immediate response, she pounded again.

'I'm coming!' The muffled voice stopped her hand just as she was about to give the door a third and even harder pounding. She waited impatiently for the several hours it seemed to take before the door opened and Kier's face appeared.

'What . . . ?'

Before he could finish, she pushed past him into the room. 'Last night. What happened?'

'It's all right,' Kier said. 'They didn't touch the Lotus.'

Alex caught her breath in relief. Her mind had been conjuring the most appalling images of sugar in the petrol tank, or some other invisible but devastating damage. 'Tell me everything,' she demanded.

In a few succinct sentences he told her everything she needed to know. Nodding as she listened, Alex began to calm down. She realised that the room was quite dark. Kier was little more than a shadow. Without thinking about it, she turned to the window and drew back the heavy curtains. When she turned back, Kier was running his hands through his sleep-tousled hair. He was wearing nothing more than a pair of dark boxer shorts. Standing with his arms raised, the muscles of his chest and his stomach were flat and taut. He was tanned, but then he always had been, even when they were just kids. But he wasn't a kid any more. This was a mature man, who showed every sign of an active outdoor life. His body was firm and sloped gracefully down to slim hips. She had to look. Not even a saint could have turned away from the picture of sheer masculine beauty he presented; even his mussed hair simply added to his appeal. As did the smile slowly forming on his lips.

'Oh!' With a sudden start she realised two things. First, that he was well aware of her lingering scrutiny of his near-naked body. And the second was that she was not the only one this morning who had woken feeling the ache of unfulfilled desire. Her first thought was to turn away, but to do that would be to admit what she was feeling.

'I'd better go to the stewards' meeting,' she said, aware that it was well over an hour away.

Kier glanced at the bedside clock and his mouth twitched with humour. 'All right. They are going to delay the start of the race, to give people a chance to check their cars. I wouldn't mind getting a little more sleep. I was up pretty late last night, making sure the Lotus was all right.'

'Oh. Yes. Thanks for checking the car. You go back to . . .' Alex kept her eyes firmly off the rumpled bed, which would no doubt still be warm from his body, and steeped in the warm, masculine scent of him.

'I'll see you later.'

'All right.' She began backing towards the door. 'Sleep well.' She twisted the handle and almost ran from the room. As she marched swiftly down the corridor, she took back the salutation. She hoped he didn't sleep well. She hoped he wouldn't sleep at all. He should toss and turn on that bed, restless and disturbed as she now was.

The crowd around the stewards' office was big, and growing by the minute. Lyn stood slightly to one side looking for Alex or Kier. Looking for Paul. She couldn't spot any of them. The dark grey clouds gathering above the valley gave a feeling of impending doom, as the buzz of voices grew ever louder. News of the night's sabotage was spreading, and people were flocking to the office in search of news. Lyn could have joined in with her version of events, but she didn't. She hovered in the background, not wanting to draw attention to herself. She spotted Dee Parker on the edge of the crowd. The woman still looked worried. The Porsche brothers, who were worst affected by the events, were complaining loudly about lack of security. Lyn was beginning to think that they had earned their unflattering accolade. If they hadn't started their engine in violation of the rules, they wouldn't be any worse off than anyone else. Maybe they really were pricks.

Lyn tugged at the neck of her race suit. It didn't feel quite straight this morning. Like most of the other drivers, she had only one suit for the entire race, and it was beginning to feel a bit . . . lived in. Despite her best efforts at airing it every night, it was also developing a distinctive odour of sweat and petrol fumes. Not that she was looking exactly her best right now. The leather race gloves had left her nails chipped and rough. Her complexion, normally model perfect, was showing the effects of days inside a fire-retardant balaclava and race helmet. And as for her hair! What would her agent think if he could see her now? The designers she modelled for would start an immediate search for her replacement.

'Good morning, Lyn.'

It was the voice she had been waiting to hear. Wishing she looked more like a model and less like some racetrack wannabe, Lyn turned to greet Paul.

'Hi.'

'Have the stewards said anything yet?'

'Not yet,' she said. 'There have been a lot of rumours about last night floating around. A few people are a bit upset.'

'Let me guess . . . the Porsche brothers?'

Lyn nodded, marvelling at how Paul's mere presence was enough to make her smile.

'I guess they'll delay the race start by at least an hour,' Paul mused. 'I just hope that nothing else happens.'

'What do you mean?' Lyn asked. 'What else could happen?'

'I don't know. I hope they haven't got anything else planned. They could be dangerous. You take care out there today.'

His face creased with concern as he spoke, and Lyn

felt a tiny frisson of pleasure that in some small way he cared. 'I will,' she reassured him.

Any further conversation was interrupted by a sudden surge of noise, marking the arrival of the chief steward. He climbed on to the bonnet of a car, and waved his hands for silence.

'Listen up,' he yelled. The crowd stilled. 'We're pushing the start time back, because of an incident last night.'

All around Lyn, the crowd erupted into renewed clamour. It took a few minutes for the steward to restore order, and then he recounted the events of the previous night, without mentioning Kier or Paul's role.

'So, drivers, check your fuel,' he said in closing. 'Remember to observe fire safety rules. We don't want any spills. No fuel on the car park. If anyone finds anything – report to the stewards' desk immediately. If we have to, we can reschedule some cars for an even later start. Be ready to start your engines and line up at . . .' he looked at his watch, 'eight thirty.'

The crowd rapidly dispersed.

'He should have given you and Kier credit for what you did.' Lyn was a little miffed. 'You deserved it.'

'I'm pleased that he didn't,' Paul said. 'I don't want either team singled out . . . just in case.'

'In case . . . ?' Lyn didn't know what he meant.

'That might make us targets,' Paul said quietly.

'Oh!' Lyn felt a sudden flash of fear. She hadn't thought of that. 'You don't think—'

'No.' Paul spoke quickly. 'Don't worry about it. I'm being over-cautious. You'll be fine. Just keep your eyes open. That's all.'

Lyn studied Paul's face, wondering if he was just trying to reassure her. As always, all she saw was open, honest concern. She wrapped her arms around her body, feeling a little chilled. She put it down to the rising breeze.

'There you are.' Alex suddenly appeared at their side.

'Did you hear the chief steward?' Lyn asked.

'Yes.'

'You don't have to worry,' Paul offered. 'Last night Kier—'

'I know,' Alex said. 'I spoke to him earlier.'

Was Lyn imagining it, or did Alex's cheeks colour just a fraction, and just for one brief moment? She tried to catch her friend's eye, but Alex turned to Paul. 'They didn't damage the Alfa?' she asked.

'No. It's fine,' Paul told her.

'That's great,' Alex said. 'Thanks for what you did last night. If it wasn't for you and Kier . . .'

'I'm not convinced that this is all over.' Paul shook his head slowly, his frown deepening. 'Just be careful.'

Alex nodded.

'Where's Kier?' Lyn had to ask.

'He was up half the night with the Lotus,' Alex said. 'When I left him, he was going to try to get a bit more sleep.'

'Oh?' Lyn raised an eyebrow. She wasn't going to let that pass.

'But it looks like he's awake now.' Paul unwittingly rescued Alex from further questions.

They spotted Kier walking towards them. His hair was still wet from a shower, and he was dressed in blue jeans and a light cotton shirt, despite the cloudy skies. His eyes were on Alex as he approached. For her part, Alex looked as if she had been carved from marble as she waited for him, her focus entirely on the man walking towards her.

Lyn could almost feel the air between them crackling with electricity that had nothing to do with the storm clouds above them. Alex hadn't said much about the past, but it was pretty clear that something was happening between her and Kier. It was also pretty clear that they had about as much chance of controlling it as they had of controlling the weather.

Lyn took half a step away from the charged aura around Alex and collided with Paul. He put his hands on her shoulders to steady her, and she felt a flash of the same electricity that was sparking between Alex and Kier. She looked into Paul's face. Did he feel it too? His eyes were unreadable as they looked steadily into hers. For a few seconds the four of them seemed frozen, then the sky erupted with light as a mighty crash of thunder seemed to shake the mountains around them.

'Whoa!' Alex gasped.

Lyn shook her head, feeling a little dazed. The wind had risen and was snapping flags and posters on the fences, and chasing papers across the car park.

'I think we're in for a storm,' Paul said. 'That's going to make racing difficult.'

Lyn looked up at the roiling sky, as another lightning bolt flashed, followed almost immediately by a crash of thunder. 'Will this delay the start even more?'

'I don't think so,' Paul said. 'But between this and the fuel problems, I think the race has just been thrown wide open.'

As he spoke, the first huge drops of rain fell around them.

12

'Damn it – I wish it would either rain or not rain,' Alex swore. 'I can't stand this.'

She reached out to flick the windscreen-wiper switch one more time. The blades sliced across the screen, clearing the large drops of rain, and for a few seconds she had a clear view of the starting line, and the two cars queuing ahead of her. The wipers stopped moving. Then a large drop of water plopped on to the windscreen. Then another. And another.

'Why didn't I install better wipers for the race?' she growled as her view slowly dissolved into a watery blur.

'I thought keeping the car original was part of the deal,' Lyn said. 'Where's the fun if you have wipers with five different speeds?'

Alex didn't reply. There was a lot about this rally that was supposed to be fun – and wasn't. Most of that could be traced to the moment five days ago when she looked up and saw Kier standing next to her. The capricious god who had put him once more in her path was still delighting in making her life a misery. The downpour hovering in her immediate future was just one more torment. She could hear a steward shouting and wound down her window to listen.

'The road's wet,' he was saying. 'Take it easy out there.' Alex wound the window up again. Take it easy, indeed!

Almost immediately there was a tap on the window on the other side of the car. When Lyn opened it, a steward in a raincoat was standing there shaking raindrops from a clipboard.

'There's water across the road at one point three kilometres,' he said. 'And again at four kilometres, just past the left downhill. It's several centimetres deep. Likely to be getting deeper. Once you start the long downhill past the ranger station, it's clear until the end of the stage. But there's no guarantee it will stay that way.'

Lyn was nodding as she wrote on her notes. 'Got it.'

'Good luck.' The steward's face disappeared and Lyn wound the window back up.

'It's going to be a slow day, at least till we get out of the mountains,' she said.

'We can't take it too slowly,' Alex said.

'Just don't kill us. That's all I ask,' Lyn replied.

'I'll try not to.' Alex gunned the engine and pulled forward. They were on the starting line. She turned the wipers on once more and listened to Lyn's voice counting down the seconds. The light turned green and she planted her foot on the accelerator. The Lotus fishtailed on the damp road as it sped away.

'Five hundred metres, then a dip. Then three hundred and a long slow left.' Lyn slipped into navigator mode.

Alex almost didn't see the first water on the road. The clouds chose that moment to open and dump a heavy downpour right on top of the car. The Lotus was moving far too fast when it hit the water.

'Shit,' she exclaimed as she felt the wheels lose

traction. 'Hang on!' The car started to drift to the left and there was nothing she could do about it. To touch the brakes would invite disaster. The car aquaplaned across the top of the water, and just as Alex was beginning to think she was in real trouble, the tyres gripped the road surface again and held.

'About not killing us . . .' Lyn yelled.

'Yeah. Got it.' Alex eased back on the accelerator. The rain was getting heavier now. Visibility dropped as the clouds sank lower over the mountains. 'Lyn, there's condensation on the screen. Wipe it,' she instructed.

Lyn grabbed the cloth she had ready. 'I guess these old windscreen de-misters are part of the fun too?' She wiped the moisture off the screen, and Alex's vision improved.

Alex was tense and frazzled when they pulled into the checkpoint at the ranger station next to the park entrance.

'We've got another four stages still in the mountains,' Lyn said. 'After that the road gets better. As for the rain . . . I guess there's one good thing about it. If those protesters were planning any more trouble today, I guess they've cancelled it.'

'We don't need them to slow us down,' Alex said bitterly. 'The rain is doing it for them.'

She let her head fall forward. The cold, hard plastic of her helmet cracked against her knuckles. She took a long, deep breath. She wasn't driving well, and today of all days she had to be at her best. It wasn't just a matter of winning the race. If she drove badly today, she was risking her life, and Lyn's. She had to get herself together.

'Are you all right?' Lyn asked.

It was a good question, and Alex wasn't sure of the answer. She was fine, if tired and tense. But was she all right? The answer was that she was disturbed and distracted, and there were no prizes for guessing why. She should never have walked into Kier's room. Should never have let herself remember . . .

'I just need a couple of minutes,' she said.

'We've got a transport stage next,' Lyn told her. 'You can take it a bit easy. We are looking good for time. We have two minutes in hand, so if we're a little slow it won't matter. Considering the weather, that's pretty amazing.'

Lyn was right. Alex should be feeling good about their performance.

'You! Lotus. Number fifty-three. You've got four minutes. Pull into line.'

Alex nodded to the steward and slipped the car into gear. She forced herself to focus on the road and on the race. A transport stage would give her time to get herself together. She had forty minutes of easy driving ahead. She glanced at the sky, looking for just a hint that the rain was easing. She almost convinced herself that the clouds were lifting, and felt her heart lighten a little.

By the time they were lined up for the next race stage, the skies above them had cleared to a brilliant shade of storm-washed blue. Alex had almost managed to push Kier to the back of her mind. Almost. Her problems, however, were far from over.

'There's a lot of water coming off the mountains,' the steward told them as they took their place in the starting line-up. 'It's flowing across the road in too many places to track. Just be aware and don't do anything stupid!' He waved them forward.

He was right about the water. Although the rain had stopped, water was gushing off the mountainsides, looking for the easiest way down. Alex's hands ached from gripping the steering wheel. Her eyes didn't leave the road for one second. Lyn's course notes were some help, but there was no way of predicting when they would come around a corner to be faced with a river instead of a road.

About halfway down the mountains, Alex thought the volume of water on the roadway was easing. They were driving down a cut in the steep mountainside. On their right was a high rock wall. To their left, tall trees marched down into a deep gully.

'I think we might be ahead of the water now,' she shouted above the engine noise.

'Maybe.' Lyn didn't sound convinced. 'But you've got a sharp right, a three right coming up. Don't go too wide – the edge of the road is broken.'

Alex flexed her fingers and steered the Lotus into the bend. They were halfway around the curve when she saw it. The red Mini was on its roof, lying across the road at right angles to the oncoming traffic. The wheels were still spinning. The crash had happened mere seconds ago.

'Shit!'

Alex instinctively steered the Lotus between the crashed car and the trees lining the road. She winced as branches scraped down the side of the car. Beside her, Lyn yelled something, but she didn't know what. Carefully she touched the brake to ease back her speed, aware that a fraction too much pressure would see her repeat the other car's accident. Sliding just a little on the wet road, she brought the Lotus to a complete stop about fifty metres in front of the other car. She made sure she was as far off the road as she could get, and turned off the engine. Then she leaped out, tossed her race helmet on to the seat behind her and started to run back the way she had come. Lyn was just a step behind her.

The red Mini had started this leg a minute before them. Alex had talked to the driver once or twice. He was young and friendly. He'd admired her Lotus. But she couldn't remember his name. That suddenly seemed very important, as she knelt down beside the overturned car and looked fearfully inside. The driver and navigator were still in their seats, held there by the racing harness. They were hanging upside down, their race helmets inches from the crumpled car roof. Neither was moving. The windscreen and windows had shattered during the crash, and broken glass was strewn for some distance along the road, crunching under Alex's feet as she tried to reach out to touch the driver's shoulder.

'Are you all right?' It was a stupid question, but what else was she to say?

'Don't move him.' Lyn was at her side.

'I won't.' Alex withdrew her hand. 'Guys?'

There was still no movement from either man.

'You've got to stop the race,' Lyn said. 'If the next car hits this one . . .'

Alex didn't need any more explanation. She stood up and reached into her pocket for her phone. She held it high for a few seconds. 'No service.'

Lyn tried her own phone, but shook her head.

'Stay here,' Alex said. 'If they wake up, talk to them. But don't—'

'I know what to do. Don't worry. I'll be fine. Stop those cars. And send for help.'

Alex nodded and looked back the way they had come. The next car couldn't be more than a minute away. She started to run. The back of Lyn's course notes were designed to act as a red emergency flag for moments just like this – but she didn't have time to go back and get them. She kept to the side of the road, knowing that any second a car could appear around the bend. Her soft leather racing shoes weren't much protection on the rough road surface, but she ignored that and just ran. As she rounded the corner, she saw a car approaching. It was close. If it took the corner too fast, it would collide with the Mini. Lyn was there too. Alex had to stop it. Now! Without a second thought she stepped into the middle of the road, waving her hands. For a few terrifying seconds she thought it wasn't going to stop. Her body seemed to freeze as the blue shape hurtled towards her. Then her brain seized on the fact that it was slowing down, veering across the road as the driver fought to control it under heavy braking. Suddenly realising the danger she was in, Alex flung herself off the road. The blue car slid past her and stopped halfway around the corner.

Alex leaped to her feet and ran towards the vehicle, realising with relief that it was Paul.

'There's been an accident,' she panted.

Paul looked further down the road, where the overturned Mini was now visible. 'Bloody hell,' he said. 'How bad are they?'

'I don't know. We have to get help. The phones don't work here in the mountains.'

Paul nodded as he moved quickly to the rear of the Alfa. He opened the boot and pulled out a rucksack. 'Medical kit,' he said in answer to Alex's unspoken question.

'I'll go back up the road,' Alex said, 'and stop the oncoming cars.'

'Good.' Paul leaned in through the window of his car and spoke to his navigator. 'Jack, you drive on to the next checkpoint. Alert the stewards. We need an ambulance.

And they have to stop the race.' Jack nodded and started to move into the driver's seat.

Very aware that the next car couldn't be far away, Alex set off back up the road at a run.

Lyn tugged at the buckled car door, but it was jammed solid. The Mini had obviously rolled more than once. Every panel was twisted and torn. Every piece of glass broken. The driver and navigator were well and truly trapped inside. She dropped back to her knees and peered through the broken window. Both men appeared to still be unconscious. Feeling totally helpless, she could only be thankful. They were better off like that – when there was nothing she could do for them. She looked around the twisted interior of the car, and was horrified to see blood dripping from the driver's inert body. Dimly she heard a car drive past, then running footsteps.

'Lyn. How are they?'

Paul dropped to a crouch next to her, a rucksack in his hand. Lyn had never been so glad to see anyone in her life.

'They're both unconscious. At least, I think . . .' Lyn didn't want to even think about the other possibility.

'I need to get in there,' Paul said.

Lyn stood back as he quickly moved around the vehicle. The front of the cabin had crumpled when the Mini rolled, and the car was now tilted slightly forward. The front windscreen had shattered, but there was no way anyone was going to be able to climb in that way. The back of the car was relatively intact, making the rear windscreen more accessible. Paul dropped to his hands and knees.

'Be careful . . .' Lyn felt her heart contract as Paul lay

on his back on the roadside and eased his head and shoulders into the car. There were a few moments of terrible silence before he spoke.

'They are both alive, but the driver is badly hurt.' His voice was incredibly calm. 'I have to stop the bleeding. Get my bag.'

Lyn did as she was told. She unzipped the bag and saw an assortment of medical supplies. 'What do you need?'

'There are some absorbent dressings. Big ones. White packets.'

'Got them.' Lyn ripped the first package open and placed the dressing in Paul's outstretched hand.

'Another one. Then a bandage.'

As Lyn did as she was instructed, she heard a groan from inside the car. She moved around to peer in the passenger's window. The navigator was moving feebly.

'It's all right,' she said in the calmest voice she could manage. 'We'll help you.'

The navigator moved his arm, and Lyn reached through the broken window to close her hand around his. She squeezed gently. 'Try not to move.' The fingers inside hers twitched slightly in response.

'Lyn, we need to get the driver out. He'll bleed to death if he stays like that.' Paul was sliding back out of the car.

'The doors won't budge,' she told him.

'Is there anything in the Lotus we can use as a lever?' Paul asked.

Lyn stood up and ran back to the Lotus. She flung open the boot, and looked inside. Like most race drivers, Alex carried not one kilo of weight more than she absolutely needed. She did however have a spare tyre and a small jack. There was a nylon bag that rattled when Lyn lifted it. Tools. She grabbed the wheel brace, jack and bag and ran back towards the Mini.

'The navigator's coming round,' Paul told her. 'Talk to him while I see what I can do with these.'

Lyn nodded.

'You'll have to go through the back windscreen,' Paul added. 'We'll never get the driver's door open – but I might be able to do something with the passenger side.'

Lyn lowered herself to the glass-covered road and edged her head and shoulders towards the back of the car. Both the navigator and the driver were starting to move.

'You're going to be all right,' she said again, hoping that she wasn't lying. 'There is more help on the way. Just relax. Try not to move . . .' She reached out to touch the driver's shoulder, hoping that might give him some comfort. As she did, she saw with horror that blood was already seeping through the dressing Paul had placed over the wound in the man's leg.

'Paul!' she called. 'The driver's bleeding again.'

'Put pressure on the wound,' Paul called. She could hear him bashing the torn metal of the passenger-side door.

Pressure? How was she supposed to do that? She wriggled further forward into the wrecked car, then twisted on to her side and reached between the seats and the two injured men. She could just get at the injured man's leg. Tentatively she spread her hand over the reddening dressing and gently applied pressure.

'Harder!' Paul called.

Wincing, Lyn increased the pressure on the wound. She could feel the blood seeping through the dressing on to her hand. She pushed even harder.

'Got it?' Paul called.

'I think so.' She wedged her back against the seat and increased the pressure even more. The driver had stopped moving. 'I think he's passed out again.'

There was a hideous grinding of metal from the passenger side. She looked over. Paul had some kind of metal bar against the door and was levering it open. Only a few centimetres. It wasn't enough.

'Hang on.' She could hear the strain in his voice.

The navigator started moving again, his arms flailing about. With only one hand, there wasn't much Lyn could do. She took hold of his nearest hand and squeezed the fingers tightly. 'I'm here,' she said. 'We're going to help you. Just try to stay still.'

The man's eyes flickered open. He looked at her in an unfocused fashion. Lyn remembered all those times with Lorna. The times she had held her sister's arms to stop her hurting herself as she thrashed about. The blank expression on Lorna's face when she looked at the sister she didn't recognise. Lyn closed her eyes for just a heartbeat, let the memories and the pain wash past, then squeezed the navigator's hand once more.

She could hear voices coming from outside the vehicle. Someone was banging on the crumpled metal door again.

'Lyn, watch your eyes,' Paul shouted.

She turned her face away and closed her eyes. The sound of tearing metal drowned out the laboured breathing of the two injured men. When she looked up again, the door was half open. Paul was peering anxiously in at her. She could see other people moving behind him.

'We're nearly there,' he told her. 'Just another minute or so.'

The passenger door gave way under the combined assault of many hands, and Paul appeared again. 'Lyn, I'll support his neck and head. When I give the word, can you release the harness?'

'Yes.'

The car rocked as Paul manoeuvred himself into position. 'Okay. Do it.'

Lyn let go of the navigator's hand. Careful to keep her other hand pressed down hard on the injured driver's leg, she grabbed the buckle of the navigator's harness. The man's weight had pulled the straps tight, and she fumbled for a minute before she heard it click open. The navigator dropped, but Paul was ready for him. Holding the man by the shoulders, he pulled him towards the door. Willing hands reached in to cradle the man's head and neck as he was slowly dragged free of the wreck. In a flash, Paul was back, ready to help the injured driver.

'All right. I'll take him now.' He placed his hand over Lyn's, which was now stained with blood.

She pulled her hand free and slithered out of the car. As she stood, she was startled to see a small crowd of men surrounding the Mini. They were all wearing race suits and they had all come to help. As she watched, Paul and the others pulled the driver free and laid him gently on the roadway.

'Lyn, my bag!' Paul called. She took it to him. In an instant he'd found a plastic bag of clear liquid. 'Hold this, please.'

As she took it, he reached for a needle. Lyn had seen this done many times before. It was the work of just a few moments to get the drip in place. Paul applied another dressing to the man's leg, which was still bleeding, but more slowly now. Then he sat back on his heels.

'That's all I can do for him.' He turned his attention to the navigator.

Lyn nodded, and as she did, her hands started to shake. She felt the road spin, just a little. Then Paul's arm was around her shoulders. He passed the saline bag she was still holding to another of his helpers, and then guided her away from the two injured men. Someone thrust a bottle of water at her. Gratefully she went to drink from it, and then stopped in horror, looking at her bloodstained hand holding the bottle. Gently, Paul took the bottle and poured water over her hands, rinsing the blood away. Then he held her shoulders as she held the bottle and drank deeply.

'It's just the shock. You'll be fine.'

Lyn shook her head. 'You should be worrying about them, not me.'

As she spoke, they caught the faint clamour of an ambulance siren. It fell silent, then after a few seconds they heard it again, sounding much closer this time, before once again the mountains blocked the sound.

'They'll be here any second,' Paul said. 'I'll just talk to them . . .'

'Go.' Lyn nodded. She felt stronger now, but was very glad when Alex appeared at her side.

'Are you all right?' Alex asked.

'I'm fine.'

With the arrival of the ambulance and the stewards, all responsibility was lifted from Lyn and Alex's shoulders. Paul spoke to the ambulancemen, and stayed with them while they loaded the injured men into their vehicle. One of the paramedics came to check Lyn, but she assured him she was fine.

'You're not driving?' he asked.

'I am,' Alex answered for her.

The ambulanceman nodded and turned away. He hesitated for a second, then turned back. 'I thought you might like to know – you probably saved that man's life.'

Alex gave Lyn's shoulders a gentle squeeze. 'See. You're a hero. Or is it heroine?'

'Paul's the hero,' Lyn said gently, her eyes seeking out the familiar figure still standing by the ambulance. 'Why don't they get going? That man needs to get to hospital.'

'They know what they're doing,' Alex reassured her.

Lyn took a deep breath and tried to calm her shattered nerves. 'What do you think happened? Was it the protesters again?'

'I don't think so,' Alex said. 'The silver Porsche was in front. It seems to have made it through. I guess the Mini just took the corner too fast.'

Lyn nodded, very much aware that it could so easily have been the Lotus lying in the roadway, and herself and Alex in that ambulance.

A race steward approached them. 'Are you all right to drive on to the next checkpoint?'

Lyn looked around, taking in her surroundings for the first time since this nightmare had begun. A line of race cars lined the road back towards the starting line. Of Paul's Alfa, there was no sign. Several stewards had somehow found their way to the scene, along with the police and ambulance, which was now moving away. The overturned Mini still blocked part of the road. Lyn wondered just how the stewards were going to turn this mess back into a car rally.

13

'... Cross to our newsroom for a special update on the Snowy Mountains Classic car race, which is currently in its fourth day.' The voice from the radio seeped into Kier's brain, past the turbulent thoughts of Alex that had robbed him of his extra hour of sleep that morning. He reached for the volume control on the car radio.

'Word is just coming through of a serious accident involving rally competitors.'

Kier glanced down at the radio, as if by doing that he could change the news that it was about to deliver.

'Details are still sketchy at this time, but we do know that the third leg of today's race has been stopped. Cars are being held at the start line. We also know that an ambulance and stewards have set out from the next checkpoint and are heading up the mountain.'

Kier's eyes were drawn to his left – towards the mountains still cloaked in cloud. Like the other support drivers, he had been held at the Perisher resort until the rally cars had cleared the first race leg. While the competitors had headed west, along the Alpine way and deeper into the mountains, the support teams had formed an impromptu convoy and turned east, out of the high country, to circle the great man-made lakes of the Snowy River Scheme. Their plan was to arrive at Tumut well before the competitors taking the slower route through the mountains. Ahead of Kier, cars were pulling to the side of the road. People were getting out of their vehicles and gathering to listen to the news. Kier did the same.

'. . . I'm at the Clover Flat picnic area,' said the voice on the radio in the front car as Kier approached. 'This was the start point for the third leg, a race through the twisting mountain roads towards Cabramurra. Now I've driven that road many times in the past. There are some dangerous hairpin bends and some very steep grades. That road can be treacherous in the wet.'

'Don't tell us what we already know,' one of the listeners muttered. 'Tell us what's happened.'

'As you know,' the reporter continued, 'mobile phone reception is bad in the mountains, so we don't have a lot of detail. But I can tell you that word came through from the stewards at Cabramurra to hold all traffic here at the checkpoint. That's competitors and support teams and stewards. No one is driving up that road. We know there's been an accident, but we don't know how bad it is or who is involved. We've got a lot of concerned people here at the starting line, waiting for news.'

'They're not the only ones,' someone said.

A few people were reaching for their phones. 'Don't bother,' another man said. 'He's right about the phones. I can't get through.' A couple of others nodded their agreement.

'We have got our reporter at Cabramurra on the line,' the radio announcer declared in an excited voice. 'Bill, what can you tell us?'

'Well, as you say, details are sketchy,' a new voice

began. 'But I am at the stewards' office at Cabramurra. Only two race cars have arrived at this end of the course. The first was the Porsche, car number one-two-one.'

For once the assembled listeners didn't mutter the traditional abuse.

'The second car, a blue Alfa Romeo, car number seventy-one, arrived about five minutes later.'

'That's Paul White's car,' one of the listeners said.

'. . . only one person in that car,' the voice on the radio continued. 'The navigator. Apparently the driver stayed behind to help.'

'Paul's a doctor,' Kier added.

'. . . went straight into the stewards' office. He hasn't . . .' The reporter's voice was lost in a wave of crackling static. '. . . ambulance with it, suggesting someone is hurt . . .'

Kier decided that was enough. He spun on his heel and strode back to his car. Standing here wouldn't help. He pulled a map out of his glove box, looking for the best route to the place he needed to be. He had to get to Cabramurra. He had to find out if Alex was all right. He opened the map across the bonnet of the car. There were few roads in this wilderness region, and most of them were marked with a yellow highlighter. Those were the roads closed to traffic because of the rally. He traced the possible routes with his finger, then folded the map again in disgust. There was no way he could get through. There was only one road and that was closed. He had no choice but to head for Tumut – the next checkpoint after Cabramurra and the only place he was likely to get to. As he turned the ignition key, the car radio sprang back into life, informing him that a helicopter had been dispatched to bring at least one badly injured person to hospital. He pushed that information to the back of his mind as he reached for the gear shift.

He pushed the car to the limit as he sped along the highway, leaving the other support crews behind. A short time later, he spotted a road sign pointing left towards Cabramurra. His first instinct was to take that road. He was already slowing for the corner when he saw the traffic barrier. His car slid to a stop a few metres past the barrier, and Kier leaped out. Two men were standing by the roadside. One was the race steward, the other a police officer. The policeman held up a warning finger as Kier approached.

'You need to take it easy,' he said sternly. 'You were travelling much too fast.'

'I need to find out about the rally crash,' Kier said.

'There's nothing I can tell you,' the officer said firmly.

'But I'm part of the rally. Alex . . . my driver is out there and I need to know what's going on.'

The policeman must have heard the tension in Kier's voice. He relented. 'I don't have that much information,' he said. 'There was an accident on the third race leg. The race was stopped.'

'I know that.' Kier couldn't hide his frustration. 'You must know something more.'

'Sorry.'

As the officer spoke, the steward's phone rang. The man stepped to one side to answer it. Kier strained to hear what he was saying. The call didn't last long.

'Any news?' Kier asked.

'They are sending all the competitors through to Cabramurra. They'll restart the race from there. Support crews are to drive on through to the next checkpoint at Tumut.'

'That must mean the accident wasn't too bad.' Kier felt his hopes rising.

'Apparently not,' the steward said. 'There were only a couple of cars involved. The first two or three.'

'No!' Kier felt as if the earth under his feet was giving way. The first two or three! Alex had been number three on the start line that morning. If anything had happened to her . . . Before the startled steward could say another word, he had turned and run back to his car. Ignoring the policeman's shouted warning, he leaped behind the wheel and started the engine. The spinning wheels flung loose gravel back at the barrier as he raced away towards Tumut.

The radio in the car was still on, but the announcer had run out of things to say about the accident. He was playing a song. A golden oldie. Kier let the gentle guitar melody flow through his mind. How Alex had loved that song back then . . .

Kier was humming as he strode down the street. He'd just finished the tape that morning – the mix tape, with all Alex's favourite songs on it. It had taken a long time for him to gather all the right tracks. He'd spent weeks borrowing records and CDs, attracting a certain amount of teasing from his friends along the way, when he'd asked to borrow girlie records from their sisters. But it was worth it. Alex would love the tape and that was all that mattered. Her seventeenth birthday was just a few days away. He was planning a picnic for her in their special spot down by the river. Now all he needed was her present.

The shop assistant looked up as Kier walked through the door, and frowned slightly. He knew why. This shop probably didn't get a lot of teenage customers in faded blue jeans and stockman's boots. She probably thought he was going to steal something. He was out of place here. He looked it . . . and felt it. His instinctive reaction was to walk back out the door, but he didn't. He took off his Akubra, and twisting the hat between his hands, began looking in the display cases. At first he saw nothing but the glitter of gold and diamonds. He was well aware that the bundle of hard-earned and even harder-saved cash in his pocket was not going to be enough for this glittering display. But that was all right. Tom Reilly would buy his daughter something flashy. Kier was looking for something that said he knew her – as herself. Something that told her that he—

'Can I help you?' The shop assistant's voice was clipped and harsh, as if she was flinching away from something unpleasant.

'Not right now,' Kier said. 'I'm looking for something special. I'll let you know if I find it.'

The assistant stepped back, but not too far. She was keeping a pretty close eye on him. Trying hard to ignore her, Kier moved slowly around. He ignored the displays of rings. One day he would buy Alex a ring, and when he did, it would hold the sort of brilliant diamond that she deserved. For now, he was looking for something that spoke of shared dreams.

He found it lying on a piece of dark blue velvet. There were a dozen silver charms there, but the one he wanted seemed to leap out at him. He bent and put his face close to the glass for a better look.

'Can I show you something?' the assistant asked at his elbow.

'Yes, please. That charm.'

Pulling a key from her pocket, the assistant unlocked the display case. 'Nice choice,' she said, picking up a piece of silver worked into the shape of a horse.

'No. Not that one,' Kier said. 'The one next to it.'

'This one?' The assistant sounded bemused.

'Yes.'

Kier hesitated to touch it when she laid it on the counter. The silver charm was in the shape of a sports car. If he tried really hard, he could almost imagine it was a Lotus. The Lotus that Alex desired above all things, but had told no one about but him. The car that for her was the symbol of freedom. At last Kier picked it up. It seemed very delicate in his big worker's hands. He turned it over, marvelling at the detail it showed. He could even see the little petrol cap near the rear wheel.

'How much?' he asked.

She told him. He could afford it!

'And would you like a bracelet to put it on?' The shop girl was smiling now. 'We have some very nice ones . . .'

'No. Not a bracelet.' If Alex wore the charm on a bracelet, everyone would see and it would no longer be their secret. 'Do you have a chain? A necklace? Something she could wear around her neck?' Then the charm would lie close to her heart.

'Of course.'

Kier left the jewellery shop with a small velvet bag in the pocket of his jeans and a smile on his face. He had enough money left over to buy a bottle of champagne and two of those fancy glasses he'd seen in another shop window. He could almost see the smile on Alex's face. He was so caught up in the picture in his mind that he didn't see the woman standing on the footpath until he was level with her.

'You're Kier Thomas?'

Kier recognised her immediately. He had seen Alex's mother many times from a distance. Never this close. And he had never spoken to her.

'I am,' he said.

'I am Jacqueline Reilly.'

'I know.' She was carefully groomed and wearing a lot of make-up. Her face was closed. Hard. Kier saw nothing of Alex in her mother's eyes.

'I understand your brother has been released from hospital. How is he?'

The words should have indicated concern. Caring. Instead, Kier felt himself gripped by a cold fear. 'He's home and doing fine.'

'Yes. Your mother must be very pleased to have him back.' If anything, her voice became harder as she spoke.

'She is,' Kier said warily.

'It was a terrible thing. The crash during the police chase. Of course, if it hadn't been for their attempted robbery . . .' Jacqueline's eyes narrowed. 'I imagine your mother is worried about the court case.'

Rob had already made one court appearance and been released on bail to recover from his injuries at home. He'd be back in court next month for trial. Kier's mother was terrified, certain her son would end up in prison. Kier shared her belief, and still carried the extra burden of the guilt that he couldn't shake. If he had acted that night, he might have been able to stop Rob. Everything would have been different.

'With his history, he will almost certainly go to jail,' Jacqueline continued.

Kier dropped his gaze to the pavement, avoiding her eyes. He knew what she was thinking. Alex had told him *about their fight. In Jacqueline's mind, Rob and Kier and all their family were just trash. Nothing would ever change that, and he was beginning to wonder why she had stopped on the street to have this conversation.*

'Perhaps if someone spoke up for your brother,' she said slowly. 'Someone of influence in the community. Perhaps the judge might be . . . lenient.'

Kier looked up at her. 'Who would do that?' he asked cautiously.

'Perhaps I could.'

Her face was unreadable, but Kier knew one thing for certain: this offer wasn't about kindness. There would be a price to pay.

'You would do that?' he asked.

'I might.'

Something about the way she looked at him caused a cold dread to settle around his heart.

'Think how pleased your mother would be if he didn't have to go to prison.'

Kier couldn't bring himself to speak. He knew what was coming, and it was more than he could stand.

'As a mother, I understand how she feels.' Jacqueline's voice was quiet – but not soft. Nothing about her at this moment was soft. 'A mother will do anything to help her child.'

'This is about Alex.' It wasn't a question.

'Yes.'

An icy fist was closing around his whole being. She wouldn't ask him to . . . She couldn't.

'Just as the right words from me can keep your brother out of jail, so the wrong words from me can see he stays there for a very long time.'

'And you want me . . .'

'I want you out of my daughter's life.' Jacqueline wasn't mincing words. 'She has such a bright future ahead of her, and you are not going to be a part of that.'

'No! I won't do it.'

'That's a shame. It will break your mother's heart to know that you could have helped your brother. And you didn't.'

The words cut through Kier's defences, reigniting the guilt that was just too close to the surface. Could he let his brother down a second time? But ... what about Alex? He couldn't leave her. It would break her heart ... and his own. He put his hand in the pocket of his jeans to clasp the velvet bag.

'Please. Don't make me choose.' It was a cry from the deepest recesses of his soul.

'That is exactly what you must do.'

He was gripping the soft cloth so hard he could feel the metal biting into his flesh. Two days until Alex's birthday.

'And don't think you can have it both ways.' It was as if she was reading his thoughts. 'You have to leave town and stay away. Don't try to write to her, or contact her, or your brother will be behind bars so fast your mother will never understand what happened. You know I can do it.'

Each word was like a knife in his heart. He felt the future come crashing down around him. He saw the satisfaction on Jacqueline's face as she realised that she had won ...

Kier parked the car amid a dozen other support cars at Tumut. The radio announcer had not been able to shed any more light on what had happened, and for a few moments Kier was almost afraid to get out of the car. He had lost Alex once, through his own betrayal and stupidity. The pain then had almost destroyed him. He could not bear to think that it might be happening again – and that this time, she was . . . He shook his head. He wouldn't think that. Couldn't think that. He opened the car door.

There was a crowd gathered around the stewards' table. Kier glanced at his watch, then realised he had no idea when the first race cars were likely to appear. He didn't know when they had started the race – if indeed that was what they had done. If the accident had taken a life . . .

'Any news?' he asked as he approached the crowd.

'Not much,' someone offered.

'But they did start the next leg,' another man pointed out. 'That has to be good news.'

'I heard there was only one car involved.'

'I heard two – the Mini and the red Lotus,' added another voice.

Kier didn't see who had spoken. He spun around. 'The Lotus?'

'So someone said.' The speaker saw the look on Kier's face. 'But hey, I might have got it wrong.'

Before Kier could respond, a steward appeared. He climbed on a chair and waved his hands for silence.

'Listen up,' he called. 'You all know there's been an accident. Only one car was involved. Car number one-oh-seven, the Mini, driven by . . .'

Kier no longer heard the words. The Mini – not the Lotus. Alex wasn't involved. Alex was all right! He looked around wildly as if expecting to see her standing next to him.

'. . . that leg is cancelled. The race started again at Tumut. We expect the leading cars to reach this checkpoint in the next ten minutes. So, crews, it's business as usual. Get to it.'

Kier was oblivious to the wave of people washing past him. Alex was all right. He hadn't lost her!

'Hey, mate? Are you all right?'

Kier looked into the concerned face. 'Yes. Yes. Everything is fine.' And it was. He glanced at his watch. She would be here soon. Just a few minutes. This checkpoint included the lunch break. They would have an hour. That might almost be enough to convince him that she was all right. He looked down the road, willing the red car to appear. The waiting was intolerable.

The Lotus was the first car to arrive. It crossed the line and came to a halt in the lunch parking area. Kier had already started moving towards it when he saw the scratches running down the side panels. He felt his heart actually stop beating for a few long moments of total fear. Something was wrong. Alex! Her name was a silent prayer inside his head. Then the driver's door opened, and there she was. Kier froze as she pulled her helmet off, and ran her fingers through her hair. She looked tired, but she was unhurt. She was also the most beautiful sight he had ever seen. Without thinking, he broke into a run. He pushed his way through the gathering crowd, ignoring the questions they were asking Alex, and pulled her to him. For one long second he gazed down into her lovely green eyes, and then he kissed her.

14

His lips were soft and strong and sensual. He was the feel of a warm fire on a freezing night. The taste of chocolate and the sound of laughter. He was the scent of rain in the air at the end of a hot day, and the sparkle in the eyes of a friend. He was a promise fulfilled. A wish granted. He was . . . Kier. Alex put her arms around him and welcomed him with every fibre of her being.

After an eternity that was far too short, his lips moved away from hers, just a breath. 'I thought you . . .' His voice was a whisper of pain. 'I couldn't lose you again.'

Before the words could touch her, before he could kiss her again, the real world intruded. They were surrounded by a crowd of laughing, teasing, whistling men. Someone was cheering and hooting encouragement. Someone else was clapping. She was beginning to feel like the half-time show at some football match. She dragged her eyes away from Kier. Lyn was standing beside her – the surprise on her face slowly giving way to a grin. In the distance she caught a glimpse of television crews heading their way. Then the crowd was scattered by the high-speed arrival of a blue Alfa Romeo. Paul pulled up next to them, and got out of the car. He moved swiftly to Lyn's side.

'Are you all right?' His voice was full of concern as he placed one hand gently on her shoulder.

'Still a bit . . . you know . . .' Lyn answered softly.

Alex knew exactly what she meant. She too was a bit . . . but her reasons were altogether different.

'What the hell happened out there?' a voice shouted from the crowd.

'Who was hurt?'

'How bad are they?' The journalists had reached them and were adding their voices to the clamour.

Alex felt herself beginning to panic. She couldn't cope with this. First the accident, and now Kier. She was shattered. She needed to get away. She needed a few minutes to try to regain her grip on a world that was spinning out of control. One look at Lyn's face told her that she felt the same way. Alex reached out to close her fingers around her friend's hand.

'Give us a minute.' Paul raised his voice above the clamouring crowd. He turned to Kier. 'Take the girls somewhere quiet. They don't need this.'

Kier nodded. He put an arm around Alex's shoulders. 'Come on, guys. Give us some room.' He raised his other arm as if to push back the crowd. The shouting didn't stop, but the men did move back a little.

'I can answer a few of your questions!' Paul said loudly.

His words had the effect of immediately drawing the attention to himself. As the curious crowd turned to Paul, Kier was able to lead Alex and Lyn away. They moved swiftly to a sheltered spot behind a brick toilet block. It wasn't exactly pretty, and the smell left a lot to be desired, but it was a haven away from the peering eyes and questioning voices. Alex dropped on to a grassy bank.

Lyn joined her, while Kier remained standing – almost as if he was on guard.

For a few moments, none of them spoke. Alex closed her eyes and took several deep breaths, feeling her panic lessen with each one. She wasn't sure what had caused it – the accident, the pressure of the crowd, or Kier's kiss.

'God, Lyn, are you hurt?' Kier had seen the blood-stains on Lyn's clothes.

'No. The blood isn't mine. I helped Paul with the injured driver.'

Kier didn't ask anything more. When Alex looked up at him, she could see the questions in his eyes. He was desperate to know just what had happened out there on the race course, but he wouldn't put any more pressure on them. He'd hold his tongue until they were ready to talk.

'You two wait here,' he said. 'I'll be right back.' He vanished back in the direction of the race camp.

When Lyn spoke, breaking the silence, her voice was shaky. 'I wonder where Paul is?'

Alex glanced across at her. She saw the glint of tears in Lyn's eyes. 'Hey,' she said, sliding closer to put her arms around her. 'He's keeping the reporters and cameras away from us. He's fine. What about you?'

'I am feeling a bit . . . So much happened so fast.'

Alex knew exactly what Lyn was talking about. As soon as the ambulance had left with the injured men on board, the stewards had started getting the race going again. Lyn and Alex had barely had time to catch their breath when they were instructed to drive on to the next checkpoint at Cabramurra. The other race cars followed in a convoy. They had lost track of Paul. He must have got a lift with someone, because barely had they reached Cabramurra than he was back with them.

That stop had lasted just a few minutes. The officials were keen to get the accident behind them, and had restarted the race almost immediately. Alex and Lyn hadn't really had time to think before they were at the starting point, listening to the countdown. On the course, instinct had taken over and they had raced as they always did. A couple of times Alex was aware that she was driving more slowly than she might have done before the accident. But that was the least of her concerns. She had kept going until they reached the Tumut checkpoint and the one-hour break for lunch that she knew she wouldn't eat. And Kier . . .

'Paul was pretty amazing,' Lyn said softly. 'I was so glad he was there.'

'You were pretty terrific yourself,' Alex said. 'How did you learn to be so calm in a crisis? And as for climbing in that car to help . . .'

'I've had a few crises to deal with,' Lyn said. 'My sister has bad days. And there are other kids in the home. You learn to cope.'

Alex nodded. Lyn didn't often talk about her sister, but Alex knew her well enough by now to understand what she was saying.

'And what about Kier – or you and Kier?' Lyn's voice was stronger, almost like her old self. 'That was some welcome. What was that all about?'

Now was the time for Alex to tell Lyn about her past with Kier. No doubt she had guessed some of it. She might be blonde, but she wasn't stupid. But Alex just didn't have the emotional strength to talk about it. Not with the taste of Kier's kiss on her lips, and the sound of his heartbeat still echoing hers.

The sound of approaching footsteps saved her any

need to answer. Kier appeared around the corner of the toilet block, a cardboard box in his hands. He dropped to the grass beside Alex.

'Here. I thought these might help.'

The box contained bottles of water, paper cups of strong dark coffee and sandwiches wrapped in plastic.

'You are a lifesaver,' Lyn said, as she reached for a bottle of water and a cup of coffee.

Alex didn't say anything. She avoided Kier's eyes as she took the water he offered, but shook her head at the offer of a sandwich.

'You should eat something,' he said.

'I don't think I could,' she replied.

Kier put the box down on the grass within easy reach. 'Paul told me what happened,' he said. 'You are both very lucky you didn't hit the Mini.'

'That would be down to Alex's great driving.' Lyn was starting to regain her composure. 'I couldn't have done it.'

'The Lotus . . .' Alex remembered. 'I guess there's a fair bit of damage.'

'Nothing that can't be fixed,' Kier told her. 'Better the Lotus than . . .' He couldn't finish the sentence.

'Is there any word on the condition of the guys from the Mini?' It bothered Alex that she still couldn't remember the driver's name.

'Apparently they are in hospital in Gundagai. They're going to be all right, thanks to Paul and Lyn's first aid.'

'Where is Paul?' Lyn wanted to know.

'He's with the stewards. And the police.'

'I guess we'll have to answer a lot of questions too,' Alex said.

'Yes. But you can hide for a while if you like.'

Hide. Alex thought that was a great idea. She could

hide from the police. The stewards. The media. But much as she wanted to, she couldn't hide from Kier. Or from herself. Not for long.

'I think I'll go and try to wash.' Lyn got to her feet, and looked down at the stains on her race suit. 'If my agent could see me now . . .' She smiled and shook her head.

Alex forced a small smile on to her own face, but that was the best she could do. After Lyn had vanished into the ladies' toilet, she and Kier sat very still and very quiet for what seemed a long, long time.

'Are you going to finish the race?' Kier asked at last.

'Yes.'

'Are you sure?'

'Of course I'm sure. I'll be fine. So will Lyn.'

She made to get to her feet, but Kier put a restraining hand on her arm. 'Alex. About . . . well . . . when I saw you. Until that moment, I was so afraid you were the one . . .'

Alex turned to look into his dark eyes. She saw the echo of his fear still lingering. She saw something else too. Something she couldn't deal with right now.

'It's all right,' she said. 'Kier, I just need to get through the rest of the day. Please don't . . .'

'I won't,' he responded instantly. 'I'm here to help you, remember. I crashed my car – you saved yours. I guess that means we are both in the right places.' He smiled.

As jokes went, it was a poor attempt, but Alex smiled back. They had an afternoon's racing ahead of them. She had to hold it together. She paused for a second, and reached deep inside herself for the reserves that just had to be there. 'All right then. Let's get Lyn out of the loo, and get ourselves ready to race.' She glanced down. 'And

I guess you should bring the sandwiches – I probably should eat something.'

They raced.

At first Alex wasn't sure that she could. As they lined up at the starting point, she felt her hands shaking. She almost turned the engine off and walked away. But she couldn't do it. She wouldn't do it. Alex Reilly wasn't a quitter. And there was Lyn to think about. She had an awful lot riding on the race. Alex wasn't about to tell her that it wasn't going to happen. As for Kier . . . She wasn't going to let him see her back down. She was still the Alex who had helped tame a wild colt. Who had defied her father and gone joyriding in his car. Defied her mother and loved—

That wasn't helping. There was only one way to rid herself of those thoughts. She gripped the wheel firmly and focused all her attention on the thing she did best – taking control and winning. She wouldn't let fear beat her. In fact she wasn't even about to let another driver beat her. She was Alex Reilly, and she was going to win this race!

When she finally parked the car at the end of the day, Alex was so exhausted she could barely speak. She saw the same look in Lyn's eyes, and by mutual agreement they locked the car and walked away from it. There was no sign of Kier, and Alex was secretly glad. What she needed right now was space. The night's stopover was the Gundagai showgrounds. There were no hotels nearby, but the rally organisers were running a shuttle bus. Alex and Lyn jumped aboard and were soon at their hotel. Kier had already checked them in. Their keys were waiting at reception. Their bags were in their rooms. The two girls parted company, agreeing to meet up later at the showgrounds to check the results of the day's racing.

Alex stood for a long time under the shower, letting the warm water run over her body as if it could wash away the tension of the day. It didn't. Feeling only slightly refreshed, she slipped on a pair of jeans and a light cotton top and paced the tiny room for a couple of minutes.

'This is no good,' she said out loud. 'I've got to get out of here.'

The rally shuttle bus took her back to the showgrounds, but just a few seconds after alighting from the shuttle, her sneaker-clad feet were taking her rapidly away from the cars, the rally and everything and everyone connected to it. She still needed time alone.

The showgrounds were on the flat Murrumbidgee River floodplain. Alex walked slowly across the dry baked earth, the grass chewed short by cattle that were no longer around but that had left enough evidence of their passing to cause her to step carefully in the half-light of late evening. Above her, a full moon hung low in the sky. The air was very still. Even the crickets were silent. Ahead of her, two long dark shapes threw shadows in her path. The two great wooden bridges crossing the floodplain had been built to provide safe passage when the mighty Murrumbidgee was flooded. They were very old and no longer in use. The huge timbers were dark, but still strong. She leaned against one of the pylons. That timber had supported the great bridge span for more than a century. Now it was supporting Alex too.

Looking up, she caught glimpses of the deepening sky through the gaps in the bridge decking. How many cars had crossed that bridge in all those years? she wondered. How many people? How many lives and loves had been brought together by it? How many lives and loves torn apart by a simple journey?

Still feeling restless, she stepped away from the bridge and turned towards the river. The grass was sparse as she picked her way down the steep bank, to lean against the sloping trunk of a gum tree. She stared down into the water and the shimmering reflection of the moon. She could almost see his face – that old man in the moon. Was he smiling? Or was he crying, as she had cried so many times under his bright gaze . . . ?

The dining room of the Reilly homestead was huge, as was the table that dominated it. Two candelabra sitting on the gleaming wood were also suitably large, the flawless silver glinting in the light. Why did her mother insist on candles? They only made the room hotter and more oppressive. In fact, Alex didn't know why her mother had insisted on this dinner at all. No one was enjoying it. Her father was talking business to Jim Cassidy and a couple of the male guests at one end of the table. Her mother and her female friends were talking fashion at the other end, and in the middle, Alex wasn't talking to anyone. It was supposed to be her birthday party, but no one she really cared for was there. It was just another chance for her mother to show off. And for her father to ignore her. Oh, he'd bought her an expensive present. The diamond hanging around her neck on a fine gold chain had been admired by everyone in the room. But Alex didn't like it. It was simply another demonstration of her father's wealth and power. She didn't want it any more than she wanted to be sitting at this table, being served food that she didn't want, making conversation with people she didn't like. She wanted to be down at the river with Kier, watching the stars overhead and . . .

A small frown creased her forehead. She hadn't seen Kier since the previous weekend. Not that it mattered. The two of them had made their plans for a picnic by the river weeks ago. Alex had also made her own, private plans. Tonight was going to be special. The most important night of her life. Tonight she and Kier would—

'. . . replace the Thomas brothers.'

Jim Cassidy's words caught her attention. She turned her head slightly to listen to the conversation between her father and his manager.

'Both of them?' her father asked.

'Yes.'

'What about them?' Alex demanded.

Tom Reilly looked askance at his daughter. 'Jim was just saying he has found two men to replace the Thomas brothers.'

'Replace . . . ?'

'Well, obviously the older one can't work any more. He's still recovering from his injuries and he'll probably be going to prison in a couple of weeks anyway,' Jim said. 'And as for the younger one – he's run off.'

Alex heard the words, but for a few seconds she struggled to grasp the meaning. 'Run off?' Her voice was a whisper.

'Vanished,' Jim said. 'Hasn't shown up for work the last couple of days. No one knows where he is. Not even his father.'

No. That couldn't be right. Kier wouldn't just run off. Alex could not – would not – believe what she was hearing.

'I figure he was involved in that robbery too, and has disappeared to avoid going to prison with the others.'

'No!' Alex leaped to her feet. 'He was not involved. He's not like that.'

'Alexandra.' Her mother's soothing voice cut through the tense silence that followed her outburst. 'It's time to cut the cake.'

'He hasn't gone,' Alex declared defiantly. 'He wouldn't leave me.' She looked from her father to her mother. Jacqueline's face was a frozen mask.

'Alexandra, do sit down,' she said calmly.

'No.'

Alex pushed her chair back. She turned and fled the room, almost colliding with the cook, who was waiting outside, her arms laden with a huge silver tray, and a birthday cake covered with lighted candles. She ran to the front door, and down the shallow staircase. She kicked off her impractical sandals as she raced across the grass. The soles of her brown feet were as tough as leather from years of just this sort of behaviour. She ran past the stables, and the empty yard where the black colt had once resided. As she did, the lines of trees that marked the river came into sight. Her eyes sought the gap in the trees, looking for a light, or some movement. Anything that would tell her he was there, waiting for her. That everything was as it should be. As she needed it to be. But as she ran, she began to be very afraid that nothing would ever be as it should be . . . not ever again.

'Alex? Are you all right?'

Of course he had found her. He knew that she would be drawn to the full moon and the river.

Alex lifted her eyes from the water. Despite the moonlight, his face was in shadow, but that didn't matter. She knew every line of it as well as she knew her own. She knew the way his forehead creased when he was puzzled. The way his lips curled when he smiled. The way his eyes flashed when he looked at her and his thoughts turned to . . .

'Why did you leave?' Too many years and too many tears had passed, but the words were still a cry of pain.

'I . . .'

'My seventeenth birthday, Kier. Why did you leave me? Why then?'

'I had no choice.'

'I don't understand.'

'You should ask your mother . . .'

Her mother? 'I'm asking you.'

'I did it to stop my brother from going to jail.'

Of all the things he could have said, she would never have thought of this.

'I know Rob was in trouble, but what did that have to do with us?'

'Alex.' Kier's voice was as gentle as she had ever heard it. 'This isn't going to do either of us any good. You always had enough trouble with your parents. I don't want to add any more. You should talk to your mother.'

'I don't think my mother and I have said anything meaningful to each other for years. So why should I—' Realisation was like a splash of cold water in her face. 'My mother? She made you leave.' It wasn't a question. Even as she said the words out loud, Alex understood that they were true.

'I didn't want to. You have to know it was the hardest thing I have ever done. But . . .' Kier hesitated.

'My mother threatened Rob,' Alex finished for him.

'She said she could use her influence to keep him out of jail – or get him sent down for a longer time. I believed her.'

'That was after the accident.' Alex spoke slowly,

remembering. 'You were already feeling guilty about that night, I remember. You thought you should have tried to stop Rob.' She was fighting to understand the emotions this revelation was sending in shockwaves through her. It wasn't Kier who had betrayed her. It was her mother. Her mother had threatened Rob – and made Kier face an impossible decision. A decision no one that young should ever have been forced to make. She had made him choose between Alex and his brother. Kier hadn't walked away from her. He had been driven away.

'I am so sorry,' he said. 'I had to save Rob, or at least try to save him!'

'That night. The night of my birthday. I was going to . . .' She couldn't put it into words. She felt Kier stiffen beside her, and knew she didn't have to. He moved closer to her, so that she could see his face and his eyes. She saw the boy she had fallen for all those years ago. The boy who understood how trapped she felt in her father's big house. The boy who shared her dreams of adventure. Who loved fast cars and fast horses . . . and her.

Her hand shook ever so slightly as she raised it to touch his face. She didn't feel the man's dark stubble. Her fingers touched the boy's softer cheek. There was no grey in the hair that ran through her fingers. No lines around the eyes that held hers. When she kissed him, they were seventeen again, on a riverbank a lifetime ago. It was a gentle kiss that tasted of innocence and yearning. In the darkness, beneath the towering gum trees, time faltered. The years fell away. Two hearts remembered. Two bodies remembered.

Alex didn't feel the bite of the tree's rough bark on her skin as Kier melded his body to hers. She caught her breath as his lips found the pulse beating at the base of her neck. He slipped the thin strap of her top down her shoulder, his fingers trailing across the soft satin of her skin, ice on fire. She pulled at the fabric of his shirt, desperate to touch him. He moaned as her fingers slid up his chest, revelling in the feel of strong muscles taut beneath his skin. She closed her eyes and gave herself up to the touch of his hands and lips on her body, and the sound of his heart beating in time with hers.

She almost whimpered when his body pulled away from hers just a fraction. She opened her eyes and looked into his dark face. She wanted to tell him she understood. That everything was all right. That they could be together now. Give in to the need that was still so powerful. But knowing why he'd left wasn't enough. She couldn't just forget. As she looked at him, the boy faded, and she saw the man he had become. And suddenly, all those missing years crashed down on her. Everything wasn't all right. She had spent too many nights sobbing into her pillow. It wasn't that easy.

Hating herself for what she was doing, Alex gently pushed Kier away. She saw the hurt in his eyes, and the pain and loss and regret – the same things that had stared back at her from her own mirror for so many long, lonely nights.

'I'm sorry,' she whispered. Then she turned and walked away.

15

'I'm fine, Mum,' Lyn said into her mobile phone. 'You shouldn't worry.'

'It was on the news. Of course I worry. They mentioned that you were the first car on the scene after the accident. They said you helped.'

The voice in her ear sounded a little fragile, and Lyn cursed herself for adding to the burden her mother already carried.

'It was the car in front of us,' she said. 'It ended up in the middle of the road, but Alex was great. She avoided it really easily. We were never in any danger.' It wasn't exactly true, but it wasn't much of a lie either.

'And the injured men?'

'They're going to be fine.' Lyn went on to describe to her mother how Paul had treated the trapped driver. She made very little mention of her own involvement.

'Would this be the same Paul who helped fix the car that time?'

'Yes. That's him.'

'The same Paul who rescued you from the steward?'

'Yes.'

'The one who is related to the engineer who built all those dams and tunnels and things?'

'Yes.' Lyn hadn't realised she'd told her mother that much about Paul.

'So, tell me everything. How old is he? What does he look like? Where does he live?'

'Mum!' Lyn said in mock horror. 'It's not like that at all.'

'And why not? He sounds wonderful!'

'Stop it, Mum,' Lyn chuckled. 'Now, more importantly, how is Lorna?'

Lyn listened as her mother talked for a while about her younger daughter. The care centre was following Lyn's progress in the rally with great interest. The patients might not understand what was happening, but they enjoyed the air of excitement among the staff and parents. A lot of hopes were riding on Lyn's fund-raising.

'I hope I don't let them down,' Lyn said.

'You won't, darling,' her mother assured her. 'Now, go and find that nice doctor and get him to buy you dinner.'

Lyn was laughing as she hung up. Her mother was an amazing person. With all the problems she had, she retained the most positive outlook on life. Lyn loved her for that.

The next job was her blog. Lyn spent a lot of time on it. She couldn't ignore the accident, but it was important to find the right tone as she wrote about it. She put a great deal of emphasis on how other drivers had helped out, and assured her readers that the two injured men would be all right. She replied to some of the comments, all the time encouraging her readers to donate to her cause. The fund-raising had suffered a setback when Kier crashed the Ferrari. Without the car to auction, they weren't going to reach their target. But there were still some generous donations being made. Every dollar mattered.

Blog done, Lyn was wondering how to get back to the showgrounds when her phone rang. It was her agent. Could she leave for a modelling assignment on Monday? The job was a three-day photo shoot in North Queensland. Lyn hesitated. After the trials of the race, she had been looking forward to a few days at home, relaxing. She wanted to spend some time with Lorna, and maybe give her mother a chance to have some time for herself. She was about to say no when her agent mentioned the money. It was a good offer. A very good offer indeed. Lyn agreed. As she hung up, she realised the job offer had also solved one more problem. The final day of racing was Friday, followed by the ball and awards ceremony on Saturday night. On Sunday morning, she would have to go straight back to Sydney to be ready to fly north on Monday morning. There could be no suggestion of spending any more time with Paul. That was good, because it was a tempting thought . . . if he wanted her to stay, which of course he didn't. At least, he hadn't said anything about wanting her to stay.

When she left the hotel room a few minutes later, Lyn wasn't sure what she should do, but she knew she was going nowhere near the showgrounds, the rally, and everything and everyone to do with it. She was heartily sick of cars and the smell of petrol. Sick of thinking about the road ahead and the cars behind. At this moment, she really didn't care if she and Alex were winning the race, or losing it. She just wanted a bit of peace and quiet. She decided to walk up the hill towards the centre of the town, and the old buildings that gave it an historic air. She would enjoy the cool of the evening and get something to eat. Something that was not a burger or a sandwich;

possibly something the rally caterers had never heard of . . . like a salad.

She turned up the hill, but before she had travelled more than a few metres, she spotted a very familiar figure. Paul was wearing his usual faded blue jeans and white cotton shirt and he was walking down the hill. Lyn forgot her desire to get away from all things rally-related. Paul was different. She raised one hand to catch his attention.

'Hi,' she said as soon as she drew close. 'I thought everyone would be down at the showgrounds, waiting for the results.'

'I was,' Paul replied. 'They're out already.'

'And?' Lyn asked.

'They have cancelled the stage where the accident happened,' he told her. 'And based on what is left, congratulations are in order.' He grinned.

'I don't get it?'

'Congratulations. You and Alex. You're winning the class.'

'Winning?' Lyn could hardly believe it. 'But what about the Porsche?'

'More than thirty seconds behind you,' Paul said. 'They must have been even more shaken by the accident. Their times this afternoon were not very good.'

'And you are . . . ?'

'A rather distant fourth, I'm afraid. The Datsun has jumped ahead of me by a few seconds.'

'Oh,' Lyn sympathised.

'That's all right,' Paul said cheerfully. 'I'm not out of the race entirely. There's still one full day of racing to go – anything could happen . . .'

'And probably will.' Lyn completed the sentence for him.

'Maybe. If I'm lucky.'

He had a lovely smile. It wasn't just the way his lips curved, and the tiny dimples formed on either side of his mouth. It was the sparkle in his brown eyes. Paul's face might not compare favourably to the male models she worked with, but right now she would rather be with him than anyone else she could think of.

'What were you doing here?' she asked quickly, suddenly aware that Paul was regarding her with as much interest as she was feeling towards him.

'Well,' he said, 'have you heard of Rusconi's Marble Masterpiece?'

'No.'

'Ah!' Paul made a dramatic face. 'You are in for a treat. You've heard of the dog on the tucker box, haven't you?'

'Of course. We sang the song when I was at school. Isn't there a statue?'

'Five miles from Gundagai,' Paul chanted. 'That's the one. It's all about our pioneering past. What most people don't know is that the artist who made the statue spent nearly three decades building a marble masterpiece – which is on display in that very building.' He swept one arm wide in an extravagant gesture towards a low brick building with a sign proclaiming it as the visitor centre.

'Well, I didn't know that.' Lyn grinned. 'But I haven't been reading the tourist brochures.'

'Guilty as charged,' Paul confessed. 'Now, let me escort you hither, that you may gaze with awe on the masterpiece.' He waggled his eyebrows at her, and held out his arm. Laughing, Lyn tucked her arm in his and allowed him to escort her to the building.

'Frank Rusconi,' Paul intoned in a serious voice as they walked, 'studied under the master marble carvers of

Europe. He carved altars for cathedrals. Funeral monuments for the rich and famous. But it was here, in the small town of Gundagai, that he laboured for twenty-eight years on his masterpiece.'

'Which was?' Lyn fell in with the tone of Paul's discourse, but her interest wasn't feigned. She loved obscure facts just as much as he did.

'A miniature baroque cathedral containing about twenty thousand pieces of hand-worked marble.'

'Wow!'

'Wow, indeed. And in a few short moments, you may feast your eyes upon this wonder.'

They were brought up short by a closed and locked door.

'Damn,' Paul said, suddenly deflated. 'I had hoped they might stay open late tonight because of the rally.'

'Never mind,' Lyn said. 'I'm sure it would have been lovely.'

'I don't think lovely is quite the word I would use,' Paul said. 'I know. There must be an shop open somewhere. There will be a tea towel with the masterpiece on it. I'm going to buy you one.'

This time, he took her hand in his. Lyn liked the way that felt. Together they walked up the hill towards the town centre, while Paul told her tales of Gundagai's past. She listened with interest to stories of floods and bushrangers. She was impressed by Paul's knowledge, and genuinely interested in what he was saying. But most of all, she listened to his voice, liking the humour she heard in it. Liking the compassion. Just liking the warm, rich sound.

'Ah – this should do it.' Paul stopped in front of an open shop. Together they walked in. The place seemed to sell everything from groceries and newspapers to elastic-sided riding boots and Akubra hats. Most importantly, it sold tea towels. Paul selected one that featured a slightly fuzzy print of a pointed structure with what looked like a clock in the tower.

'Sorry it's not gift-wrapped,' he said as he handed Lyn the plain white plastic bag containing the tea towel.

'That's fine. I'll treasure it always,' said Lyn. She was exaggerating, of course, but she was absurdly pleased by the gift.

'Have you eaten?' Paul asked as they emerged back on to the street. 'Because if you haven't, I thought maybe we could have dinner.'

It wasn't exactly a date, Lyn told herself. But it was the closest thing she'd had in quite a while. Oh, she'd been out to dinner many, many times. In restaurants far more glittering and expensive than any they were likely to find in Gundagai. But a non-working dinner? With a man she actually liked? That was a rarity.

'I'd love to,' she said.

They ended up eating at a pub. Lyn was quite taken with the old wooden building, with its wide veranda and wrought-iron railings. The restaurant area at the back of the bar was busy. They recognised a few rally people, but Lyn guessed that was only to be expected. They found an empty table in a quiet corner, and joy of joys, the menu featured food that had not been cooked on a beer-splashed barbecue.

'So, tell me. Why modelling?' Paul asked as they waited for their food.

Lyn twirled the small glass of white wine in her hands. She got asked this question so often that she had come to hate it. She had several glib answers ready. She looked at

Paul, saw the genuine interest in his face, and rejected them all.

'If I'm going to be totally honest,' she said, 'I'd have to say money. I thought it would be an easy way to make a lot of money.'

'And is it?'

'Easy? No. Not really. But the money is very good.'

'And you need it for your sister.'

Paul's soft words caught Lyn totally by surprise. 'How do you know about my sister?'

'I read your blog. I was really impressed by the fund-raising you were doing. And I asked Alex.'

'Oh.' Lyn wasn't sure how she felt about that.

'So, your sister. Tell me about her condition.'

Lyn never talked about Lorna. Or her mother and their heartbreaking struggles. Never. No one else could possibly understand. No one – except perhaps Paul. Maybe it was because he was a doctor. Maybe it was because she would never see him again after the rally was over. And maybe it was just because . . .

She told him everything. When she talked about Lorna's illness, Paul sounded like a doctor, asking questions and understanding the answers. When she talked about the day her father walked out the door, never to return, he touched her hand like a sympathetic friend. When she told him about her mother's struggle to cope, he frowned like someone who really cared.

'And the modelling was just for the money?' Paul asked.

'I want to have money set aside for when we need it, and I'm sure one day we will. Lorna's care is expensive. And at some point. I'm going to have to take care of her alone. I need to have the money to do it.'

'Your father helps?'

'No. He sent money for a while, then we just stopped hearing from him. He never comes to see Lorna. It was just too much for him. By the time she was five, he was gone. He didn't love Mum enough. Didn't love any of us enough to stay.' Lyn heard the bitterness in her own voice.

'You haven't forgiven him for leaving, have you?'

'No.'

Lyn looked across the table at Paul's face. She could see the sympathy in his eyes, but no trace of pity. No trace either of withdrawal, but it was early days yet. If her father had taught her anything, it was that no love would ever be enough to compensate for the demands Lorna's illness made on them. The care of a severely handicapped woman came at great cost, both financial and personal. No man would ever want to take on that responsibility. Add to that the chance that any child of Lyn's might suffer in the same way ... Paul was wonderful. She could so easily love him. He might even love her. But the baggage she carried was just too heavy. No, she suddenly realised. It wasn't going to happen for her.

'Would you like dessert? Or another drink?' Paul's voice reminded her that several minutes had passed in silence.

'No. Thanks. I guess I'd better get back. We've both got to be at our best for tomorrow.'

Paul nodded as if he understood. 'Of course.'

They left the pub and started to walk back down the hill, towards Lyn's hotel. This time Paul didn't hold her hand. Lyn was grateful for the breathing space, but also just a little disappointed. Accepting that something couldn't be did not stop her wanting it.

'Are you staying here as well?' she asked as they saw the hotel's neon sign ahead.

'No. I'm back up the hill. In a pub. I just thought it would be nice to walk you home.'

'Well, thanks.' Lyn turned to look at Paul. He was smiling at her in such a way as to make her heart break. 'I had a nice time. Thank you.'

For the longest few seconds, they stood there. Lyn was sure he was going to kiss her. She shouldn't let him. It would bring nothing but anguish. But oh, how she wanted him to!

That was the moment the shuttle bus from the showgrounds arrived and began disgorging rally competitors.

Lyn stepped away from Paul as several of them stopped to say hello, or to make some comment about the race. She knew her moment was lost. She should have been pleased. But she wasn't. Paul waved good night and turned to walk back up the hill, leaving Lyn very alone despite the people around her.

'Hey, Lyn.' Alex was the last person to alight before the bus started moving off, taking the remaining occupants to other hotels.

'Hi.'

'I looked for you at the showgrounds,' Alex said. 'I guess you know we're in front.'

'Paul told me.'

Alex cast a thoughtful look at Paul's departing back. 'I see.'

Lyn grinned woefully and shook her head. 'It was just dinner,' she said quickly, knowing that Alex was not the only one she had to convince.

'Of course it was,' Alex said.

'And what about you?' Lyn shot back. 'That was some welcome from Kier earlier.'

Alex's eyes clouded over. 'I don't know,' she said. 'There's so much history between us. There are times I think . . . But how can I be sure about anything? Damn it!'

Just then, a car drove up the hill at high speed. Two men leaned out the back window, yelling. Their words were lost, but the meaning was clear.

'Bloody men,' Lyn said vehemently. 'They are a waste of time, the lot of them.'

'You're so right,' Alex said. They both laughed.

'I guess we'd better get some sleep.' Lyn turned towards the motel units. 'We've got a big day ahead of us.'

'Yeah! And all those men better watch out,' declared Alex.

'The race and nothing else!'

'The race and nothing else,' Alex echoed. Lyn was right. They had to focus on the race. It was the last day, and they were just thirty seconds in front of the Porsche and its obnoxious crew. Thirty seconds was not enough, and it was too much. In the course of the next few hours and few hundred kilometres, that lead could change half a dozen times. If they wanted to win, they were going to have to focus. And damn it – Alex did want to win!

The car park around them was buzzing with excitement as the teams prepared for the final day's racing. Alex guessed some of them had been up all night, doing the one hundred and one things needed to keep a rally car fettled and ready to race. She should have been doing that too, instead of wandering along the riverbank with Kier, bringing back memories and feelings that were best forgotten. She sighed, and reached out to touch the gleaming red bonnet of the Lotus.

'Sorry, girl,' she whispered softly. 'I hope I haven't let you down.'

'I've got the latest course updates,' Lyn said, adding some more papers to the pile already on her clipboard.

'Anything I should know about?'

'Not really. Except there's something here about cows.' Lyn frowned.

'You'd think they'd have stopped that today,' said Alex.

'Stopped what?' Lyn was looking at her notes, clearly puzzled.

'The cows on the course,' said a deep voice close behind them.

When she turned around, Alex stopped thinking about cows. Kier looked terrible, as if he hadn't slept all night. His clothes were filthy and had a distinct smell of sweat and motor oil.

'What happened to you?' she asked.

'Nothing. I just spent the night here. I gave the car a bit of a once-over.'

'Oh.' Alex felt a twinge of guilt. She should have been here. Doing that. But after what had happened by the riverbank, the thought of being in close quarters under the car with Kier was just too much for her to handle. 'Any problems?'

'Not really. I topped up the engine oil. The exhaust brackets had worked a bit loose.'

'Ah, that's what the rattle was,' Lyn interjected.

'Anyway, I tightened them,' Kier added. 'She's fine. Just watch out for the cows.'

'Again with the cows?' Lyn raised her eyes to the heavens. 'Can someone please tell me what's going on with these animals!'

'It's the drought,' Paul said as he emerged from behind the next row of parked cars. 'There's no grass left in the paddocks, so the property-owners turn their cattle out on the side of the road to forage for food. The stewards are worried that not all of them have been contacted, and some might still have stock on the road.'

'Oh.' Lyn clearly didn't like the sound of that. 'Haven't they got someone out checking?'

'I guess so, but we'd still better be careful,' Alex said. 'I'd hate something to go wrong on the last day.'

'Just what I need,' Lyn muttered. 'A herd of hungry bovines.'

'I've got to go,' Paul said, grinning. 'I just came to say be careful – and good luck. I'll be right behind you.'

'You'll be eating their dust,' Kier joked as he slapped Paul cheerfully on the back.

'All right, you lot, move!' The steward's voice, heavily distorted by his loudhailer, prevented any further conversation. 'You, the Lotus. I want you first. Come on, ladies, get going. Silver Porsche – you're next. Where's the Datsun? And the blue Alfa . . .'

'I'll get out of your way,' Kier said quickly. 'I'll be at the lunch stop. Waiting, in case you need me.'

'Thanks.' Alex pulled her helmet on.

'Go get 'em.' Kier opened the car door to let Alex slip in behind the wheel, then vanished into the confusion of cars and people.

Alex started the engine. 'Are you ready?' she asked Lyn, who was buckling her harness in the navigator's seat.

'You bet!' Lyn said with a grin. 'Let's show those pricks in the Porsche what racing is all about.'

Alex slipped the car into gear, and moved forward in answer to the steward's frantic waving. As the overnight leaders, they would be the first to start. She pulled up with the front of the Lotus level with the starting post. The steward nodded and waved to someone behind her. Alex looked in the rear-view mirror in time to see the silver Porsche nose into position behind her. The driver put his hand out his window and made a gesture that, at best, was not exactly sporting.

Alex cheerfully returned the compliment.

'All right.' Lyn was all business beside her. 'We've got two minutes until we start. The first section is through the town, so we're looking at good roads, tight corners and a few hills until we hit the open road.'

'I'm ready,' Alex said.

'Once we hit the open road, it will be flat, straight and fast. You'd better be ready to really shake our tail!'

Alex grinned. She looked at her navigator. 'Whatever happens today,' she said, 'I'm really glad we got to race together.'

'So am I.' Lyn grinned back. 'Now get your act together. We start in exactly sixty seconds.'

Alex flexed her gloved hands around the wheel. She glanced out the window. People were lined up four and five deep to watch the start. She ran her eyes over the faces, telling herself she wasn't looking for anyone special. Then she saw him. He nodded, and she felt her heart lift, just a little.

'Twenty seconds . . .' Lyn's voice was clear and calm, the nervousness of her first day long past. '. . . five . . . four . . . three . . . two . . . one . . . go!'

The last word was lost in the roar as Alex thrust her foot down hard on the accelerator and the little red car darted forward. They sped under the deep shadow created by the old wooden bridge.

'Two hundred metres, out of the showgrounds, then a ninety-degree left.' Lyn began the non-stop guidance that had been Alex's lifeline for the past four days.

It didn't take long to leave Gundagai behind. The watching crowds grew quickly more sparse, until they were alone on the road. The mountains were far behind them. The road became flatter and straighter as they headed west. Alex could feel the Lotus eating up the road with easy speed. This was what she loved. This feeling of freedom and power. The road stretched out in front of her like the future, just waiting for her to make it hers.

'Shit,' Lyn almost screamed.

'What?' Alex cursed her momentary loss of concentration.

'That sign,' Lyn said, swivelling her head despite the fact that at this speed whatever she'd seen was already well behind them. 'It had a cow on it.'

'A what?'

'There was a sign on the side of the road. It had a cow drawn on it. I think some stupid farmer must have . . . Look out!'

Alex didn't need the warning. She'd already spotted the dark shapes on the road ahead of her. She jammed one foot on the brake and one hand on the horn.

The blast of sound didn't seem to perturb the slow-moving beasts one bit. As Alex fought to bring the car's speed back down, they continued their slow ambling. One turned to cross the road right in front of them. Alex swung the wheel and somehow managed to get around it, without disturbing so much as a whisker on its nose. But their speed had dropped, and there were still more cows ahead.

'I wonder if Dee Parker is standing by ready to rescue this lot,' Lyn said.

'Damn it,' Alex muttered as she wove her way forward in first gear. She glanced in the rear-view mirror. Sure enough, in the distance she caught a glint of silver. 'Just my luck. I'll clear this lot off the road, so they'll be able to fly straight through.'

'Come on, Bessie,' Lyn directed the animal they had just passed. 'Get back in the middle of the road, there's a good girl.'

The cow must have heard. With joy, Alex saw a large black shape appear in her mirror. It moved to the centre of the road and then stopped. It almost looked ready to lie down.

'Attagirl,' Lyn cheered.

Suddenly they were free of the herd. Alex accelerated again. 'How are we for time?'

'We've lost some, but so will they. We're still in front.'

'Let's keep it that way.' Alex's eyes began flicking to the mirror, waiting to see when the silver Porsche would emerge from the mass of cows. It didn't take long.

For several miles Alex drove as if her very life depended on it. From time to time she caught a glimpse of silver behind her, but she tried not to look too often. She needed all her attention on the road. They screamed into the next checkpoint, and Alex started counting time.

'There are cows back there,' Lyn yelled at the stewards. 'On the road.'

'We're on it,' someone called back.

Alex pulled forward to the starting line for the next leg, still counting under her breath.

'What about the road ahead?' Lyn asked the starting steward.

'We've had someone drive it,' he answered. 'It's clear.'

'Forty-five. Forty-six.' Alex saw the silver Porsche appear. It crossed the finish line and slid to a stop at the checkpoint.

'They've caught up some of that time,' Alex said. 'Damn those cows.'

'We're still in front,' Lyn said. 'And we've got fifty seconds to our next start.'

Alex nodded. Focus, she told herself as she joined the countdown.

Things started to fall apart, literally, on the last stage before the lunch break. They were racing down a long, straight stretch of road, towards a town with the unlikely name of Wombat, when the rattle started.

'What's that?' Lyn shouted over the noise.

For a few seconds, Alex wasn't sure. Then she felt the shudder start in the steering wheel. It was subtle, but it was unmistakable. Then she saw it.

'The bonnet!'

The long, sleek bonnet had lifted a few centimetres, and was now vibrating furiously.

'The catch must have broken,' Alex yelled. 'I can't leave it like that. We have to tie it down.'

'With what?'

'Anything.'

Alex glanced in the mirror again, looking for the Porsche. She was going to have to stop. She couldn't leave the bonnet vibrating like that.

'Have you found something?' she called to Lyn.

'Give me a minute.'

'We haven't got a minute.'

Beside her, Lyn began to wriggle in her seat. She was trying to open the front of her race suit.

'What are you doing?' Alex yelled.

'Damn it,' Lyn said. 'I'm going to have to undo the harness. For God's sake don't do anything stupid.'

Taking off her harness was against the rules, not to

mention dangerous, but Alex wasn't about to argue. She kept her eyes on the road as Lyn wriggled some more.

'Got it,' Lyn said. 'Ready when you are; just don't brake too hard. You'll have me through the windscreen.'

'Brace yourself!'

Alex braked as hard as she dared. The tyres squealed in protest as she slid into the rough gravel verge. She didn't bother turning the engine off. There wasn't time. With one hand she released her own harness, while holding out the other to take what Lyn was offering. She glanced down at it.

'A bra strap?'

'No crazier than a toaster spring for whatever that was.'

'Paul would be proud of you.'

Alex was out of the car in a flash. She leaned on the bonnet, hoping against hope that it would simply catch again. It didn't. She slid her fingers under it, and lifted it. Part of the catch had snapped, but enough remained to tie it down.

With her ears alert for any sound of the approaching Porsche, Alex tied one end of the black bra strap around the broken catch. The other she passed around the intact catch under the bonnet. She slammed the bonnet shut, then pulled with all her strength. The elastic strap stretched and stretched, until the bonnet was held tight. She was tying the end off when she heard the approaching engine.

'Pricks!' she yelled as she dived back into her seat.

The silver Porsche flashed past.

'Shit. Shit. Shit!' Alex cursed as she struggled with her harness.

Beside her, Lyn was once more strapped in, and Alex could hear her counting the seconds.

Alex's harness clicked into place, and she jammed her foot down on the accelerator. The Lotus fishtailed as she steered it back on to the road.

'How long?'

'They must be nearly a minute in front of us now,' Lyn said. 'Focus – there's a tight four right coming up. Then another long flat straight. You'll catch 'em.'

Alex wasn't so sure, but she was determined to give it a good go.

For the next hour, she drove with all the skill she possessed, and at times it seemed she drove better than she had ever done before. It did her no good. The silver Porsche remained just those few seconds ahead of her. There were times she felt she was close enough that she might just be able to slide past, but it never happened.

She was reaching meltdown point when she turned the car into the lunch checkpoint to discover they were a good forty seconds behind the Porsche.

'It'll be more than that on corrected time,' Lyn said as she pulled her helmet off. 'And it's all due to that pit stop.'

'What happened?' Kier seemed to materialise from nowhere, water bottles and sandwiches in his hands.

'Bonnet catch,' Alex told him.

Without a word, he handed over the refreshments and turned to the car.

'What's this?' he said as he looked at the black strip holding the bonnet closed.

'Bra,' Lyn said as she gulped down some water.

Kier raised an eyebrow, but said nothing more as he struggled to untie the knots pulled even tighter by the vibration of the car. He lifted the bonnet. 'Metal fatigue, at a guess. The catch just snapped. I might be able to fix it, but,' he handed Lyn her bra strap, 'don't go putting this back on until I'm sure.'

He left at a run in the direction of the spare parts van. As he did, Paul's Alfa pulled up next to them.

'So, the Porsche got you,' he said as he stepped from behind the wheel.

'We had to pull over. The bonnet catch broke.' Alex sounded as angry as she looked.

'But,' Lyn smiled cheerfully, showing Paul her tattered bra strap, 'we did some running repairs. Fangio would be proud.' The two of them laughed at the private joke.

'There's still a couple of hundred kilometres to go,' Alex said to no one in particular. 'We could still catch them.'

They could, but it would take a miracle.

'I've got a new catch.' Kier was back, armed with a selection of tools. 'I think it will fit.' He disappeared under the bonnet.

Alex stood watching. She was helpless to do anything at this point, and she didn't like that feeling at all. She accepted a water bottle and a sandwich from Lyn. She wasn't hungry, but it was something to do to keep from watching the clock, or screaming, or ripping the tools out of Kier's hands. She knew that he would do his best, but that wasn't the point. The whole point of this was that it was her race. Her win or her loss. She had let herself get distracted. Let memories of the past take her mind from the job at hand. Now other people were involved and she was no longer standing on her own two feet.

After an eternity, Kier slammed the bonnet shut and tested it.

'That's not going anywhere,' he said. 'Of course, you may never get it open again.'

Alex didn't even grin at the joke. She looked at the havoc all round her. Cars and crews. Stewards, media people and somewhere, no doubt, a woman worrying about more injured animals on the road. And right in front of her, Kier, who had her so confused she hardly knew what she was doing. She was about to fail in front of all of them. She could blame Kier, of course. For doing to her whatever it was he did by just standing there, looking at her with those dark eyes, and that lock of hair falling across his forehead. But deep down, she knew that if she failed – it would be her own fault for letting go.

'Drivers, start your engines.' The tinny voice over the loudspeaker shook her back into action.

'Thanks for fixing the bonnet,' she said to Kier, putting on her leather gloves as she did to avoid looking at him. If she looked at him, or anyone now, she'd lose it.

'Good luck.' He didn't try to catch her eye. He didn't touch her. It was as if he knew how close she was to breaking point.

Alex eased the car into the starting line-up. Ahead of her, the silver Porsche was in first place. The navigator stuck his head out of his window and waved cheerfully at them. Beside her, Lyn made a rude noise and poked out her tongue.

'If we can't win, I'd rather it was anyone else except them,' she declared.

'We can win,' Alex said in her most determined voice. 'They'd better watch out – because I'm right on their tail.'

She was as good as her word. The Porsche had a one-minute head start when Alex sent the Lotus roaring over the start line. But she was determined that wasn't going to last long. Just as the Porsche had dogged her in the morning's run, so she did the same to them during the afternoon. The Lotus was never more than half a kilometre behind them. Sometimes she drew closer, and they must be able to see her sleek red bonnet in their rear-view mirror. Sometimes they drew away and for a few minutes she'd lose them, but on the next long, straight stretch, the glint of silver up ahead would spur her to reach new speeds.

'Come on, girl,' Alex muttered under her breath. Soon they'd be on the highway heading back into Canberra. From then on, her chances of passing them were pretty slim.

When it happened, it happened in slow motion.

The Porsche was about three hundred metres ahead, coming in to a bend. The driver took it too fast. The Porsche drifted across the bitumen, then its wheels were in the gravel at the side of the road. Alex saw the driver lose it totally. The Porsche started to spin, facing back the way it had come, as it slid ever closer to the wire fence, behind which some cattle were dozing. Its tail clipped the fence as Alex hit her brakes, slowing down just enough to take the corner safely herself.

'Go, girl, go!' Lyn screamed at her side as Alex powered away from the bend.

'What's happening back there?' Alex yelled.

Lyn twisted in her seat to look back. 'They're still off the road. Wait, someone's moving to the back of the car. I think they're caught in the fence.'

Alex grinned. If the wire was caught around the rear bumper, or the exhaust, the Porsche driver would not just power his way out. That would do too much damage to the car. At best, they'd lose time checking. Time she would make the best possible use of. 'Come on, girl,' she whispered to the little red Lotus. 'It's now or never.'

'You've got five hundred metres straight.' Lyn's voice began the now familiar refrain in her ear. 'Then a right bend, not as tight as the last one. After that, plant it . . .'

Alex glanced in the mirror, checking for a silver car, as she pushed the Lotus, and herself, to the limit.

17

Waiting was hell.

Kier died a little bit each time the crowd stirred in anticipation. Any hint of movement on the road would set necks craning, desperate to see who was going to be first to cross the line. But time and time again the road remained empty. Roped into their respective viewing areas, guests and press, support crews and spectators were equally tense. From time to time a rumour would fly through the crowd. This car had spun out on a corner. That one had crashed. Another had broken down. Kier ignored them all. He had to, for each one was just another knife twisting in his gut. He should be used to waiting next to a finish line. He was a racehorse trainer, and every weekend he waited as his horses lined up in the barriers. Every weekend he cheered them on as they raced. That was nothing compared to this torment. It wasn't that he didn't care about winning horse races. It was his livelihood and the realisation of a dream. Each of the glossy thoroughbreds he cared for was, in some small way, an extension of the black colt he and Alex had trained and loved and lost.

But this time, it was Alex herself.

Kier shifted restlessly. He was sitting on the roof of

Dee Parker's wildlife rescue van, his weight resting on thin metal racks designed to support suitcases rather than humans. He had been searching for a good vantage point when he spotted the van, given a priority parking space because of its official role. Dee had been more than happy to give him a spot on the roof. It was, she said, a thank-you for helping her to rescue the eagle, which, she hastened to inform him, was recovering well. Dee was a firm believer in returning favours. According to her, people should get what they deserved.

Kier wondered if that was true. Did his brother Rob get what he deserved when he went to jail? Some people would say yes. Alex's mother, Jacqueline Reilly, would certainly be one of them. After all, she had done her bit. But what about Kier's mother? Did she deserve the pain of watching her son imprisoned? And if people got what they truly deserved – what was in store for him when the race was over?

The crowd around the finish line moved, and Kier's eyes darted down the road. Still nothing.

Of all the things he'd thought when asked to drive in the rally, of all the possible outcomes, it had never for one instant occurred to him that he would be waiting by the finish line for Alex Reilly to roar back into his life. Because if he had his way, that was exactly what she was about to do.

The accident that had wrecked the Ferrari and almost killed him was possibly the best thing that had happened to him for years. If it hadn't been for that, he would be competing against Alex, not a part of her team. He guessed he should also be grateful for her original navigator's pregnancy. Maybe he would send her something when the baby was born, because her departure had left the way open for Lyn to team up with Alex. The gods had smiled on him that day – and it was about time.

It hadn't been easy. All this waiting had brought back so many memories – many of them painful. He'd had to face up to what he'd done all those years ago. And he had. Now it was time to put right the mistakes of the past. He knew one thing now: Alex Reilly was still as much a part of him as she'd been all those years ago. They might have been little more than kids back then, but they had forged a bond so strong that neither time nor separation could break it. Lies might – and it was time he put that right.

The Alex who was at this very moment racing towards him was a very different person to the girl he'd loved all those years ago. But she was still Alex Reilly, and he could love the woman as much as he had loved the girl. He was determined that they should be together. There was just one more hurdle they had to cross.

Subconsciously his hand travelled to the back pocket of his jeans, checking the wallet that he always carried there. He didn't have to pull it out to look at the photo. He carried his daughter with him always. As soon as this race was over, and they had time to think, he would tell Alex about Katie. About what had happened. And why. Alex would understand. Wouldn't she?

Kier took a long, slow breath. Yes. She would understand. He was sure of it.

At that moment, a sudden roar from the crowd heralded the appearance of the first car. Kier rose to his feet to get an even clearer view.

The red Lotus was hurtling down the road towards them. Alex was in the lead! But even as he opened his mouth to cheer, the silver nose of the Porsche appeared through the heat haze. It was close behind her. Too close.

Kier had checked the times – Alex had to beat the Porsche by at least twenty seconds if she was going to win the rally. Twenty seconds at that speed ... No. The Porsche was only a few metres behind.

The roar of the two engines was almost deafening as both cars raced to the finish line. The Lotus crossed first. The Porsche flashed over the line just a few metres behind. Kier leaped down off the van and began to run. The crowd all around him surged forward. The two cars were clearing the stewards' area, making way for whoever was following, but the press, the officials, the guests were all clamouring to get at the Lotus and the Porsche. Kier was faced with a heaving mass of people. He was going to have to fight his way through to get to Alex.

'Alex, how did you get around him?'

'Alex, do you think you've got him – on final times?'

'Lyn – how does racing compare with being on the catwalk?'

The journalists were shouting and waving microphones. Cameras were flashing. And somewhere in the midst of all that, Kier suddenly heard Alex's voice.

'We won't know for a while what the results are,' she said in a firm voice. 'I just want to say it's been a great race – and I hope we've raised a lot of money for charity.'

He was nearing the centre of the crush when the assembled media gave way to let two men through. The Porsche brothers approached Alex and Lyn.

'Great race,' said the driver, putting out his hand.

'Thanks.' Alex took it. The scene dissolved into a flashing spectacle as the photographers went wild.

'Just hold on a second.'

'Lyn, you jump in the photo too.'

'Guys, how about you put your arms around the girls?'

'How about he doesn't?' Lyn said firmly. 'Let's wait and see who wins this before anyone starts that sort of thing.' The tone of her voice set the crowd to laughing.

'She's pretty good at this, isn't she?' said a voice at Kier's side.

He turned to see Paul, just pulling off his racing gloves as he watched the scene in front of him. 'They are both pretty amazing.'

The two men looked at each other, and Kier had a feeling they were both thinking the same thing.

'Hey – how did you do?' Kier suddenly realised Paul had also just completed a gruelling race.

'Fourth across the line. But the guy ahead of me was the Datsun. He had a bad run this morning – so my guess is that I'm number three behind them.' He nodded in towards the centre of the media scrum.

'Well done,' Kier said, slapping him on the back.

'Thanks – but I'm not done yet.'

Before Kier could ask him what he meant, there was a sudden wave of movement around them. Another driver, a movie star with more celebrity status than Lyn, was fast approaching the finish line, and the press pack set off in pursuit. Alex and Lyn were left alone, standing by the side of the car.

'Hey. Well done!' Kier said brightly as he rapidly closed the gap between them. 'First across the line.' He would have hugged Alex, but the look on her face stopped him.

'We haven't won,' she said. 'On corrected time, they'll still have us.'

'Maybe,' Paul said as he joined them. 'But if I was you, I wouldn't count on it.'

'What do you mean?' Lyn asked.

Alex shook her head. 'It doesn't matter. I can live with

second.' Her voice didn't sound like she could.

'Well, we've raised a lot of money for the home,' Lyn said. 'That's thanks to you, Alex. If you hadn't let me join you after Kier's accident . . .'

'Glad to help out.' Alex moved away from them to the other side of the car.

Kier heard her sigh as she examined the long scratches left there the day before, when she had steered around the crashed Mini. It was probably to be expected that she'd feel down. After the stress and excitement of the race, they would all start feeling a little lost.

'How about we all go out and celebrate?' he said. 'There's nothing more for us to do. They won't release today's times until after they announce the overall winners at the ball tomorrow night.'

'That's a good idea.' Paul sounded enthusiastic. 'What about it, Lyn? We'll find somewhere where the food is good and there's not another rally driver in sight.'

'I guess it would be nice not to be covered in grease for an evening. All right,' Lyn said. 'Count me in.'

'Alex?' Kier asked.

She shook her head. 'No thanks, guys. I'm tired. I think I'll just get an early night.'

'No way,' Lyn cut in. 'You are not spending tonight in some dingy hotel room worrying about the results. You're coming with us.'

Kier watched Alex's face as she sighed and nodded. She was still pretty low, and what he was about to tell her wasn't going to help. He should probably wait until after the ball tomorrow. Let her enjoy a well-earned celebration. He'd kept his secret so long now, another day wouldn't matter. Or would it? He felt a sudden urge to be finished with the lies and deception. It was well past time he was honest with Alex . . . and with himself.

'Let's get the cars through to the lock-up.' Paul's voice interrupted his thoughts.

'Hey. Wait up!' Before they could move, a steward darted towards them. 'I'm going to need the Lotus brought through to the stewards' compound.'

'What?' Alex asked. 'What for?'

'There's been a protest.'

'There's what?'

'A protest. Against the Lotus,' the steward said.

'Who by?' Alex demanded. 'And about what?'

'The Porsche protested,' the steward said. 'I don't know the details.'

Alex stepped forward, her face a mask of anger. 'What are they protesting for? They've won on corrected time, haven't they?'

'I have no idea.' The steward was starting to look annoyed. 'All I know is that you have to take this car to the stewards' compound. It'll be held overnight to ensure no one tampers with it.'

'As if I . . .' Alex started.

Kier put a gentle hand on her arm, and she slowly subsided. 'Then what?' he asked the steward in a calm voice.

'Inspection tomorrow morning. Ten o'clock. You have to be there. You'll get details of the protest then.'

Beside him, Alex stiffened, as if to argue. Just for a few seconds, then he almost felt the fight go out of her as she slowly relaxed and nodded. Without a word, or even a glance at her friends, she got behind the wheel of the Lotus and started the engine. Kier caught Lyn's eye. Lyn stepped back to let him slide into the passenger seat. Alex didn't even look at him as she put the car in gear.

'It'll be all right,' he said. 'I bet they just protested in

case you ended up in front on corrected time. You've
done nothing wrong. We'll beat this, just you wait.'

She didn't answer.

Ahead of them, the steward was directing them into a
fenced enclosure next to the stewards' office. Alex parked
where she was told and got out, still without saying a
word. She locked the car and turned away without even
looking at Kier. Then they heard the sound of another
engine. Alex stopped, and they both turned to see the
silver Porsche pulling into the compound.

'What the hell . . . ?' Alex stepped to Kier's side as
they waited for the Porsche to park. The driver was out in
a flash.

'I guess you think you're smart,' he said, waving an
angry finger in Alex's general direction.

'I don't know what you mean,' she said. 'You're the
ones who lodged a protest against me.'

'Yeah, and you lodged your own right back.' The
Porsche driver moved closer, his face a mask of fury, all of
it directed at Alex.

'Hey.' Kier stepped forward. 'Enough.'

The driver's eyes left Alex and focused on him. For a
few seconds, Kier wondered if he was going to have a
fight on his hands. Then the Porsche driver stepped back.

'It wasn't us who protested against you.' Alex was at
his side.

'Sure. I believe you,' the driver sneered.

'I can't help what you believe,' Alex said.

The driver turned and stormed away. Alex looked up
at Kier, her eyebrows raised.

'I don't know who did it,' Kier said in answer to her
unspoken question. 'But I do know this race is still a long
way from over.'

A shower, hot or cold, just didn't help. Alex wrapped herself in a towel and stomped back into her room. She flicked her wet hair back from her face, and glared into the mirror. A protest! The pricks in the Porsche had actually lodged a protest against her. And she still didn't know what it was about. The stewards had flatly refused to give her any details. She would find out tomorrow morning. Kier had offered to try again tonight, but Alex knew it wouldn't work. She had retired to her hotel room to shower and try to relax before they all went out for dinner.

She found a comb and began dragging it through her messy hair. Dinner. Now that was another issue. The four of them having dinner. Four. As in two couples. There was Lyn and Paul . . . and there was her and Kier. She wasn't quite sure if she was ready for that just yet. She tossed the comb back on the dressing table and turned away from the face in the mirror. She wasn't sure yet how she felt about Kier, and his confession . . . Was it just last night? The events of the day had pushed him not to the back of her mind, but at least away from the front of it. Now the race was over. The protest was out of her hands until tomorrow. With nothing else left to think about, he was in her every thought.

He hadn't left her! Well, he had, but not of his own choosing. He had been driven away. Alex felt a twinge of sympathy for him. His brother had been trouble for as long as she could remember. But Kier had never turned his back. She doubted that she would have been so steadfast. Rob had never deserved Kier's unswerving loyalty. Kier should never have had to choose between his love for her, and his brother. Alex despised her mother for inflicting such a decision on a boy of seventeen. For that was what Kier had been. A boy.

Alex tossed her suitcase on to the bed and flung it open. If she was going to go out for dinner, she needed something to wear. It might feel nice to be clean, and wearing something other than a hot, sweaty race suit, which was now lying in a crumpled, smelly heap in the corner of her room. She dived into the case and started rifling through the clothes. One of the first things she found was a black cocktail dress. It was scrunched into a corner, under a pair of high-heeled shoes. This was the outfit she had planned to wear tomorrow night – at the gala celebration dinner. She had expected to wear it when collecting her prize. Well, that might not happen now; which was possibly a good thing, as the dress had suffered from being pushed around her suitcase for a week. It looked like something the dog might have dragged in. She pulled it out of the bag and found a hanger in the wardrobe. The dress looked a little better on the hanger, and the creases might just drop, if she was lucky. She could almost hear her mother tutting her disapproval.

Her mother. Kier had said she should ask her mother. Alex didn't need to ask. Deep down she knew that Kier wasn't lying. But maybe she did have to speak to Jacqueline. There were a few things she wanted to say.

She was already in a foul mood – not even the ordeal of speaking to her mother could make her feel any worse.

Alex found her mobile phone. She hesitated for a moment, wondering where Jacqueline might be. Then she realised, there wasn't really any question. A few years ago her father had purchased a high-rise unit in a Queensland beach resort, with views of the Pacific Ocean and at least two television stars in the same block. He hated it, and never went there. Her mother loved it and rarely left. As she found the number, Alex wondered how long it was since her mother and father had slept under the same roof – let alone in the same bed.

'Hello. This is Jacqueline.'

'Hello, Mother.'

'Alex! It's so lovely to hear from you, dear.'

The voice was as cultured as always, but Alex could hear the censure underneath. Not without cause, she thought. It had been weeks since they last spoke. No one would call them close.

'How are you, Mother?'

'I'm well, thank you. And you?'

They exchanged pleasantries for a few minutes. Alex hated this part of the call, but her mother was firmly set in her ways. Politeness before all else.

'So, where are you, dear? And what are you doing?'

'I'm in Canberra, Mother. I have just finished competing in the Snowy Mountains Classic Car rally.'

'A car rally? Alex, you really should forget this obsession with cars. It's not very ladylike.'

How typical that her mother shouldn't even ask how well she had done. Her father's first question would have been 'Did you win?' And if the answer was no, his second question would have been 'Why not?'

'Yes, Mother. I'm here with Kier Thomas.' She held her breath, waiting for a reaction.

'Kier Thomas?'

'Surely you haven't forgotten him. After all, he and I used to be . . . quite close.'

'Yes, I remember. Dreadful family. The brother went to jail.'

'Yes, he did. And just how much did you have to do with that?'

The silence at the other end of the phone lasted for what seemed like an age.

'Come on, Mother. There's no point trying to deny it. Kier told me everything. How you forced him to abandon me, or you'd do your best to get his brother jailed.'

'I didn't have to do anything,' Jacqueline answered. 'He managed to get there all on his own.'

'Yes, he did. But you still made sure Kier left, didn't you?'

'Well, really.' Jacqueline sniffed down the phone. 'There's no need to be like that. I was just trying to protect you.'

'Protect me?' Alex almost yelled. 'When Kier left, he broke my heart.'

'Rubbish. You were just a child. I wasn't going to have you throw your life away on some handsome, sweet-talking Irishman, like I did.'

Alex blinked in surprise. 'Like you did? Are you talking about Dad?'

'They're all the same,' said Jacqueline, her voice dripping with bitterness. 'All muscles and twinkling eyes, but no class. Common, the lot of them. I wasn't having you getting involved with someone who was so far beneath you.'

Beneath her? Alex could hardly believe what she was hearing.

'Mum,' she said softly, 'did you ever love Dad? I mean really love him?'

'Love doesn't come into it.'

Alex knew that part of the conversation was over. 'I suppose you kept Kier's letters from me too.'

'Letters?' The surprise in Jacqueline's voice was genuine. 'There were no letters.'

No letters? 'He must have tried to get in touch with me.'

'No. Not once. No letters. Nor did I ever see him come back to the town.'

'But . . .'

'Alex, don't be a fool.' Jacqueline sounded testy. 'He was no good then, and I don't imagine he has changed.'

Alex hit the disconnect button. She dropped the phone on to the bed and stood staring at it as if the device itself was somehow responsible for the words she had just heard.

Kier hadn't written to her. He hadn't tried to get in touch. Not once. That didn't make sense. Surely, after his brother went to jail, there would have been no reason for Kier to stay away from her. Not if he loved her. Alex shook her head. There was something here she didn't understand. She reached for some jeans and a shirt. She needed to talk to Kier about this.

In her bare feet, she walked briskly down the hotel corridor to Kier's room. It took him a long time to answer her knock. When he opened the door, his face creased in surprise.

'Alex . . .'

She pushed past him into the room. 'I've just been talking to my mother.'

'Oh.'

Kier leaned against the dressing table. His movement caused her to really look at him for the first time since she'd entered the room. He had obviously just stepped from the shower. He was wearing a pair of jeans, slung low on his hips, the belt not yet done up. He must have slipped his shirt on when she knocked. It was unbuttoned, and fell loose around his body, exposing his fit, tanned chest. He was such a sexy man! Alex felt an all too familiar sharp longing deep inside. That was the problem, she thought. She had let her body take control of her mind. What had her mother said? All muscle and twinkling eyes. In that she had been right.

'You never wrote to me.' It wasn't a question.

'What . . . ?'

'After you left. You never wrote to me. You never came back.'

'I couldn't.' Kier spoke in a calm voice. 'Your mother said that if I did, she'd make sure Rob went to jail.'

'But he did go to jail,' Alex said. 'Just a few weeks after you left. There was no more harm she could do then. So why didn't you come back?'

'Alex, you have to believe me. I wanted to.' She could hear the tension in his voice. See it in the set of his shoulders, and the pain in his eyes.

'Then why didn't you?' she said. 'Kier, my heart was broken. I cried myself to sleep night after night. Even at university I used to lie awake at night and wonder what was wrong with me.'

'Oh God.' He stepped towards her and grabbed her by the shoulders. 'What was wrong with *you*? It was me. My failings. My weakness.'

She could almost feel his heart beating. She could feel

the strength of his pain in the vice-like grip of his fingers on her arms.

'Then why?' she whispered.

For a long time he didn't speak. He just looked at her with such pain and yearning on his face that she wanted to stop everything right there. She suddenly knew that whatever was coming would change everything between them. In a sudden surge of panic, she wanted to pull free. To run away before he could speak. Because once the secret was out, it could never be recalled.

'I couldn't come back then. It was too late for me.'

She didn't understand.

Kier let his hands fall away from her shoulders. He turned back to his dressing table and reached for something there. It was his wallet. He opened it – and held it out for her to take.

Puzzled, Alex took it and looked down. There was a photo there. Of Kier with a child. She must have been about five or six. She had his dark hair and eyes. She was quite beautiful. Both were smiling.

'Your daughter?' She didn't really have to ask; the resemblance was obvious.

'Katie.'

'She's very pretty.'

'Thanks. She's a great kid. She lives with her mother . . . my ex-wife . . . up in Queensland. I don't see her very often.'

'But I don't understand . . .'

'That's an old photo.'

Alex felt a terrible fear growing in the pit of her stomach, but it was too late now to turn back.

'How old is she now?'

'She's just turned eleven. Last month.' He said the

words as if he knew the damage they would do.

She didn't want to do the maths, but she couldn't stop herself. Kier had left her just days before her seventeenth birthday. That was twelve years ago . . . or rather – almost twelve years ago. Her birthday was still a few weeks away. And if his daughter was already eleven . . .

She didn't want to look at him. She stared at the wallet. At the photo of the little girl. Kier's daughter. Conceived . . .

'You didn't waste much time, did you?'

'Alex, it wasn't like that.' He took a step towards her, reached out as if to touch her.

'Don't.' She backed away from him as if his touch would burn her.

'Please. Let me explain. I loved you. I still—'

'No. I don't want to hear it.' The room was spinning. She felt as if she was going to be ill. He must have been with someone else . . . and just days after leaving her. She looked at him and caught the shine of what might have been tears in his eyes.

'My mother was right. You are no good. You never were.' She turned away and fled. When she reached her own room, she slammed the door and fell back against it. Then slowly she sank to the ground, as the tears began.

'Alex isn't coming.' Lyn looked up from the screen on her mobile phone.

'Oh. Is everything all right?' Paul asked.

'I don't know. Hang on a second.' Lyn's fingers flew over the keys. She didn't like doing this – sending a text while Paul waited patiently beside her. It was . . . well, it was a bit rude. But he didn't seem to mind. He was, without a doubt, one of the most patient people she had ever met.

'Do you want another drink?' They were sitting in the hotel bar, at a corner table as far away from the rally crowd as they could get. That wasn't very far. Most of the hotels in the city were full of rally competitors and officials. This particular hotel was hosting the ball tomorrow night, so it was very much race central. The bar was the natural congregating point.

'No. Thanks.' Lyn smiled. 'I'm fine.' The four of them had agreed to meet in the bar before heading out to dinner. They had decided to find some small suburban restaurant where there was a possibility, however small, that no one would know them. 'I hope Alex is—' Before she could finish the sentence, her phone beeped again.

Need sleep b4 inspection tomorrow. U have fun.

'I guess that means Kier isn't coming either,' Lyn said. 'I wonder if the two of them are . . . well . . . you know.'

'I don't think so,' Paul said. 'Look.'

Across the room, Kier was leaning on the bar.

'He doesn't look happy,' Lyn said. 'Maybe I should go over there and talk to him.'

'No. I'll go.' Paul slid his chair back. 'From the look on his face, I'd guess the last thing he wants right now is to talk to a woman.'

Lyn took a second look at Kier. She had to agree. She watched Paul join him at the bar. The two men talked for a few moments. Lyn smiled at the picture they made. Kier so dark and handsome and, tonight at least, brooding. Paul was not traditionally handsome, but she loved his face. It was calm and kind, intelligent and strong and humorous. Everything about the man he was could be seen in his face.

'Hey, are you all alone? We can't have that.'

Lyn looked at the man now occupying the chair Paul had so recently vacated. He was young and good-looking. She vaguely remembered seeing him once or twice before. He was racing a Ferrari, which probably meant he was rich. He was also pretty drunk. 'Let me buy you a drink.' His slurred voice confirmed her suspicion. 'What do you want?'

'Thank you for the offer,' Lyn said with a polite but not too friendly smile. 'But I think what I want right now is just to be alone.'

'You'll break my heart,' the young driver declared.

'I think you'll live,' Lyn assured him. Paul was walking back towards her, so she stood up. 'Good night.'

She intercepted Paul when he was still a few feet away. He understood, and steered her towards the door.

'You're good at that, you know,' she told him.

'Good at what?'

'Rescuing people.'

Paul smiled. 'Was he bothering you?'

'No. I'm sort of . . .' She stopped. To say she was used to it would be boasting about her appearance, something she had never done. Her appearance was her job, nothing more.

'Used to it?' Paul finished for her.

Lyn nodded.

'They've got it all wrong, you know,' Paul said as he guided her through the front doors of the hotel.

'Why do you say that?' Lyn wanted to know.

'Because the most beautiful part of you isn't your face.' Paul went in search of a taxi.

At the bar, Kier wrapped his fingers around his nearly empty glass.

'Would you like another?' the barmaid asked.

'Yes. Make it a double.' He pushed some money across the bar.

The drink arrived swiftly. He held the square glass in his hands, swirling the contents around gently. The light glinted on the amber liquid. The sharp odour brought memories flooding back. He remembered the smell from his childhood. His father was a whisky drinker. Rob too. Or rather, Rob had been a whisky drinker. He'd spent most of his adult life in jail. First for the robbery, and then for the violence that followed. Kier doubted there was much whisky in jail, and certainly not the expensive single malt his brother had favoured.

Irish men drank whisky. That was the way of it, according to his mother. They drank whisky and chased women and got into trouble with the law. He lifted the glass to his lips and breathed in the heady fumes. Despite the fact that he was several generations away from Ireland, and Australian to the core, she wasn't wrong. She seldom was. Look at him. Although he'd never been in serious trouble with the law ... though there had been moments back then. In those first years on his own. Those first years without Alex. When he'd drunk his fair share of whisky. And as for women ...

He paused before the golden liquid even touched his lips, then took a deep breath and set the glass back on the bar. He knew better than that. He walked away without even bothering to collect his change.

The elevator took him to the floor where all three of them had their rooms. Him, Lyn and Alex. He stepped from the elevator and looked down the corridor. His room was at the far end of the hall. To get there he had to walk past Alex's. His steps faltered. He didn't want to stop at her room, but he couldn't just walk past. He stood facing the door, one hand raised to knock. He could explain if she would just give him a chance.

He stood for what seemed like for ever, then he let his hand fall and walked away. He didn't look back as he carried on to his room.

Once inside the four walls, Kier decided that he would not pace aimlessly. He would not waste time and energy and emotion in useless recriminations or impossible hopes. He would eat, watch some television and go to bed. If he was lucky, he might get some sleep. This was the only hotel of the trip that boasted room service, and he might as well use it. Not that he was hungry. He ordered a steak and salad – but no wine. Mineral water was all he wanted. He was trying to decide whether to turn the TV on when his mobile phone chirped. He picked it up, and smiled when he saw the caller ID.

'Katie.'

'Hi, Dad!'

Kier closed his eyes and blessed the gods for the ray of sunshine that was his daughter.

'How did she go, Dad? Did Lyn win the race?'

After her initial disappointment, Katie's enthusiasm for the race hadn't waned when her father crashed out. If anything, she was more excited than ever. The thought of an all-female team taking on the men had inspired her junior rebel's soul. Then she'd seen the television stories about Alex and Lyn, including their role as rescuers after the mountain crash. Kier guessed that had scored her some serious points among her friends at school. He was beginning to think she had forgiven him for crashing out of the race.

'We don't know yet.' He explained about corrected times and the protests. 'We'll just have to wait until tomorrow to find out.'

This news was greeted with the sort of horrified wail that only eleven-year-old girls could manage. 'That's for ever!'

'Not quite for ever,' he chuckled.

'You'll ring me as soon as you know?' his daughter instructed.

He assured her that he would.

'Can't I come down there? Please, Dad.' That tone had won him over many times before, but not tonight.

'Sorry, kid. Your mum's right about this. It's too far to come all on your own.'

'But you said I would get to meet Lyn.' He could almost see the petulant pout.

'And you will. Next time you come to stay with me, we'll organise a visit. All right?'

That seemed to satisfy her, and for a while Kier just listened to her chatter about her school, and her friends, and her puppy. He loved to hear his daughter talk. He could so easily picture her bright, smiling face. For a second, the accusing look in Alex's eyes flashed back into his mind. No matter what she thought, he would never regret Katie's birth. He might be ashamed of his own actions back then – but of his daughter . . . never.

On her modelling assignments, Lyn had eaten in restaurants all over the world. Many of them were expensive, and some were almost as famous as the people she had been dining with. But never had she enjoyed a meal as much as this one.

The taxi driver had taken them to a tiny little Italian restaurant away from the city centre. It appeared to be a family affair, and every other customer seemed to be on first-name terms with the host. Not that the newcomers were treated any differently. The food was simple, but tasted wonderful. So did the wine. The service was as good as the food. Well, almost. But the best thing about it was how completely happy she was. And the reason for that happiness was currently walking back from the bathroom.

She and Paul had done nothing but talk since they sat down. They talked about food, and places they had both been. They talked about music and books. There had even been a light-hearted competition over who knew the most obscure facts. They hadn't talked about the race. Or Lyn's job. Or the fact that after the race ball tomorrow night, they would go their own separate ways. Lyn had spent years in the company of some of the world's most handsome men. Rich men. Interesting and well-dressed men. Why then did she feel this tiny frisson low in her stomach at the approach of a plain man dressed in faded denim and a crumpled white cotton shirt?

'A penny for them,' Paul offered as he sat down again.

'They're not worth that much,' Lyn disseminated.

'Don't sell yourself short.' Paul reached out to gently touch the tips of her fingers. 'I can see past the façade, you know.'

Something in his eyes told her that he was right. Something in her own heart told her the same thing. His smile invited her. The ache in her body and soul encouraged her. But the thought of putting her thoughts . . . her longing . . . into words was terrifying.

'So, you will have dessert?' A heavily accented voice saved her from having to say anything at all. 'Or perhaps coffee?'

Lyn looked up at the waiter, not sure whether to thank him or to yell at him to go away.

'Coffee, Lyn?' Paul asked. 'Or would you prefer to head back now?'

Lyn tried to read his face. Was there expectation there? Or hope?

'I think I'd like to go back,' she said.

Paying the bill took for ever. As their smiling host bade them good night, Paul's hand lightly touched the small of Lyn's back to guide her out of the door. It was a caress, not a claim. Walking down the footpath, looking for a taxi, their fingers entwined almost of their own volition, and stayed that way all through the ride back to the hotel. The corridor leading to Lyn's room was empty. As she walked past Alex's door, she wondered briefly if her friend was asleep. If she had fixed whatever was wrong between her and Kier. But she didn't have time to wonder for long. She and Paul were at her door.

She didn't know what to say. She should go into that room alone. She should post her blog. Call her mother. Do all her fund-raising and caring duties. She should. But what she wanted to do was . . .

Paul touched her cheek. His hands were worn and strong, but the touch was the caress of a dove's feather. No power on earth could have stopped Lyn from leaning ever so slightly forward, longing for the touch of his lips on hers. It was like coming home. When their lips parted, she didn't allow herself to think. Duty could wait. Tonight was for her. Her needs. Her feelings. Her life.

She unlocked the door to her room, and walked through, leaving it open for Paul to follow.

There was a crack in the plaster on the ceiling. Alex lay fully clothed, sideways across the bed. Her hands were clasped behind her head and she was staring at the ceiling. She wasn't sure how long she'd been doing that, but long enough to become intimately familiar with the crack above her. There was also a small stain near the light that might just be the handprint of some mainten-ance man who had changed the bulb. Then there was the tiny cobweb in the corner of the ceiling above the window. It was almost hidden by the curtains, but Alex had been staring at nothing for long enough to notice that too.

Staring at nothing, because nothing was safe.

Trying to think about nothing was safe too – but it was so much harder.

It was impossible.

Thinking about nothing would make the pain stop. It would make the hurt and anger go away. But try as she might, she couldn't do it. Couldn't get Kier's face out of her mind. Couldn't stop thinking about him with someone else. Just a few days after he left her. A few days after her birthday. Just a few nights after the night he and she were supposed to be together. Maybe even on that very night . . .

She felt the tears prick the back of her eyes, and sat up. No. She was not going to cry again. She'd done all the crying over Kier that she was ever going to do. She was not going to cry any more.

She slid off the bed. A room-service tray was sitting on the table, the pasta meal and the glass of wine almost untouched. The smell of it made her feel queasy, and she decided to get rid of it. She slowly got to her feet, collected the tray and opened the door. When the waiter had brought her meal, there had been a second tray on his trolley. As she deposited her untouched tray outside for collection, she wondered briefly if the person who had ordered that steak and salad had done his meal more justice than she had.

Back inside her room, Alex avoided looking at the bed. She wasn't going to lose herself in pity again. She would do something useful. There was nothing she could do to prepare for the next day. Without knowing what the protest was, she couldn't prepare to fight it. She could, however, start getting ready to go back to her real life. She hadn't been near her work e-mail all week. She had cases pending. Court dates coming up. She was a successful and busy lawyer, not a heartsick schoolgirl.

She sat at the table and hit the power button on her laptop. As she waited for it to boot, she happened to glance over at the mirror. The face that stared back at her was wan and drawn. The eyes were dark pools of pain.

Couldn't he have waited? She had. For years. But he never came back. Now she knew why. He had found someone else, and forgotten her. Given someone else the love that should have been hers. Walked down the aisle of a church with someone else.

Her laptop beeped to alert her to unread messages in her inbox.

That was her life now, she thought. She was a lawyer. A grown woman. Not some hormone-fuelled teenager with a tendency to overdramatise the littlest things. She shouldn't be wasting her time thinking about Kier. She had her own life. She had made a success of herself. Proven herself worthy. Worthy . . . of what? Of who? She still spent her nights alone.

Alex leaned back in her chair, her eyes drifting once more to the ceiling. From this angle, she could see another crack in the plaster.

Lyn was determined not to open her eyes.

If she opened her eyes, she would see the laptop and phone sitting on her desk. And that would take away the wonderful feeling that suffused every part of her body. The laptop would remind her that she had done nothing this evening to help her sister's cause. The phone would remind her that she hadn't called her mother, to help her through the strain of her long day. Opening her eyes would let the real world back in.

Keeping her eyes closed meant she could only feel. And hear. And taste. She could hear Paul's breathing and taste his lips on hers. She could hear his heart beating in his chest just where her head was lying, and feel the warmth of his body stretched next to hers. Most of all, she could feel every inch of her own body, languid and joyful.

Lyn was no stranger to sex. In her world, sex was about being seen with the right person. Keeping the right reputation. Filling the gossip columns with the right words. Making love with Paul was a whole different universe. Yes, it was physical pleasure – but enriched by giving and sharing and caring. In all her years on the catwalk and in front of the lens, no designer gowns or make-up had ever made her feel as beautiful as she did at this moment – held in the arms of a man whose slow breathing seemed to hint that he was falling asleep.

It couldn't last, of course. Paul was patient and kind, but she couldn't ask him to take on her problems. She loved her sister, but Lorna was a burden that was going to fall increasingly on Lyn's shoulders as her mother got older. She couldn't expect Paul to cope with the demands of Lorna's illness – the cost and the emotional drain. Then there was the issue of the children that Lyn would never have. Paul would be a wonderful father. He deserved that chance.

No. This wasn't going to last. But it was hers for tonight, and for tomorrow night too. After the ball was over, she and Paul would go their separate ways. But that was for the future; right now, she would lie here and keep her eyes shut. She sighed. As she did, she felt Paul shift slightly, and his lips brushed her hair. Maybe it would be all right to open her eyes again after all.

20

The crowd around the stewards' compound was thick and noisy – and getting thicker and noisier by the minute. Race teams and track stewards had nothing else to claim their time now that the race was over. There were the casual onlookers, drawn by news of the protests, and there was the media scrum. There seemed to be a wall of cameras and microphones between Alex and the stewards' compound. She wasn't the only competitor caught up in a protest, but she was the one attracting all the attention. What could be better than a protest involving the only all-girl team in the race? The fact that one was a supermodel and the other a successful lawyer just added extra spice. What would the journalists do, Alex wondered, if they knew the whole story? She stood quietly in the shadow of one of the buildings, watching the confusion in front of her. She had to present herself to the stewards for her hearing. The only way she was going to do that was to fight her way through the scrum.

'Hello, Alex.'

The whole thing suddenly got a lot tougher.

'Kier.' She didn't turn to meet him. She stayed where she was, her eyes on her goal.

He took up position beside her. 'It's pretty crazy out there,' he said.

'Yes. It is.' Her voice wasn't shaky. She was proud of that. She still didn't turn to him. Right now, she didn't want to be near him. There was no way she could avoid his presence, but that didn't mean she had to look at him.

'Alex, about last night. If you'll just let me—'

'No. I don't want to talk about it. I've got enough on my plate this morning. Dealing with the protest. And that lot.' She nodded towards the crowd.

'I understand. But Alex, we have to talk about it sometime.'

No, we don't, she thought, but she didn't say anything. Still not looking at him, she pushed away from the wall and began walking towards the compound. She heard him start after her. She could hear his boots on the dry earth. But more than that, she could feel his presence behind her. She wanted to scream at him to go away, but she wasn't going to. She was Alex Reilly, and she was in control.

'Alex, is your car illegal?'

'Alex, were you cheating?'

'Did you protest against the Porsche?'

The questions flew thick and fast as the press pack descended on her. Alex ignored them. She fixed a neutral expression on her face as she pushed her way through the crowd. She was aware of Kier behind her, holding back some of the cameras. The gate to the compound seemed a million miles away, but at last she was there. A steward opened it to let her and Kier through. The sound of the gate closing, leaving the media behind, was very sweet.

Lyn and Paul were already there. So too were the Porsche team members.

'Now that we're all here,' the chief steward gave Alex a pointed glance, 'let me tell you how this is going to work. I have two protests.

'The first is against car one-two-one – the Porsche. This alleges an illegal camshaft lift, and was lodged by car seventy-one, the Alfa Romeo.'

'Paul?' Lyn was the first to speak. 'You protested against the Porsche?'

'Yes. Remember back in Perisher, you said the engine sounded funny. I think you were right. I think they're cheating.'

'We are not,' one of the Porsche brothers protested. 'How dare you even suggest—'

'Enough!' The chief steward brought them all back under control. 'The second protest was lodged by the same Porsche, car one-two-one, against car fifty-three, the Lotus. The complaint – an illegal diff ratio.'

'What?' Alex exploded. 'You've got to be kidding. There's nothing wrong—'

A look from the steward quelled her.

'What's an illegal diff . . . ?' Lyn whispered to Paul.

'The rear axle gear converts the rotary motion of the prop shaft to the rotary motion of the wheels,' Paul began.

'In English, please,' Lyn said.

'By fixing the diff ratio, you can get a lot more power through the gears. You'd notice it in the hilly sections. They must think the Lotus showed more power than it should.'

'All right.' The chief steward took control. 'I need the engine out of the Porsche. I'll have two stewards to supervise that. When it's ready, I'll come and take a look.'

With a great deal of angry muttering, the Porsche brothers headed in the direction of their vehicle.

'As for you,' the steward turned to Alex, 'I'll do you right now. This shouldn't take too long.'

He led the way to where the Lotus was parked.

'Have you got a jack?' he asked.

'Not in the car, no.'

'No problem.' He waved to one of the other stewards, who disappeared, to return a few moments later pushing a trolley jack.

Kier stepped forward to help the steward position it, but Alex put an arm out to block his way. 'I'll do it.'

Positioning the jack was a matter of just a few seconds. She wished it would take longer. She was still trying to understand the events of the last few minutes. An illegal diff ratio would put her out of the race. And she would have no one to blame but herself, because she'd made all the decisions and done most of the work while preparing the car for this race.

'Why doesn't he just ask her?' Alex heard Lyn's whispered question from the other side of the car, where she and Paul and Kier had gathered to watch.

'He has to see for himself,' Kier told her.

Kier was right, of course, but Alex wondered if she could answer him correctly. Had she set the ratio to 4 to 1 or 4 to 8? She should know, but at this exact moment, she couldn't remember. She felt as if she could barely remember her own name. The events of the last week had left her shattered. The race alone she could have handled. But Kier too . . . it was too much. She'd held it all together for seven days now, and she was beginning to think that she wasn't going to be able to do it for much longer.

'Is it in neutral?'

'What?' She turned towards the steward who had spoken.

'I need it in neutral.' He indicated the Lotus.

'Of course.' Alex opened the driver's door to check. 'It's fine.'

The chief steward sat down, and slithered on his back under the rear of the car. Another steward crouched down by the wheel. Alex could hear them talking as the rear wheel slowly rotated. She didn't hear the exact words, though. It was as if they were coming from a million miles away. She was far more conscious of Kier standing just a few feet away. His eyes darting from her to the car to the stewards and back again, as his forehead creased in a frown.

'Right!' The chief steward slid out from under her car, and nodded for her to lower the jack. That done, his associate pulled the jack out and walked away.

'Four to eight,' the chief steward told her.

Alex wasn't sure what he wanted her to say. 'If you say so.'

He raised an eyebrow. 'My recollection is that this model should be four to one. I'm going to check some references now. If you have any documentation to prove your case, you should bring it to me as soon as possible.'

'All right.'

'You can take the Lotus to the display lines now,' the steward said as he turned away.

'Alex!' Lyn was at her side. 'Have you got the proof he needs?'

Alex just shook her head. 'I . . . I don't know. No.'

'There might have been a racing model with four to eight,' Paul offered. 'I've got some books that might help, but they are at my place back in Sydney.'

'The internet,' Kier offered. 'We'll be able to find something on the net. I'm sure of it.'

The three of them turned to Alex, as if they expected something of her. She wasn't sure what.

'Are you all right?' Kier asked softly.

She turned to him and looked at him for the first time that day. His face was exactly as it had always been. Handsome. Those lovely dark eyes. His hair, showing the first signs of grey now, but still as thick and wild as it had always been. She was surprised. She had almost expected some sign of his betrayal to show. If there was any justice in the world, he would have become ugly overnight, so that her treacherous heart and body would stop longing for him.

'Yes. I'm fine,' she replied automatically. But she wasn't.

'They've started on the Porsche,' Paul said.

All four turned towards the other side of the stewards' compound. The brothers had the rear of the Porsche jacked up so high, it almost looked like the silver car was standing on its nose. They were standing between the rear wheels, working on the engine.

'What are they doing?' Lyn asked Paul.

'They'll have to take the engine out,' he replied. 'That'll take them a couple of hours. Then they'll need to undo the camshaft cover and measure the height of the cam lobes.'

'I have no idea what that means.' Lyn smiled up at him.

'Well, if they are as little as a millimetre higher than they should be, that would make an enormous difference to their horsepower.'

Alex ignored Paul's explanation. She knew exactly what the stewards were looking for. Paul was probably right. The pricks in the Porsche probably had cheated. Not that it mattered any more. She had lost the race.

More than the race. Suddenly she just couldn't stand it any more.

'I'm taking the car back,' she declared.

'Shall I come with you?' Kier said, his eyes asking so much more than his words.

'No!' Alex said in a fierce whisper. What she needed more than anything else in the world right now was to be alone.

'If you're sure?' Kier said hesitantly.

She couldn't say another word. She just turned back to the Lotus.

'I'll look on the internet for diff specifications,' Kier called after her. 'If I find anything, I'll give them to you.'

The last thing she wanted was for him to come after her. Today, or any other day for that matter. She didn't even bother to buckle her harness. She turned the key in the ignition and was rewarded by the smart burbling of the engine as it started. She quietly slipped it into low gear and began moving towards the display lines, where all the entrants were now supposed to be available for the public to view. To crawl over and envy. Alex decided she wanted none of it.

'You're supposed to have the car on display,' the steward on the gate said to her. 'I'm not supposed to let anyone out.'

Remembering Lyn's past success, Alex smiled in what she hoped was a flirtatious way. 'Please. I've just done some work on her, and I really need to take her for a quick run.'

'Well . . .'

'I won't be long. I promise.'

'I shouldn't.' The steward smiled. That was all Alex needed.

'Thank you!' she called as she engaged first gear and drove through the gate.

She chafed with impatience as she wound her way through the city streets, hampered by traffic and very conscious of how noticeable the Lotus was. But once she was out of town, she put her foot down. The little red Lotus responded as she always had, leaping forward like an eager horse. Alex sped down the country road she had raced over . . . was it really less than a week ago?

It was a lifetime ago.

She wound down her window to let the wind whistle through the car. This was her greatest comfort, the pleasure of driving with the wind in her hair and the feeling of total control. It had been since those first few times she had taken her father's Jaguar and gone joyriding. Alone at first, and then with Kier . . .

She thrust her foot down ever harder on the accelerator. Her tyres squealed as she rounded a corner just a bit too fast.

Kier had loved the speed and the excitement as much as she had. He had loved the power and beauty of the cars. He was the one she'd told about her dream of owning a Lotus, and he'd understood, because he knew her. Because he loved her . . .

Her foot drew back from the accelerator. The car instantly began to slow. She steered it gently off the road on to a patch of short grass, and turned off the engine.

He hadn't loved her.

All those years. All those dark, painful nights. She had imagined a hundred reasons for his leaving. Made a thousand excuses for him. And the simple truth had never occurred to her.

He hadn't loved her. Not the way she'd loved him.

He had been the most important thing in her world. There was nothing she would not have sacrificed for him. But he hadn't even waited a month to find someone else. To share with her an intimacy he had never shared with Alex. There was nothing more to say or do or think.

He had never loved her. It had all been a lie. Every moment that she had held in her heart as a treasure, all these years, had been a lie.

Alex lowered her head to rest on the steering wheel, and wondered how long the pain would take to fade this time.

21

The phone clicked through to voicemail. Lyn frowned and hit the disconnect button. She had left a message for her mother about an hour ago, when she called for the first time. This was the third time her mother hadn't answered the phone. That was unlike her, particularly when Lyn was away. Her mother knew how much she worried. Lyn looked at the phone again, called up her contact list and selected a number.

'West Sydney Care. Can I help you?'

'Hello, this is Lyn Stanton.'

'Oh, hello, Lyn.' All of the nurses knew her. 'How's it going in the rally? We've been following you on the web and on TV. Do you know if you've won yet?'

'No. We'll get the official results at the ball tonight,' Lyn said. 'I don't suppose my mother is there with Lorna, is she?'

'No. She's not.'

Lyn felt a twinge of anxiety. 'Has she been there at all today?'

'Oh, yes, dear. She was here this morning.'

'And Lorna's fine?'

'Yes, she is.'

Lyn took comfort from the words as she ended the

call. Just because her mother wasn't answering her mobile didn't mean she should be upset. There could be any one of a dozen good reasons. Maybe her mother was having a break, just like the one Lyn was giving herself. She smiled at the thought. If her mother did take a break, Lyn doubted there would be anyone like Paul White in it. Her mother hadn't been on a date since her father walked out all those years ago. Lyn couldn't blame her. If she had trouble believing that a man would stay around because of her sister, she could imagine how much worse it must be for her mother, with a disabled daughter totally dependent on her.

Lyn decided she should simply leave it alone, and continue getting ready for the evening. If she spent much longer in this towel, she'd feel like she had to take it home with her. She opened the door of the wardrobe, into which she had emptied her suitcase last night. One of the good things about being a model, she mused, was how easy it was to accumulate clothes. Designers just gave them to her. Not all the time, but often enough. She couldn't remember the last time she had bought anything other than lingerie.

Because of her fund-raising role, she had come prepared to dazzle at tonight's gala ball and prizegiving. She'd tossed no fewer than three designer outfits into her bag. There wasn't a lot of material in clothes like that, so they didn't take up much room. The same could be said of the ultra-high heels that were already waiting for her by the door. She had worried about those, in case they made her taller than Paul. But then she realised that Paul wouldn't care. Just like he wouldn't care what she was wearing. He would appreciate it – he was, after all, a man. She'd learned that last night. But he would feel the same towards her no matter what she wore. And that was something very special.

It was such a shame that tonight was all they had.

Lyn pushed the thought to the back of her mind, and glanced at the bedside clock. For some reason Paul had asked her to be ready early. Perhaps he wanted a drink before they went on to the ball. Or maybe he would have some news about the protest. Whatever the reason, Lyn was more than happy to oblige. She had so little time left in his company, she would gladly take every minute she could. She slipped into the familiar routine of getting herself ready. The dress she chose was Versace silk, with one shoulder bare and a flirty hem that bounced around her knees. The ultra-high gold sandals finished an outfit that had felt pretty good when she wore it on the catwalk. It felt even better now she was wearing it for Paul.

She was just applying some lip gloss when someone tapped on her door.

He was still wearing blue jeans and a white cotton shirt. By now, Lyn had come to realise he never wore anything else. In honour of the event, his jeans were stylish and well-fitting. Not at all faded. To her expert eyes, the fine cotton shirt looked tailor-made, as did the dinner jacket that completed the outfit. On anyone else it might have looked foolish. Or contrived. On Paul it looked just right, but Lyn had the feeling that tonight she would think everything about Paul was just right.

'You're beautiful.' He said the words as he smiled into her face. Then he let his gaze fall over the rest of her. 'Wow!'

'Ah, at last you noticed,' Lyn said with a grin. 'I was beginning to think you only wanted me for my mind.'

'Oh, I do.' Paul took her hand, and lifted and turned it so he could gently touch his lips to the soft skin of her wrist. 'But I think I can cope with the rest of you too.'

Lyn almost shivered. 'Keep that up, and we won't get to the ball.' The words were a low whisper.

'Then I shall desist immediately.' Paul carefully tucked her hand under his arm. 'Because you, my lady, are going to the ball.'

Walking down that plain hotel corridor with Paul felt so much better than the fanciest runways in Paris or Rome.

'I don't suppose you've heard anything about the protests,' she said as they neared the elevators.

'No.' Paul pushed the call button. 'I doubt we'll hear anything until the big announcement tonight.'

'I hope Alex isn't disqualified. She deserves to win.'

'I admire your loyalty,' Paul said, 'but there's nothing you or I can do to help her, and there is something else we need to attend to right now.'

'What something else?' They stepped into the lift.

'You'll soon find out.'

The first-floor landing was deserted when they left the elevator. To their right, a wide, elegant staircase sloped down to the hotel foyer. Soon guests would be streaming up those stairs, but Lyn and Paul were alone as they approached the big ballroom doors. Faint noise floated up from the downstairs bar, where no doubt some of the rally teams were indulging in an enthusiastic pre-dinner drink. When they reached the doors, Paul knocked loudly on the polished wood.

Before Lyn could ask what was going on, the doors opened a few inches. The face that appeared nodded and stepped back. As the doors swung open, light music floated towards them. The ballroom was brilliantly decorated in silver and blue. Flowers and flickering candles adorned the tables. Balloons floated around the ceiling, as spotlights waltzed across the dance floor. In the middle of that floor, a young woman sat in a wheelchair, her face turned upwards and shining with delight. Her hair was blond, and she was wearing a pale pink dress. One could almost believe she was about to stand up out of the wheelchair and begin to dance. Instead, she laughed so gaily it brought tears to Lyn's eyes.

'Lorna?'

A woman was standing behind the wheelchair, slowly spinning it in a circle as the lights from the mirror ball danced like butterflies around her.

'Mum?'

Lyn almost ran across the room to hug her mother. Then she dropped to her knees in front of her sister. Lorna didn't recognise her; she never did. The child who would never grow any older saw only a beautiful woman in a pretty dress. She laughed some more and clapped her hands. Lyn clapped her own hands too, and was rewarded by another laugh.

Lyn looked up and saw for the first time that her mother was also dressed for a ball. Over the years, Lyn had given her several designer dresses, but this was the first time she had ever seen her wear one.

'What . . . ?'

She saw her mother's tear-bright eyes move to look at someone approaching from behind. 'Ask him.'

Lyn rose slowly to her feet. She turned around to see Paul watching her with a look of immense pleasure on his face.

'You did this.' It wasn't a question.

He nodded. 'I thought they might like to share in the fun.'

'But when . . . ? How?'

'It wasn't that hard.'

Wasn't that hard? He had to be kidding. No one knew better than she did just how hard it was to deal with her sister. Lorna could be difficult at times. Her care was costly. Her father hadn't been able to cope. Yet Paul . . .

A burble of laughter from beside her tore her attention back to her sister. Lorna was waving her hands cheerfully around, trying to capture a balloon that some errant breeze had sent wafting towards her.

In an instant, Paul had seized the strip of silver ribbon training from the balloon. Slowly, so as not to frighten her, he moved closer to Lorna. He knelt down beside her and brought the balloon within her reach. Giggling, Lorna stretched out her fingers to touch the shiny silver orb.

'He's a really surprising person.' Lyn's mother was at her side, watching as Paul tied the balloon to Lorna's chair.

Her mother was right. Paul was surprising. But at the same time, Lyn shouldn't have been surprised. He was the most generous soul she had ever met. To give this gift, not just to Lorna, but also to her mother . . .

'I'm sorry, but we have to open the doors now.' A waitress standing behind them was watching Paul with something like adoration on her face.

'Of course.' Paul got to his feet.

'I'll take her back up now,' Lyn's mother said.

'I'll come too . . .'

'No, Lyn. You stay here.' Her mother smiled. 'I'll make sure she's all right.'

'But you will be back later,' Paul said. 'You did promise to dance with me.'

Lyn had never seen her mother blush like that before.
'Yes. As soon as she's settled.'

Lyn frowned.

'Paul found a nurse to sit with her,' Lyn's mother
whispered as she kissed her cheek. 'He really is
something.'

Yes he is, Lyn thought as she watched Paul kiss first
her mother, then Lorna, on the cheek.

The waitress went to open the door for the wheelchair,
leaving Paul and Lyn alone on the dance floor, with the
fairy lights still whirling around them.

'Thank you.' Lyn felt tears prick her eyes. 'That was
really something special. How on earth did you organise
everything?'

'It did take some doing,' Paul admitted sheepishly.
'But it was important to me.'

'Why?'

He took both her hands in his. 'Because I knew what
your father had done. And it occurred to me that you
might think all men were the same. That I was the same.'

'No, I wouldn't . . .'

Paul raised a finger to her lips to stop her speaking.

'I was afraid you might decide that we couldn't be
together. Because of Lorna.'

She didn't say anything.

'And I wanted to show you that someone who really
loved you would love everything about you. Not just your
face and figure. Everything – and that includes Lorna.'

Lyn felt as if her heart was about to explode in her
chest.

'So, if you were thinking that tonight was all we have,
you can stop thinking that now, can't you?'

How she wished she could.

'There's something else,' she said. 'You're a doctor. You know that Lorna's condition is genetic.'

'Of course, but how does that—'

'Kids,' Lyn said quickly before she could change her mind. 'I can't have kids. The risk that a child of mine would . . . suffer like Lorna. I just won't do it.'

'I understand that.'

'But if you . . . we . . . If we were together, that would mean you would never be able to . . . It wouldn't be fair on you.' The final words came out in a rush.

Paul's face was incredibly gentle as he spoke. 'Lyn, if the choice is to have you but no children . . . or children with someone else . . . I choose you.'

Lyn blinked back the tears. She didn't trust herself to speak. Paul kissed her hands.

'You know I mean that,' he said.

She nodded.

'Good. Now, I think I'd better get you a drink. You look a bit shaky.'

Suddenly she was laughing. She threw her arms around his neck, and kissed him, a bright, happy kiss that quickly began to develop into something far deeper . . . something hungry and passionate.

'Ahh . . . excuse me!' The voice finally parted them. A waiter was hovering, trying to hide the grin that was tweaking his lips. 'If you are having trouble finding your table, perhaps I can help.'

'No. No trouble at all,' Paul said as his arm encircled Lyn's waist. 'We were just about to find some champagne.'

They headed for the bar, but had taken only a few steps when Lyn suddenly stopped.

'It's just occurred to me,' she said. 'It must have cost a

fortune to get them here. And hire the nurse and everything.'

Paul shrugged deprecatingly.

'Paul.' Lyn put on her sternest voice. 'Have you been hiding something from me? Are you rich or something?'

'Not rich,' he said. 'Not really. But I guess something close. Close enough that you don't have to worry about Lorna again. But like you, I didn't want people judging me for the wrong reasons.'

Any words she might have found in response to that were lost, as a few yards away, the great polished doors were flung open and brilliantly clad people streamed into the room to celebrate.

22

Kier searched the crowded ballroom, but he couldn't see Alex. He wove his way through the cheerful throng that was already dipping enthusiastically into the champagne. He spotted Dee, the wildlife lady, whose wave suggested to him that she had forgiven him for injuring the kangaroo when he crashed the Ferrari. He saw Paul and Lyn at their table. Paul's navigator Jack was with them, along with an older woman who Kier guessed was Lyn's mother. Paul had confided his plans to Kier, and it looked like it had all worked out. Paul and Lyn positively glowed with happiness, whereas Kier felt like something that had crawled out from under a rock.

Responding in monosyllables to the greetings from other competitors, he made his way to the bar. He ordered a beer, and slowly sipped from it as he surveyed the crowd again.

He'd spent most of the day on the internet, trying to help Alex. He'd failed. He couldn't find a single reference anywhere that would swing the protest her way. She had got it wrong. She was going to be disqualified, and there was nothing he could do. He had let her down, again. That was the story of his life. He pushed away from the bar, taking his drink with him. He had to find her. Some time this evening, the stewards would announce their findings. He didn't want her to have her dream shattered in front of three hundred drunken motor sport enthusiasts who would no doubt take great delight in the downfall of the only woman driver. She should hear it from him. It wouldn't be the first time he had shattered her dreams.

He set out for another lap of the ballroom. Surely she was coming to the dinner. Unless she already knew about the result of the protest. She might have decided to stay away. Maybe he should try her room. He turned to walk back to the elevators, and it was then that he saw her.

She took his breath away. Her dress was black and simple and elegant, outlining a sleek and sexy figure. She was too short ever to have been a model like Lyn, but she moved with enough poise and grace to shine on any catwalk. Her hair shone like gold, and her face ... It wasn't that she was the most beautiful woman in the room. She probably wasn't – at least to other men. But to Kier, she was perfect. For a few seconds, all other thoughts were driven from his mind. He just wanted to take her in his arms and kiss her and tell her that he would never, ever let her go. Then she looked at him. Her eyes were like ice, a cold wall to hide what she felt inside. But Kier could see through the façade to the fear and hurt behind. Afraid that she would turn away, he moved quickly to her side.

'Would you like a drink?' He was hiding too, finding safety in convention.

'No. Thank you.' Her voice was quiet, but hard, like a knife.

'I spent the day on the internet,' Kier said. 'I'm sorry.

I couldn't find anything to help you overthrow the protest.'

'There never was anything you could do,' Alex said. 'I made a mistake and I'll have to wear the consequences. I'm just going to apologise to Lyn. She worked hard for this. She deserved better.'

He put one hand gently on her arm to stop her from walking away. 'Before you do, we need to talk.'

She looked down at his hand. Kier let it slowly drop away from her.

'There is nothing to talk about,' she said.

'Yes, there is.' He wasn't going to give up. 'I made a mistake a long, long time ago. I'm not going to repeat it now. I walked away because your mother threatened me. I will walk away again if you tell me to – but not until you've heard what I have to say.'

Her eyes were glacial as she stared at him, but she didn't say no. He steered her across the room, towards a series of glass doors that opened out on to a large balcony on what Kier guessed was the roof of the ground-floor reception area. The balcony looked out over the city's famous man-made lake. He could see the moonlight glinting on the water.

Alex stopped next to him, also looking out over the water. Was she thinking, as he was, of moonlight on a river so many years ago?

'When I left,' Kier began, 'I went to Scone and got a job at a racehorse spelling farm. I was always good with horses. Remember the black colt . . .' His voice faltered. Of course she would remember. 'Eventually I moved on to a training stable. And . . .' He stopped. This wasn't what she needed to hear. But he needed to confess.

'A week after I left, the police came for my brother. He

was out on bail on one charge and at home with Mum, recovering from the crash. He was still on crutches, but they came for him anyway. It almost destroyed her . . .'

'Mum. Please!' Kier closed his eyes. The sound of his mother crying at the other end of the telephone was almost too much for him to bear. 'Tell me what they said.'

'They . . . they said there were other charges against him. Other robberies. They searched his room, and they took some stuff.'

'What stuff?'

'I don't know. I think there was some jewellery. Then they took him. They wanted to handcuff him. They would have, if it wasn't for the crutches. Oh Kier, please come back!'

His mother's cry was like a kick in the guts. She needed him, and he wanted to be there for her. But the moment he went back, Rob was doomed. He had not the slightest doubt that Jacqueline Reilly would carry out her threat.

'Mum, I'm sorry. I just can't.'

'I don't understand. I need you here. Why can't you come back? Just for a while. Just until this is over.'

But that was exactly how long he had to stay away. 'Mum, I'll explain everything one day. I promise.'

He hung up the public phone in the back bar of the pub where he was living in a small cheap room. He'd walked almost straight into the job the day he arrived in town. He hadn't looked for his own place. He wasn't planning to stay long. As soon as his brother's trial was over, and there was no more harm Jacqueline Reilly could do, he was going home. Back to help his mother. Back to Alex. In the meantime, the pub offered cheap meals and a clean bed. It couldn't provide a remedy for the aching loneliness and *shattering guilt that were his constant companions. There were plenty of people around, but the laughter and voices only made his world seem even more empty.*

Each day he would drive to work as the sun came up. The hours that followed were filled with shovelling muck out of spelling yards, feeding and grooming horses, checking fences and cleaning tack. He was surprised to find that he loved the hard work, and he certainly loved the fine horses he cared for. Maybe they were just an outlet for feelings that left him tormented and sleepless, night after night in the tiny hotel room.

Kier had been away for almost three weeks, when they charged his brother with attempted murder.

He had returned from a long but satisfying day's work, and was looking forward to a burger and beer in the bar. The beer, of course, would be illegal. His eighteenth birthday was still a few weeks away, but the publican didn't know that, and an underage beer was the least of the Thomas family's problems with the law. His brother's trial had started that day, and that meant it wouldn't be long before Kier could go home again. Home to Alex. That thought was the only thing that kept him going.

'Kier. Phone home,' the publican said as he walked through the door.

Kier was surprised. He had called his mother almost every night since Rob had been arrested. She knew where he was, but she never called him. Why today? He had been thinking about buying one of those new mobile phones – but they were very expensive, and still not for the likes of him. He walked to the public phone at the back of the pub.

'Mum, what's wrong?' he asked as soon as she answered.

'It's Rob! He attacked a policeman!' His mother broke into hysterical sobbing.

During the next ten minutes, as Kier fed coins into the phone, he heard how his brother had lost his temper at the courthouse and attacked one of his guards with the metal crutch he still needed to walk. The guard was seriously hurt and in hospital.

'Why?' Kier asked, but his mother had no idea.

Kier let the information sink in. His brother had attacked a policeman. Almost killed him, according to his mother. Rob was going to jail. Nothing and no one could help him now. Kier felt a weight of guilt lift from his shoulders. It wasn't his fault. None of it was. Nothing he could have done would have stopped Rob from breaking into the shop that night. He couldn't have saved his brother from the high-speed crash that almost killed him, just as he couldn't have stopped him from attacking that cop. Rob was a lost cause and his own worst enemy. Kier was not his brother's keeper. And now he was free of his deal with Alex's mother. Rob had crossed the line. Jacqueline Reilly couldn't keep him out of jail any more than Kier could. Not now. That meant Kier could go home. Tonight. He'd have to tell his boss; the man had been good to him, but he was going home to give his mother the support she needed. He was going home to be with Alex. She would be angry at him, but he'd explain everything and she'd understand. She had to. Despite the bad news he'd just heard, Kier felt the darkness begin to lift.

'Is Dad there with you?' he asked his mother.

'Of course not. He's down the pub drinking, where else.'

Kier mentally cursed his father. His mother needed someone right now.

'Have you spoken to Rob's lawyer?'

'Yes, I have. He said things don't look too good. But there is one small bit of hope. Mrs Reilly came to the office.'

Kier felt icy fingers close around his throat. 'What did she want?'

His mother was too upset to notice the tone of his voice. 'She said she could help. Wasn't that nice of her?'

'What can she do?' Kier asked bitterly.

'She said she'd speak up for him. Give him a character reference.'

Kier didn't believe it for an instant, but his mother sounded so hopeful. He couldn't destroy that.

'It must be because you all worked for her husband. She asked after you, too. Asked where you are.'

I'll bet she did, Kier thought.

'Anyway, she said she'd do what she could for Rob. Rob's lawyer says it will help. I thought that was very kind of her.'

No it wasn't, he wanted to shout. It was evil. And manipulative. She was simply making sure he realised that she was still a threat, and he had better stick to their deal. Mrs Reilly might not be able to save Rob from his latest stupidity, but Kier had no doubt that she could make things far, far worse for him. He fought to keep his voice calm as he continued to talk to his mother. It almost broke his heart to tell her that he couldn't come back to help her. He would have given a year of his life to be able to tell her why. Her wounded voice was like a knife in his gut.

His hands were shaking when he finally hung up.

Damn that woman! He was so grateful his mother hadn't perceived the threat in Jacqueline's words. God, how he wished he and Alex were free of her. That wasn't *going to happen yet – but it would. Kier reached under the neck of his T-shirt, and felt the silver charm that he wore. The charm he had bought for Alex. One day he would give it to her. One day they would be together, and there was no way that Jacqueline was going to stop them. For a moment he could feel himself losing control. This shouldn't be happening to them. They were only seventeen. This should be the happiest time of their lives. Damn it! It was not fair.*

He spun on his heel and walked back to the bar.

'Scotch,' he told the barman.

The man raised an eyebrow. He had been holding a beer glass, but he put it back and reached for a spirit glass. 'What'll you have with it?'

'More Scotch.'

The barman put the drink down without a comment.

It didn't help. Nor did the second, but he still ordered a third. Eventually the Scotch would numb the pain. Wouldn't it?

'Hey, are you all right?'

Kier looked at the girl who was standing next to him, her hand on his arm. He'd seen her before. He searched his suddenly fuzzy brain for her name.

'Pam,' she offered helpfully.

He knew her now. There weren't too many teenagers in the town, and she'd already indicated she would like to see a bit more of him. He'd ignored the hints; after all, he had someone. He had Alex.

But he didn't.

'Hi, Pam,' he said. 'Would you like a drink?'

'All right.' She slid on to a stool next to him. 'But just the one.'

She was a pretty girl. Not at pretty as Alex, of course.

Her hair was dark, not gold. Her eyes were blue, not green. Her voice was not the whisper of a gentle breeze across a field of ripe wheat. She wasn't the first golden rays of dawn after a stormy night.

Kier signalled the publican to bring two more drinks. When Pam smiled at him, he smiled back. When she rested her hand on his arm, he didn't shake it away. And when she walked back to his room with him, he opened the door and let her in.

As he said the words, Kier heard Alex's sharp intake of breath beside him. He looked down at her, but her face was hidden in the shadows as she stared out across the lake.

'It was just that one night,' he told her, knowing that it really didn't make any difference. 'I was trying to stop the pain.' It hadn't helped; it had simply added to the increasing burden of guilt that he carried.

'Rob's trial took two weeks. Then another two weeks before the sentencing was done. I don't know if your mother was involved at all, but he got five years. Not that it mattered. As soon as he got out, he was in trouble again. He's back there now.' Kier took a steadying breath. The next words would be the hardest he had ever spoken. 'The day he was sent down, I was planning to come back . . . but I couldn't. Pam was pregnant.'

He wouldn't tell her that he had walked down to the river that day. A different river, a long way from their special place. He had taken the silver charm from around his neck and thrown it into the water.

'We were married a few weeks later. The day that Katie was born, I felt happy for the first time since I left you.'

He stopped talking, waiting to see if Alex would speak. She was as still as if carved from ice.

'We tried to make the marriage work, but it was never going to. All we really had in common was Katie. We divorced when she was five. Pam has remarried and she lives up in Queensland. I don't see Katie as often as I would like. Of all the regrets I have, the one thing I don't regret is my daughter. She is wonderful and I love her.'

He couldn't stand Alex's silence any more. He took her by the shoulders and forced her to face him. Her face was devoid of any emotion. Her eyes were cold, but somewhere inside, he knew she must be feeling ... something.

'My biggest regret ... the one that haunts me still ... is that it wasn't you.' His voice broke as he spoke. He could say nothing more. He stood, his hands still on her shoulders, and looked down into her face, realising as he did that this moment was going to define the rest of his life. His future was in her hands. He saw a tiny frown crease her forehead, as he waited for her to speak.

'There you are.' The loud voice from behind them was almost a physical thing as it tore them apart. Kier wanted to cry out in frustration.

'It's time to announce the final results.' The race steward was oblivious to the tension in the air. 'We can't do that without you there. Come on!'

The steward hustled Alex away. Kier stood by the rail, watching her go, willing her to turn to look at him. Just for a moment. He needed to see her face. To know what she was thinking.

She walked back through the glass doors without turning around.

The room was a swirling mass of movement, with no sense to it. Alex allowed herself to be ushered through into the midst of it all, because she was incapable of doing anything else. Having achieved his goal, the steward promptly vanished, leaving her rudderless in a sea of noise and colour. She looked around hoping to see a friendly face. Hoping to see Kier?

No! Kier was the last person she wanted to see.

There was a sudden upsurge in the volume of noise around her. At nearby tables, people were standing and cheering. Glasses were clinking and the sudden explosion of a cork from a champagne bottle made her duck. She turned, desperately looking for a way out.

'Alex!' Lyn suddenly appeared at her side. 'We've been looking for you.'

Alex grabbed hold of Lyn's arm like a drowning person might grab a life-preserver.

'Alex, what's wrong?'

She couldn't answer. She couldn't explain what she felt to herself, far less to Lyn.

'They're announcing the awards,' Lyn explained, starting to steer her across the room. 'Our class is next. Paul says the Porsche will be disqualified. We might win!'

'No,' Alex said.

'What?'

Alex stopped in her tracks. 'No. We won't win. I made a mistake. I'm so sorry.' She turned and fled.

Ignoring everyone around her, she pushed her way through the crowd towards the doors. She pushed one open and stepped through into the foyer. It was blessedly empty. Not willing to wait for the lift, she started down the long staircase. For one panicked moment, she thought she heard voices behind her, and she started to run. Once at the bottom, she turned towards the glass doors that led out of the hotel. A few minutes more and she was outside, taking long, deep breaths of the cool air.

Her heart stopped pounding and she began to think. She needed to get away from everyone. Away from Lyn and Paul, who had done nothing wrong except to fall in love and be happy. Away from Kier. She needed to find herself again. There was only one place where she could do that. She held out her hand, and was rewarded by the immediate appearance of a taxi.

The showgrounds were almost deserted. Everyone connected to the rally was at the ball. Except Alex. She approached the gate, and found herself facing the burly shape of a security guard.

'Sorry, miss,' he said. 'The showgrounds are closed to the public now.'

'I'm not public,' Alex said briefly. She pulled her rally passes out of her black evening bag.

The guard examined them, then looked at her closely. He raised an eyebrow at her sexy little black dress and high heels. 'You're a driver?' He didn't even try to mask his surprise.

'Yes, I am,' she replied, carefully taking back her ID.

The guard shook his head and opened the gate for her.

She walked through, and felt a strange sense of relief when she heard it clang shut behind her. She walked down the silent line of race cars, glad to be alone at last. She needed to think. The rough ground was hard going in her Jimmy Choo heels, but she didn't care. Just ahead she saw the gleam of red paint in the dim glow of the security lighting. Her beloved Lotus.

When she reached the car, she unlocked the door and slid inside. It wasn't quite so easy in a cocktail dress with a pencil skirt, but she managed. The heels she left on the dirt outside. Lovingly she ran her fingers around the gleaming polished wood of the steering wheel. She was safe here. She was in control. There was nothing to confuse her. Or frighten her. The Lotus was her lifeline . . . it had been right from the day she found it. It was on her twenty-third birthday. A birthday when she didn't cry. The first since she was seventeen . . .

The corrugated-iron machinery shed was huge, and it had seen better days. Red rust stains ran down the walls, and in places the metal sheets were hanging at crazy angles, held on by just a single nail.

'Are you sure it's safe to go in there?' she asked the property agent.

'Safe enough.' The man walked purposefully towards the rusty iron doors that enclosed one end of the building. He just wanted to get this over with, another part of his job done.

Alex shrugged and followed him, wondering if this really was the find of a lifetime. She'd seen the story on the back of a newspaper clipping her mother had sent. The clipping was about the wedding of one of her school classmates, but Alex had been far more interested in the story about the collection of ancient vehicles found in a dilapidated farm shed when its reclusive owner died. The report had included a photograph taken inside the same shed she was now approaching. It had shown a dusty collection of unrecognisable vehicles, some whole and some in pieces. There were cars and trucks and tractors. Even an old motorbike. But in one corner of the photo, something about the curve of a piece of metal struck a chord with her. It had taken her three days to organise the visit, fearful every day that someone else might get there before her.

The shed wasn't locked. There was no one within a hundred kilometres to steal the contents – if indeed they were even worth stealing. The agent took hold of one of the large iron doors and pulled it back. The hinge didn't so much squeak as scream in pain. The second door was the same. The agent waved her through, then went to sit in the shade. Alex was glad to be alone.

It took a few minutes for her eyes to adjust to the gloom. The only light fell in bright beams that speared through the holes in the roof and walls. In between, the darkness was almost a physical thing. Gradually shapes began to emerge from the gloom. It was even more chaotic than the photograph had suggested. The shed housed decades' worth of rusty junk. It was all buried under a deep layer of dust. Birds had found their way in to build their nests in relative safety. Several generations of their offspring had made their own contribution to the filth. Ignoring the smell, Alex spotted the remains of a tractor. It looked familiar. As she approached, she recognised part of the photograph. She stood for a minute, trying to picture the clipping in her mind. The vehicle she was interested in should be over to her left.

She was still picking her way through the litter on the floor when she saw it. Some small furry animal, possibly seeking shelter for the night, had brushed away a layer of dust. The light falling through a hole in the roof glinted on something that was unmistakably chrome. Alex stepped carefully over the rubble, noting as she did so a graceful curve of metal, almost covered by rotting cardboard boxes. She tentatively reached out her hand, and brushed the dust away. The metal was stained. The paint cracked and faded. But it was the bonnet of a car.

Alex began to shift the boxes. One crumbled to dust, showering the front of her clothes with foul-smelling rotten newspaper. She brushed it aside, unconcerned. Ignoring the spiders, and the possibility of snakes, she began clearing more of the rubble around the car. At last she could see it all.

It was a Lotus Elan. The 26 R. A car so rare, even her father had been unable to buy one. It was the thing she wanted more than anything else in the world. She had found one that could be hers and hers alone.

She took a deep breath and tried to open the driver's door. It was stiff, the window so coated with dust she couldn't even see inside. But at last it relented. The interior of the car stank of animal droppings. The leather seats were torn, the stuffing no doubt used as a nest by rats and mice. But the gear shift was still intact, and the steering wheel. Her heart in her mouth, Alex released the bonnet. She lifted it slowly. The engine was there. It was dirty and rusty, and parts might be missing, but there was enough! With a great deal of time and money and love, the car could be restored, and she was the person to do it.

Reverently she lowered the bonnet, then ran her fingers over the scarred paint. It had been red, the little

Lotus, and she decided then that it would be red again.

'Hello, little girl,' she whispered, as if to a living creature. 'I think you'd better come home with me.'

The car didn't answer, of course. Well, not in any way that another person would recognise. But Alex felt it. She smiled.

'Happy birthday to me.'

It was one of her most precious memories. A memory totally without pain. It usually made her smile. But not tonight. Too many other thoughts were racing through her mind, as she struggled to absorb everything Kier had told her.

For the first time she knew the whole story. Knew why he had left and why he had never come back.

The girl in the pub. His daughter. Katie. Alex could still see the smiling face in the photo he carried in his wallet. His daughter's face.

My biggest regret . . . is that it wasn't you.

It should have been me! The silent cry rose from the deepest recesses of her soul. It should have been me and you! It could have been, if not for her mother's interference. If not for Kier's brother Rob, and his unwavering talent for getting into trouble. And now it was too late. They would never recapture what they had as teenagers. There was something about first love that was precious beyond measure. Once lost, it would never return. That breathless love. That desperate yearning. She would never, ever feel that again. That had been taken from her. She wanted to scream at the unfairness of it all.

She lowered her head to the steering wheel and closed her eyes. She pictured Kier's face. The dark eyes that could see right into her heart. The smile that brightened even the darkest day. The touch of his lips and hands that made her body glow. How she wanted everything to be as it once was. She wanted to run her fingers through his hair, and laugh with him, and know that she was loved.

She could almost see the boy she had loved so much. The cheeky smile. The laugh lines at the corners of his eyes. The wavy hair – with just a hint of the first touch of grey. The fresh white scar on his forehead, the legacy of his accident. She wanted to weep for the love of that face.

That face!

Not the face of the boy she had loved with all the tumultuous passion of a teenager. The face of the grown man. The Kier of the present – not the past. The Kier who had suffered as she had. The Kier who had grown and learned from the past, as she was beginning to. As a teenager she had loved the boy. As a woman . . . ?

Alex slid out of the Lotus, shut the door and twisted the key in the lock. She paused for just a few seconds, running her fingers lovingly over the shiny red paint.

'Thanks,' she whispered. Then she slipped her feet back into her shoes.

'Is everything all right, miss?' asked the security guard as he let her back through the gate.

'Almost,' she replied.

The street was dark and deserted, but the main road was just a block away. She reached it in mere seconds and looked about wildly for a taxi. She had to get back to the hotel. She had to find Kier.

The night was totally devoid of anything resembling a taxi. Alex wanted to scream in frustration. She dived inside her handbag for her mobile phone, only to discover she had left it behind in her hotel room. She was just contemplating heading back to the showgrounds and begging the guard to let her take the Lotus when she saw a yellow light approaching. She held up her hand.

'Are you connected to the rally?' the driver asked after she'd told him her destination.

'Yes,' she confirmed distantly. Why were taxi drivers always so talkative?

'I went by the showgrounds before my shift,' the driver continued. 'I had a look at the cars. They were pretty cool. There's nothing better than a really nice car.'

'Oh yes there is,' Alex said as they pulled up in front of the brightly lit hotel foyer. She thrust a twenty-dollar bill at the startled man, and went to find it.

I n the ballroom, the party was in full swing. The
presentations were over. The band was rocking.
People were drinking and dancing and celebrating.
Groups of competitors were reliving every inch of the
rally, their voices louder than their engines had ever
seemed during the race. Alex looked at the smiling faces
as she pushed her way across the crowded room.
Someone grabbed her and swirled her in a crazy waltz
step, before dancing off, none too steadily. They were all
so happy, yet all they were celebrating was a car race.

She hadn't expected to find Kier there, and he wasn't.

At last she spotted a friendly face. Or rather, two of
them. Lyn and Paul were just leaving the dance floor,
hands firmly clasped as they made their way back to their
table.

'Alex!' Lyn greeted her. 'Did you see – Paul won our
class!' She looked up at him with such love shining from
her eyes that Alex was afraid she might be blinded.

'Congrats, Paul,' she said. 'Have you seen Kier?'

'No,' Paul said. 'I'm sorry you lost the protest.'

'It doesn't matter,' Alex said, realising that it really
didn't. 'But I am sorry, Lyn, that your fund-raising hasn't
been as successful as you wanted it to be.'

'I think it's been all right,' Lyn said. 'It would have been a lot better if Kier hadn't crashed the Ferrari. We had banked on raising a lot of money by raffling it. But despite that, we've done pretty well.'

The answer was so obvious, Alex wondered why on earth she hadn't thought of it before. She reached into her bag and took out the keys to the Lotus.

'Here.' She held them out. 'Take these.'

Lyn didn't move. 'What do you mean?'

Alex took her hand and pressed the Lotus keys into it. 'The Lotus. Auction that instead.'

'No!' Lyn looked shocked. 'Alex, you love that car. You can't—'

'I can. I will. I have.'

Lyn enveloped her in a hug. Over her friend's shoulder, she saw Paul smiling. He nodded as if he understood.

'Now, I've got to find Kier.'

Leaving a stunned Lyn staring after her, Alex made her way out of the ballroom. She felt good. Everything was going to be all right. She didn't really have to wonder where Kier might be. She turned her steps towards the lake.

The light on the lake was beautiful. Kier had found a secluded place, surrounded by trees and bushes. There were no nearby buildings. No roads. No people. Just beautiful silence. He sat on the grass, looking out into the night. In the distance, a fountain shot jets of water high into the night air, the lights playing on the water making it sparkle like jewels. This was a long way from the muddy creek that he and Alex had made their special place. They had both come a long way too, and there was no going back. Not that he wanted to go back. He was proud of what he had made of his life. He had taken a menial job and turned it into a successful career. He had a beautiful daughter. In so many ways, his life now was much more than he had ever hoped it could be – except for one thing.

Alex.

If only Jacqueline hadn't been such a scheming woman. If only Rob had been different. If only . . .

Kier shook his head. If only wasn't good enough. Had those things been different, something else would have come along to destroy what he and Alex had had back then. It had to. He didn't doubt that she had loved him, as he had loved her, but they were too young. Too different. It would never have worked. Somewhere along the line, something would have torn them apart.

But now something had brought them back together. And this time . . . this time he had only himself to blame if he walked away. He wouldn't. Not again. At least not without trying.

Kier got slowly to his feet. When he turned around, she was there. She was still wearing her sexy black dress, but her high-heeled shoes were in her hand, and she was barefoot. In the moonlight, she was almost the girl he had left behind on the riverbank all those years ago. Almost – but not quite.

Alex tried to read what was written on Kier's face. Was he pleased to see her? Now she was suddenly uncertain. Restoring a car. Driving in a race. These things suddenly seemed so much easier than what she was going to do now.

'Hi,' she said softly.

'Hi.'

'Did you know Paul won the class?'

'I thought he might,' Kier said. 'I'm sorry you were disqualified.'

'I'm not.' She smiled softly. 'I just did a good thing.'

'What did you do?'

'I gave the Lotus to Lyn to auction.' She heard his sharp intake of breath.

'But you love that car. You worked so hard on it.'

'I know.'

'It was your dream.'

'It was, yes.' She stepped closer to him. In the stillness of the night, she could almost hear his heart beating. 'But that was another place. Another time. Another Alex. I don't need that dream any more.'

'You don't?'

She shook her head. The air between them seemed almost to vibrate.

'I am so sorry for what I did, back then,' Kier said. 'I can only imagine how you felt. You must have hated me.'

'I did for a while,' Alex admitted. 'I wondered what was wrong with me, that you didn't love me.'

'Didn't love you?' The words were a strangled cry. 'Alex, never think that. Not for an instant. I loved you more than was good for either of us.'

'I know that now.'

Alex raised a hand to stroke his cheek. He covered her hand with his own, and turned his head to kiss the soft skin of her palm. He didn't let her hand go, and she didn't want him to.

'In some ways my mother was right,' she said. 'We were so young. Everything was so intense. I think we needed time to become the people we were supposed to be.'

'And now that we are . . . ?'

His words hung in the air.

'Well,' said Alex, 'I think next time I set out to restore a race car, it might be nice to have some help.'

He nodded slowly. 'And next time Katie comes to visit, I think she'd prefer to go shopping with another girl – rather than her crusty old father.'

Alex felt the tears prick the back of her eyes. 'Crusty – maybe. Old – I don't know. Let me see . . .'

She stood on tiptoe and kissed him, a gentle brush of her lips against his. Before she could pull away, his arms were around her, and he pulled her to him. His kiss tasted of love – years of love and longing pouring into her like a golden flame. When at last he released her, she thought she saw something very like tears in his eyes.

'A long time ago, I didn't show up for a date,' he said. 'You had special plans for that night.'

'I did.' It was barely a whisper.

'Maybe tonight I can make it up to you.'

Carefully Alex reached out to touch his chest. She undid the first few buttons of his shirt and slipped her hand inside to touch his skin. Kier's breath caught in his throat, as she laid her hand over his heart.

'I think it's going to take more than one night,' she said, a smile twitching the corners of her mouth.

'That's all right,' Kier said as he pulled her close again. 'I'm not going anywhere.'

Pick up a *little black dress* – it's a girl thing.

978 0 7553 4715 5

THE FARMER NEEDS A WIFE
Janet Gover
PBO £5.99

Rural romances become all the rage when editor Helen Woodley starts a new magazine column profiling Australia's lovelorn farmers. But a lot of people (and Helen herself) are about to find out that the course of true love ain't ever smooth . . .

It's not all haystacks and pitchforks, ladies – get ready for a scorching outback read!

HIDE YOUR EYES
Alison Gaylin
PBO £5.99

Samantha Leiffer's in big trouble: the chest she saw a sinister man dumping into the Hudson river contained a dead body, meaning she's now a witness in a murder case. It's just as well hot, hard-line detective John Krull is by her side . . .

'Alison Gaylin is my new must-read' Harlen Coben

978 0 7553 4802 2

Pick up a *little black dress* – it's a girl thing.

IT SHOULD HAVE BEEN ME
Phillipa Ashley
PBO £5.99

When Carrie Brownhill's fiancé Huw calls off their wedding, running away from it all in a VW camper-van seems an excellent idea to her. But when Huw's old friend Matt takes the driver's seat, could fate be taking Carrie on a different journey?

978 0 7553 4334 8

'Fulfils all the best fantasies, including a gorgeous, humanitarian hero and a camper van!' Katie Fforde

TODAY'S SPECIAL
A.M. Goldsher
PBO £4.99

When chef Anna Rowan and boyfriend Byron Smith are asked to star in a reality-TV show about their restaurant, TART, they find themselves – and their relationship – under the hot glare of the TV cameras. Do they have the right recipe for love?

A.M. Goldsher serves up another deliciously quirky and original romance.

978 0 7553 3996 9

You can buy any of these other
Little Black Dress titles from your
bookshop or *direct from the publisher*.

FREE P&P AND UK DELIVERY
(Overseas and Ireland £3.50 per book)

Nina Jones and the Temple of Gloom	Julie Cohen	£5.99
Improper Relations	Janet Mullany	£5.99
Bittersweet	Sarah Monk	£5.99
The Death of Bridezilla	Laurie Brown	£5.99
Crystal Clear	Nell Dixon	£5.99
Talk of the Town	Suzanne Macpherson	£5.99
A Date in Your Diary	Jules Stanbridge	£5.99
The Hen Night Prophecies: Eastern Promise	Jessica Fox	£5.99
The Bachelor and Spinster Ball	Janet Gover	£5.99
The Love Boat	Kate Lace	£5.99
Trick or Treat	Sally Anne Morris	£5.99
Tug of Love	Allie Spencer	£5.99
Sunnyside Blues	Mary Carter	£5.99
Heartless	Alison Gaylin	£5.99
A Hollywood Affair	Lucy Broadbent	£5.99
I Do, I Do, I Do	Samantha Scott-Jeffries	£5.99
A Most Lamentable Comedy	Janet Mullany	£5.99
Purses and Poison	Dorothy Howell	£5.99
Perfect Image	Marisa Heath	£5.99
Girl From Mars	Julie Cohen	£5.99

TO ORDER SIMPLY CALL THIS NUMBER

01235 400 414

or visit our website: www.headline.co.uk

Prices and availability subject to change without notice.